ABOUT THE AUTHOR

Originally from Northern Ireland, Jacqueline Harrett has lived in Cardiff with her husband for over thirty years. Her two grown-up children also live in the capital city.

A multi-genre author, Jacqui has published non-fiction; *Exciting Writing*, (Sage), *Tell me Another...* (UKLA); children's stories; and short stories in anthologies. She has co-authored a novel with Janet Laugharne, *What Lies Between Them*, (Dixi, 2022) as well as flash fiction and blog at www.jlharland.co.uk.

The Nesting Place is her debut novel, a police procedural set in South Wales with Mandy Wilde as the feisty detective.

Published in Great Britain in 2021
By Diamond Crime

ISBN 978-1-8384026-7-9

Diamond Crime is an imprint of Diamond Books Ltd.

Thanks to...

The dream team at Diamond Books for their help, support and enthusiasm in bringing The Nesting Place to publication. Phil, Steve and Jeff have been both professional and a pleasure to work with.

The wonderful writing classes at Cardiff University with Katherine Stansfield which provided the knowledge base for constructing a novel.

During lockdown, a further course on crime writing with James McCreet which provided invaluable feedback and the confidence to send DI Mandy Wilde out into the world.

Thanks to both for the constructive feedback and well-designed courses.

Thanks also to my readers and friends, whose comments and criticism helped shape the story. A special thanks to Fliss, Jan, Abbie and Linda in particular, who not only commented but proofread while doing so. The support of two writing groups, The Criminal Fairies and Writers Enjoying Words, has been a blessing. Lovely people and talented writers, all of them.

I also want to thank the lovely group of people who make up Crime Cymru. I am delighted to join their ranks and look forward to many more meetings as we emerge from the pandemic.

Finally, sincere thanks to my family, Doug, Douglas and Felicity. Without their love and support it would not have been possible.

Cover photo: Triad Schulz
https://tiard-schulz-fotografie.jimdosite.com

Book cover design:
jacksonbone.co.uk

And coming soon from Jacqueline Harrett:

The Whispering Trees
The second D.I. Mandy Wilde Novel
To be published by

DIAMOND
CRIME

For information about Diamond Crime authors
and their books, visit:
www.diamondbooks.co.uk

Dedicated to

The memory of my parents, Andrew and Norah Montgomery, whose unconditional love was the foundation of my life.

The Nesting Place

A DI Mandy Wilde Novel

JACQUELINE HARRETT

CHAPTER ONE

SUNDAY

The body was found about the same time as Mandy Wilde was buttering a slice of wholemeal toast to accompany her morning tea. A weak sun was trying to filter through the grey skies and a soft drizzle had started. Typical Welsh Sunday. Satan, next door's cat, was meowing and pawing at her kitchen window. The unexpected sound of Oasis filled the room. Her ringtone.

A call in the early morning was never good news.

"DI Wilde." A pause as she listened. "Right. Ring DS Jones and tell him I'll pick him up outside the station in fifteen minutes."

She was alert now. It wasn't Joy, her first thought. A body in a field in the Vale of Glamorgan. Minimal information. Woman reported missing and then a body, matching her description, found within a couple of hours. It wasn't usually that easy.

A creak on the stairs told her Tabitha was awake. Her niece, dark hair mussed and face creased from sleep, appeared. She yawned, bleary-eyed.

"Mmm. That toast smells good. I heard your phone. Work?"

"Help yourself. I've got to go out. Sorry Tabs. I thought we could have a nice Sunday together but duty calls. Well, a body anyway."

"It's not..." Tabitha had paled, eyes and mouth wide open.

"No. It's not your Mam. A young woman went missing late last night. The body fits the description."

Shit. She should think before opening her mouth. Of, course Tabitha would think it was Joy. Same as she did every time the phone rang. Although she'd know if Joy was dead, wouldn't she? Didn't twins have a special bond?

Tabitha still appeared stricken. Her mouth wobbled a little. Fifteen going on five at times. Mandy gave her a hug.

"Have you got plans for today? God knows when I'll be home. Probably just an accident but," she shrugged, "you never know what's going to happen until you get there."

"I've homework to do and maybe Kelly will come over later, if that's alright?" Anxious eyes. Always wanting to do the right thing. Not a typical teenager. How had her bonkers sister managed to produce such a lovely kid?

"Sure. There's food in the freezer. Maybe you could pop to Lidl and grab some bits? I started a half list somewhere and there's twenty quid under the tea caddy. Usual stuff. Fruit, veg, milk, cheese and some popcorn. If I'm home in time we can have a Netflix movie."

Tabitha beamed. "Sounds good. Thanks Auntie Mandy. And I'll empty the dishwasher."

Desperate to be helpful. Always aware of her responsibilities as a long-term guest. Well, Mandy didn't see her that way, though she knew how Tabitha's mind worked. She dropped a kiss on the top of her niece's head.

"Got to dash. Josh is meeting me at the station in three minutes. Go back to bed for a bit. You look tired."

"Make sure you don't speed." Tabitha grinned. "See you later."

Sunday morning and Cardiff was still asleep. No traffic, so she ignored the twenty mile an hour signs and got to the station in time to see Josh getting out of his battered Corsa. She pulled up alongside and he got into the passenger seat.

"Well, you look like shit. And the mints don't cover last night's curry."

DS Josh Jones yawned. "Anything before mid-day on Sunday is the middle of the night as far as I'm concerned. What's it all about? They just said there was a body in the Vale."

"Young woman. Reported missing just before dawn. Found a couple of hours after. Could be an accident or not. I've put the postcode into the sat nav so let's hope we can find it. Uniform's there, the coroner's been informed, and Rishi should be on the way. We'll see what he has to say." She glanced sideways at Josh. "With luck it's an accident and we'll be home by lunch."

Josh grunted and peered out through the window. "Any chance of stopping to pick up a coffee on the way? I didn't have time."

"Sorry. Nothing will be open. Bad for you anyway, all that caffeine. If you're thirsty there's a couple of bottles of water in the back and I grabbed some fruit on my way out as well."

"Rabbit food. Coffee and doughnuts preferred."

Mandy laughed. They were heading out of the city now, through Ely to Culverhouse Cross and then away from the urban expanse and into the countryside. They bypassed Cowbridge and then turned towards the coast. Sprawling veins of narrow roads. The Vale of Glamorgan. A combination of coast and country, little villages and market towns. A diverse mix of places and people. Mandy was swearing under her breath as the roads became narrower and more twisted.

"Where the hell are we? I hate the countryside." The sat nav seemed to be taking them on a wild goose chase. All the roads seemed the same, weaving between high hedges.

Then, "You have reached your destination."

Mandy hit the steering wheel with her fist. "Bloody sat nav. There's nothing here except more road. Ring the station. See if anyone can give us a more precise location."

"No signal, boss."

"Hell's bells. What next?"

There was little sign of anything or anyone. Then, at last, they turned a corner and saw a uniformed officer standing by a temporary roadblock. Mandy stopped the car and got out. There was an earthy smell after the rain and she wrinkled her nose. Fresh air. Over-rated. She flashed her badge at the officer.

"DI Wilde. DS Jones. Where's the body?"

The officer looked about twelve and uncertain of himself. Just out of training she expected. He probably

4

thought policing the Vale would be easy; all parking tickets and farmers polluting rivers with the odd road accident thrown in for good measure. He pointed to a farm gate which was covered in police tape. "Over there, Ma'am." Another uniformed officer was further up the field and Rishi, the pathologist, was already in situ, booted and suited.

"How the hell did you get here before us, Rishi?"

"I live around here. Not far from Sigingstone."

"Another country freak." She bent her head towards Josh and rolled her eyes. "So, what's the verdict?"

"Hard to tell. Dead about six or seven hours. Could have fallen, tripped. No sign of any injury or defence wounds. Some vomit spilling from the mouth. Smell of alcohol. I'll know more when I do the post-mortem."

"And when will that be?"

Rishi hesitated. "I was supposed to be visiting my mother-in-law this afternoon…"

"But a dead body is a much more attractive proposition?" A glimmer of understanding passed between them. Mandy knew what was coming.

Rishi coughed, appeared to be thinking and then said, "Of course, if it was urgent, if you required speed in this case, I could do it later today. About two? You'll want the results as soon as possible, I expect."

"Nice one, Rishi. That would be most appreciated. My apologies to your mother-in-law." She winked at him before turning to Josh.

"Josh, see if you can find a mobile signal so we know if the SOCOs are on the way. They should be here. We can't leave this poor woman for long. Once the press gets a sniff of it, they'll be swarming here. Let's keep things quick and quiet."

Mandy spent a moment gazing at the body. Manicured nails, glossy hair and, now mud-splattered, expensive dress. Designer. A Rolex watch and a Clogau ring on the middle finger of her left hand. Pink pumps, one slipped off her foot revealing toe nails the same candyfloss pink as her fingers. What had happened to her? An accident or something else?

"Who found the body?" She asked the uniformed officer.

"Local man. Retired. Lives on the outskirts of Cowbridge. I've taken details. He's coming into the station later to give a proper statement." The officer flicked open a notebook.

"He came out here to take the dog for a walk. There's a right of way and, as the field is usually empty, he can let the dog off the lead. The dog was whining and then he noticed the body."

"Did he touch her? Move her? Let the dog at her?"

"No Ma'am. He's ex-army so he says he could tell from a distance that she was dead. He went home and rang 999."

"Went home?" Mandy frowned. Why the hell would he do that?

"He doesn't have a mobile and, even if he did, the signal out here is variable."

Mandy rolled her eyes. Yeah, so they'd found out. Another reason why she hated being out of the city.

"What time was that?"

"Just after seven this morning. He says he's an early riser. Often out tramping the fields with the dog."

6

"And what time did you say this woman was reported missing?"

"About five. Just after dawn."

"Rishi says she's been dead six or seven hours. It's after eight now, so time of death about one or two am." She paused a moment. "What else? Did he see anyone else or pass a car on his way? Anything unusual?"

"No Ma'am. I called him to make sure I had the right location. We'll take a fuller statement this afternoon. After the body's been moved."

"And this report about a young woman missing. Where had that come from? Who rang? What did they say?"

"A Sophie Grant called with a concern about her friend, Megan Pritchard. It seems a group of young women were staying for the weekend in a house about a mile or so from here. Megan had wandered out about midnight. When she didn't come back, they phoned the police to report her missing."

"Five hours later? Hmmm. Okay, thank you. We'll see those reports as soon as possible, please."

The sun made a fleeting appearance and Mandy spotted something glinting in the ground. With her gloved hand she picked it up, pulled an evidence bag out of her pocket, and dropped it in. Gold earring. Simple stud. Could it have come out in a struggle? There seemed to be several sets of footprints muddying the way to the body. She hoped the SOCOs, when they arrived, managed to get some prints. It would be good to know who else had passed this way. She handed the bag to Rishi.

"You might want to check this out as well. In the mud, over there."

"Well, it's not hers. She got little diamond studs. In both ears."

Mandy could see that, now she was close to the body.

"See if there's any DNA or prints. Just in case. Could have been dropped by anyone but it's fairly clean so may have happened recently. Could be nothing though you never know, do you?"

Josh was on his way back to meet her.

"Managed to get a weak signal. SOCOs on the way. Should be here any minute."

"Good. We don't want to leave her out here any longer than we have to. It was raining last night, yeah?"

"Yes."

"And Megan didn't have a coat or proper shoes on. I mean, who goes out, even in May, in the rain, at that time of night without a jacket of some sort? And who goes walking with little ballet pumps on? Think about it? Why would she do that?"

"Maybe it hadn't started raining when she left. Drunk. She got lost. Wandered off, tripped and passed out. Choked on her vomit." Josh shrugged his shoulders.

Mandy shook her head. "I want to know what her friends were doing. Why did they wait five hours before they thought there was something wrong? Where the hell did they think she'd gone? Why not ring earlier?" She shook her head. "There's something that doesn't feel right here. Let's go and speak to them. Have you got directions?"

8

"Yeah. It's not far back the way we came and then off to the left somewhere, I think. I spoke to the officer on the roadblock. He said it was a bit off the beaten track and there was a signpost in the hedge. We'd see it as we approached. The house isn't visible from the main road."

"Main road? A bit off the beaten track. Bloody hell. It's all off the beaten track out here, if you ask me. Come on then. Let's see what these young women have got to say. It could be an accident, I suppose. There are too many questions hanging about. And I'd like some answers.

CHAPTER TWO

"The house should be off here. On the left somewhere. There. On the side. There's a sign." Josh pointed to a wooden post with one word painted on it. Nythfa.

DI Wilde slowed and turned the 4x4 into the narrow lane. "Hell's bells. I thought getting this far was bad enough. This isn't a road. If Bertha was an inch wider, we'd be eating the hedgerows. Bloody countryside."

"It's not that bad. It's got a tarmac surface, hasn't it? Some of the farm roads are little more than dirt tracks. This is okay." Josh's voice had a defensive tone.

"Well, you'd know, country boy. What's Nythfa mean anyway?"

"Nesting place, I think."

"Hmm. Not much of a nesting place for that girl we found in the field. Anything from Rishi about the time for the post-mortem?"

DS Jones checked his phone. "No signal."

"Typical. No bloody Wi-Fi. Who the hell would want to live out here in the arse-end of no-where?"

"It's not that bad. I'd live out here if I could afford to move. Better than a flat in the city, that's for sure."

Mandy's eyes softened. Oh, sod it. She'd forgotten he'd split with his wife. Rented flat and still paying the mortgage on the house. No wonder the poor bugger was miserable. Always broke and no one to go home to. Not even a pet.

She glanced at him. "No progress on the home front then?"

"Nuh. We're seeing a counsellor…" He shrugged and swiped the screen of his phone again.

"Hey. What the hell do I know about marriage but, if you love each other there must be a way."

Josh grunted. Not much of a response. Buggered that one up then. Mandy was annoyed with herself. Why couldn't she have a normal conversation without putting her foot in it? Josh Jones could be a pain at times, but he was a bloody good detective, when he wasn't moaning about his marriage problems. Just as well he had no children. If the marriage ended it would be a clean split at least. Complications. No time for complications in her life. Apart from Joy, her twin. She shook her head. Every time a female body was found there was that fear.

The road veered. A sharp turn to the right and they found themselves in a large open space with an imposing house and garden.

"Well, that's not what I expected," said Mandy.

The building in front of them was nestled in between two rolling fields, cocooned between bushes and trees. The immediate surroundings had been landscaped and there was a paved space with several cars already parked there, including a marked police car. The house itself was not a typical country cottage. Architect designed. It looked modern yet constructed with traditional materials. A stone façade, like pebbles on a beach glistening in the soft rain, slate roof and a high glass atrium to the front of the building.

Mandy whistled. "Phew. Somebody's got a pound or two."

She got out of the car and stretched. At nearly six foot tall, DI Wilde was an impressive figure. Her hair had frizzed in the drizzle adding another inch. Lithe and fluid of movement she had the poise of a dancer. She took a moment to look around, sniffing and wrinkling her nose in distaste. Josh slammed the car door shut as he got out to join her. He was shorter and stockier than Mandy. It was easy to identify him as a rugby player for the division team. He sniffed the pungent air.

"Silage."

"That's what I thought. Smells like shit. So, how far away was the body found from here? As the crow flies. Half a mile? Which direction?"

Josh shrugged. "I could check on Google maps if I had a signal."

Mandy suppressed a sigh of frustration. Surely a country boy would be good at distances. They'd only travelled a couple of miles along that road, but it had felt like forever with all those bends and the constant thought that the next one could see something coming the other way. And that phone of his. Sometimes she thought it had been super-glued to his hand.

She turned her back on the house for a moment, getting her bearings and taking in the surrounding countryside. A couple of magpies chattered in a nearby tree, watching, waiting. Two for joy. Not much joy here. Not much joy for the dead girl either.

The house wasn't visible from the road, and they hadn't passed another dwelling on the way here. Well, not that she'd spotted anything, being careful to keep her eyes on the narrow road running like a varicose vein through the hedgerows. Why couldn't the farmers keep the hedges low so people could see if anything was coming? She squinted, turning her head right and left before pointing.

"I reckon over there. Probably no more than half a mile. Where the devil was she going? It's away from everything. If she'd wanted to go to the nearest village, she could have followed the road. I don't get it."

"Maybe she didn't have much of a sense of direction. Maybe she thought she was taking a short cut."

Mandy raised an eyebrow and Josh looked at the ground.

"That's your theory, is it? About why she didn't stick to the road? She left her friends in the house and wandered out in the middle of a bloody storm and decided to have a little ramble in the fields for fun. She had to climb the gate to get into the field in the first place. I daresay we'll know more when we've spoken to the others."

"Do you think it was an accident?"

Another raised eyebrow. "We'll see. It looks that way although there are things that don't fit. Not just the fact she was found in the field but that no one thought to report her missing until early light. She wasn't wearing a coat either and those shoes were not designed for country walks, even on sunny summer days. Something's not right. I'm keeping an open mind... we'd best go in and see what's what."

A uniformed officer was at the door waiting for them. He pointed towards the interior.

"They're waiting for you, ma'am. Door to the left."

Mandy frowned. She refused to let her team call her ma'am. Smacked of deference and while she expected some acknowledgement of her authority, she preferred to be called boss, or just Mandy on nights out.

The hallway was filled with light, even on such a dull day. A female officer was just coming out of the room indicated. She closed the door behind her, smiled and inclined her head towards it.

"They're all in there. I'm just making tea. Would you like some?"

"If there's green tea, please. And a strong black coffee for my sergeant. He needs something to get his brain going."

Josh winced.

Must stop it, Mandy reminded herself. Not a joke. He could report her for harassment or something. She attempted to smooth things over.

"Sorry, Josh. You just look a bit bleary, and we did have an early start."

He brightened at that. "I could do with a coffee. Let's see what we've got shall we? After you, ma'am." The deliberate use of the title made her smile. He was getting his own back at her.

The room they entered was big enough to hold two large sofas, a couple of lounge chairs and a coffee table at one end, clustered around a woodburning stove in a chimney breast made of the same dappled colours as the exterior wall. The other end of the room had a solid oak dining table and eight chairs. Someone had lit the stove and the smell of burning wood permeated the room. It reminded Mandy of bonfires. But this wasn't November. It was late May and the hawthorn blossom on the hedges outside had already faded to brown. Through a glass bi-fold door on the right they had a glorious view of fields rising to a copse at the top of a small hillock. The Vale was mainly flat with some undulating lowland hills. Nothing like the majestic Beacons or rugged moorland landscape of the Preselis. The walls of the room were painted a pale grey. The sofas were steel coloured with rugs and cushions in primary colours. Large canvas oil paintings in vivid hues made the whole room more vibrant.

Mandy stood for a moment taking in the full picture. Apart from a handbag tucked under one sofa and an empty glass on the coffee table, the room was show home perfect. On one sofa sat three young women, huddled together. One strawberry blonde, one dark-haired and one Asian. On the chair another blonde. Four pairs of eyes watched her, silent, wary. Mandy looked from one to the other, waiting, observing, making mental notes. The friends of the dead girl. They had a lot to tell her, but instinct told her to tread softly here. It could just be a terrible accident and she didn't need the Super on her back nagging her about protocol. Bloody protocol. What about gut feelings? There were secrets here. She could feel it in the air. A certain tension in the room. Secrets she meant to find out.

Taking her badge out of her jacket pocket Mandy waved it in the air. "I'm DI Wilde, Cardiff CID, and this is DS Jones. I believe you've been told that we've found a body. We think it's your friend, Megan Pritchard. It fits the description you gave to the police earlier." A gasp from the strawberry blonde. "We know this has been a terrible shock. We'll need to speak to each of you in turn in due course, however, perhaps, for now, you could tell us why you were here this weekend."

"It's just so awful. Poor Megan." The strawberry blonde sniffed, twisting her hands. Irish accent. Another unexpected. She tucked a lock of curly hair behind one ear, then dabbed her eyes. "It was supposed to be a fun weekend and..." The sniffs started again, and she grabbed the hand of the girl next to her.

Mandy turned her gaze on the other blonde, sitting upright and still in the chair. She was stick thin with eyes too big for her face and seemed to be making an effort to keep calm by gripping the arms of the chair so tightly her knuckles were white. She stared at Mandy with eyes the colour of storm clouds and took a deep breath. When she spoke, her voice was so quiet they had to strain to hear.

"It was a reunion. We were all at uni together in Cardiff. Ten years ago. I organised it. I thought we needed to get together and have some fun. We've all had... problems... over the last couple of years and Meg, that is, Megan, was talking about going to Australia so... it was... sort of a last chance for a get-together."

"Yes. Well, it was her last chance. That's for sure." Mandy paused. Let that sink in. "Why out here? I'd have thought a group of young women would have wanted a bit of a fling in the city. You know, clubbing and all that."

"I'm Sophie. Sophie Grant. This is our house. Well, the family house." She swallowed. "There was an old stone cottage and outhouse here. Dad had it knocked down and this house built. The idea was they'd come and live out here when he retired." A deep sigh. "I think he fancied the idea of keeping animals and living in the countryside. Mum hated the thought of it." She seemed to be rambling, working hard at staying in control.

"So, the house is usually empty?" Josh asked.

Sophie bit her bottom lip. "They had it all sorted. All the furniture, everything new. Everything ready to move. Then Dad had a massive heart attack. Last year. Neither Mum nor I could face doing anything for a while. It's going on the market next week. The estate agents have been to take measurements and stuff."

"So, an empty house equals a cheap weekend?" It wasn't really a question. It seemed a logical explanation and none of the young women disagreed. "Do you mind if I have a look round? My sergeant here will take a note of everyone's details, and we'll want to speak to all of you later. Which room was Megan's?"

"Top of the stairs. First on the left, beside the family bathroom."

Mandy turned and was about to leave when the other blonde spoke. "I...I'm Siobhan. I'm supposed to be on the ferry to Rosslare this afternoon. Em, I live there, you see. What do you think I should do?"

Mandy hesitated. At the moment she had no reason, other than a gut feeling, that there was something underneath the surface with this little reunion. She gave Siobhan one of her scornful looks, eyebrows raised, and lips pursed. The young woman flushed under the scrutiny.

"It's up to you. Unless you have pressing business in Rosslare, I'd have thought you'd want to hang on for a day or so to see what happened to your friend. We'll need your details in any case. My sergeant will make some notes and, as I said, we'll need to speak to you all again. Find out what happened here."

With a nod to Josh, Mandy left them to it. Four attractive young women. The thought of Josh dealing with them amused her. That should raise his spirits.

Mandy stood in the atrium for a moment, taking in her surroundings. It was all very modern. A stark contrast to her little house in Brithdir Street, with its overgrown patch of garden and view of the backs of other terraces.

The staircase was open tread, a pale oak with glass panels. The whole impression was of light and space. Her steps sounded hollow on the stairs as she made her way to the bedrooms. Everything in Megan's room was neat and tidy. A small suitcase and handbag sat on the floor by the door and a pile of clothes, neatly folded, with an open wash bag and a matching makeup bag, on the bed. The bed had been made. Everything looked pristine. Putting on gloves, Mandy, prodded in the wash bag. Toothbrush, toothpaste, various face creams and two blister packs of tablets. Migraine relief tablets and something else. Something she didn't recognise. She took a photo, bagged it, then checked in the suitcase and handbag. Usual stuff, but no mobile phone. She peeped into the other rooms. Everything was immaculate. Almost as though no one had been staying there, or the 'help' had been in and tidied up. There was something strange about the set-up here. Something very odd.

CHAPTER THREE

Diane Grant couldn't believe it. A police car at her door and Sophie and Siobhan being escorted from it by a policewoman. What on earth was going on? She opened the door, tight-lipped and straight backed with a smile that would have frozen lava. This was not the sort of thing that happened in Lisvane and certainly not in her cul-de-sac of six large, detached dwellings. She could see Mary in the house opposite peering out of the window, eager for gossip. As the party approached, she shook her head a little and pushed a strand of hair out of her eye.

"For goodness' sake, Sophie. Why are the police here? Where's your car?" The words were spoken in a quiet voice although there was no mistaking the frustration.

The police officer intervened.

"Your daughter and her friend have had a bit of a shock. We thought it best to bring them home. If you need help retrieving the car later, please let us know."

Diane looked at Sophie. She was pale, her arms wrapped around herself. She didn't meet her mother's eyes. Siobhan looked dazed with black shadows under her eyes.

"What on earth has happened? Your message didn't make any sense. Something about Megan. What's that girl done now?"

"She's dead." Sophie started shaking.

Diane's eyes opened wider, but she maintained her poise.

"I think we'd better continue this conversation inside. We're giving the neighbours a proper show here." She turned to the police officer. "Thank you, officer. I can manage from here. How kind of you to help."

"The DI will want to talk to the two of them later, though, as I said, they've not had a great start to the day." Her dark eyes were full of sympathy and concern.

Diane Grant blinked and gave a slight wave with her hand. What had happened? Megan dead? It didn't make sense. A car accident? Maybe Sophie's car wasn't fit to be driven. Once inside the house, she turned to Siobhan.

"I thought you were going to be catching the afternoon ferry from Pembroke Dock." Her tone made it seem more like an accusation than a question or statement.

"I was that, then the detective said she'd want to talk to us and, well, she didn't actually say, 'Don't leave the country' but it sure felt like it."

"I said she could stay here until things were sorted." Sophie's voice was a whisper.

"Things?"

"There'll be a post-mortem and stuff, won't there?"

Diane felt as though someone had slapped her face. "I hadn't thought about that." She hesitated for a moment. "What happened?"

Sophie exchanged glances with Siobhan before she answered. "We don't know. She went out and didn't come back. We'd had a bit to drink and, well, when it got daylight and she still hadn't come back we went to look for her." She stopped for a moment and took a deep breath. Diane noticed she was picking her nail varnish off as she was speaking. "We drove to the pub because we knew we'd have a signal around there, so we rang the police and reported her missing. Some bloke found her a couple of hours later and... and she was dead."

"That's awful. An accident then. How unfortunate. You both look washed out. I'll brew some coffee and I've some croissants to heat. I suggest you have a nice bath and then go to bed for a couple of hours after breakfast. You must be exhausted if you've been up half the night." Diane was aware she sounded imperious, yet someone needed to take charge. They could talk later when they were rested. What a dreadful thing to have happened. And at Nythfa too. That wouldn't help a potential sale. The police hanging around. Not good news at all.

"That sounds grand, Mrs Grant. Would you like a hand?"

"It's fine, Siobhan. Relax. We'll put you in one of the guest rooms. Did you have a reservation on the ferry?"

"Yes, I'd better ring them and let them know. I'll see if they'll change the ticket. Maybe if I explain..."

"You do that. I'll only be five minutes."

22

Diane's head was buzzing. She put a hand to her chest and exhaled when she got to the kitchen. Dear God, what next? Hadn't she had enough to deal with over the last couple of years without this? She didn't know what had happened at Nythfa, although she knew she needed to protect her daughter. Once the girls were resting, she'd make a telephone call. Superintendent Ross Withers was an old friend of David's. He'd be able to advise her and might even be able to smooth things along. She didn't know what he could do. Still, she'd talk to him anyway. Yes, that's what she'd do.

* * *

"I'm sorry," Sophie said to Siobhan as they made their way upstairs, "Mum's not been exactly welcoming. I'm sure she'll be alright later."

"Oh, don't worry about me. I won't hang around and get in her hair. God I'm exhausted though."

They made their way upstairs and Siobhan stared open-mouthed at the guest bedroom Sophie indicated.

The room was spacious with a bay window overlooking a landscaped garden. Although furnished with just a bed and bedside tables a row of glossy white fitted wardrobes ran the length of one wall. The carpet was the colour of clotted cream, so deep Siobhan's feet seemed to sink an inch, and the curtains were shot silk in the colour of a Blue Jay's wings. The bed had a runner along the bottom in the same colour and the pure white duvet and pillows looked crisp and expensive. The whole house, like Nythfa, breathed money.

"It's like an ideal home or a luxury hotel bedroom. Are those real paintings on the wall too?"

"Yes. Mum is quite talented herself, but in the circles my parents moved, collecting artwork was a bit of a thing. Some of them are worth thousands I suppose. I don't like most of them,' she shrugged, "but then what do I know?" Sophie opened a door to the left of the bedside table. "The bathroom is through here. All the rooms have their own so you can soak for as long as you like. No one will bother you."

Siobhan whistled. "Sure, the bathroom's as big as my kitchen. It's all so gorgeous. What in heaven made you leave all this luxury for a one bed box in London?"

Sophie raised an eyebrow. "Do you really need to ask that?" She turned slightly towards the landing.

"What will she do when she finds out?"

"I dread to think. I hate secrets and we seem to be caught up in something none of us expected. I just hope that the post-mortem is, well, over quickly I suppose."

An anxious frown creased Siobhan's forehead. "I wonder if they'll ask us any more questions. Do you think we should have told them about … you know?

"No. We've given the facts. The less we say the less they have to twist. We didn't do anything to Megan." Sophie sounded less than confident.

"I still feel a bit guilty. I mean, we should have tried to stop her wandering off into the dark. It was a bit weird, even by Megan's standards."

"It's your Catholic upbringing. Ditch the guilt. She was an absolute bitch to you. What you said was justified."

"But I was pissed. I'd never have said those things sober."

"No, that's true." Sophie said, her face softening. "Best to keep quiet about all that. Just ride it out. My mother has contacts in the force, well everywhere actually. I'm sure she'll make a few noises if she feels it's necessary."

Siobhan gazed into space. She looked as if she was thinking about it all.

"That DI was a bit full on, wasn't she? Scary. Made me feel worse."

"You haven't seen my mother in full flow."

Siobhan chuckled. "All Mams are like that. They know how to press all your buttons, don't they now? Do you think those croissants would be ready? I've still got the munchies. I'll just wash my face and hands and see you down there."

As Sophie made her way down to the kitchen her stomach was churning. That cool exterior of her mother's hid a furious temper. Diane was all about appearances. Mary would have already been to the village shop to spread the gossip. Looks would be exchanged the next time either of them was seen and there would be concerned calls to the house. Enquiries her mother would respond to with an air of insouciance, the calm façade. Sophie would be interrogated by her mother again. Still, she hadn't told her the truth about why she'd left London and as for Megan, well, they didn't really know what happened there, did they? She just hoped that DI didn't probe too deeply. Sometimes things were best left buried.

"Where's your friend?" Diane was putting china and cutlery on the table in the kitchen.

It was a light and spacious room, illuminated by bi-fold doors and Velux windows. The rain had stopped and a hazy sun was filtering through the clouds. On the lawn a group of sparrows was engaged in searching for worms or seeds or something. How much simpler a life they had. She spotted next door's cat creeping along under the hedge towards them, so they had danger in their lives, too. Why was life proving to be so difficult? She'd thought getting away from Cardiff and leading her own life would be, if not easy, at least enjoyable. Wrong. It had been a disaster of her own making. If her mother knew the consequences, it wouldn't be pleasant. Siobhan came in before Diane had a chance to ask anything.

"Ah, there you are, Siobhan. Do sit down. I've made the coffee." Diane bestowed another of her icy smiles on Siobhan as she fussed with plates, napkins, cups and saucers.

Sophie could feel Siobhan's eyes on her as Diane poured coffee. Sophie sipped it without saying a word. She'd found that the less she said the better. If she kept quiet, she was less likely to annoy her mother and less likely to slip up and say something she hadn't meant to. When had she learnt that? Siobhan was chattering away oblivious to the tension in the air, or so it seemed. Sophie was never so grateful to have a friend who could talk for Ireland and Wales put together. A constant stream of words. Siobhan asked about the garden, the paintings, the house, all the time eating and drinking her coffee. Diane was polite and responded although the air was fraught.

"Are you going to eat that or just play with it?" asked Diane.

Sophie dropped the piece of croissant she had in her hand and stood up. The chair scraped on the tiled floor.

"I'm not hungry. I'm going to have a bath and then a nap." Her mother couldn't control everything, could she?

"Isn't that a grand idea. I'll just put these cups and things in the dishwasher first." Siobhan got up and started to gather the crockery together.

"Oh no. I can't allow my guests to do that." Diane took the plates from Siobhan's hands. "A nice bath will help relax you, too. I'll be cooking dinner for seven-thirty. I'll see you then."

Dismissed. Siobhan raised her eyebrows at Sophie, and they left Diane clearing up in the kitchen. Stifling a yawn Siobhan said, "I don't think even that coffee will keep me awake. I hope I don't fall asleep and drown in the bath. I don't think your Mam would be too keen on clearing up after that."

Despite herself, Sophie giggled. No, her mother wouldn't like that at all.

* * *

"Are you alright, Bethan?" Aisha was sitting in the passenger seat of Bethan's blue Fiesta as they drove back to Cardiff. Bethan yawned, tiredness catching up.

They were all washed out by the effects of the night they'd just experienced.

"Yeah. I'm just a bit overwhelmed. I can't take it in. I don't believe she's dead."

"That detective said they'd want to speak to us all again. Make statements and stuff. They didn't say much about what they thought had happened, did they?" Aisha twisted the bangles on her wrist and peered out of the window as the greenery of the fields gave way to the shops around Culverhouse Cross.

Bethan just grunted and seemed intent on the road. Aisha felt the need to talk. This wasn't one of those things you could stick in a drawer and forget about. She'd lost family members, elderly people, but someone her own age – that was hard to come to terms with.

"She was in line for the job I wanted in London. She knew I wanted it. I was stupid enough to tell her so she went all out to prove she could do better than me."

Bethan waited to hear if there was more to the story. It was obvious Aisha was upset.

"I don't know why she thought she had to big herself up all the time. She was always telling everyone what an amazing account she'd clinched, or what a fantastic life she had. It was wearing." Aisha sighed.

At last, Bethan was moved to speak. "Yeah. I know. I've had years of it. That's why I didn't compete with her. There was no point. I could have done accountancy too, I had the grades, but I knew that she'd do anything to be top dog."

They were winding their way through Ely at a slow pace. It seemed every set of traffic lights changed to red as they got to them. Bethan tapped her fingers on the steering wheel. She turned her head towards Aisha.

"What about the London job now?"

"I expect they'll offer it to me. I was second choice."

"Will you take it?"

"Yes, if it's offered. Huge salary and perks. Travel. Opportunity. A dream come true."

At what cost? It made Aisha uncomfortable thinking about it. Dead woman's shoes. A shiver passed through her body.

CHAPTER FOUR

"Pass this on to Rishi, will you please?"

Mandy handed the evidence bag with the blister packs to Josh as they got back into the car.

"What are they?"

"Painkillers and something else. Not sure what it is. Rishi will know. No sign of her mobile phone but everything else neat and tidy. Nothing out of place in that house and I mean nothing. It doesn't look as if any of them stayed there for the weekend. You'd think after a party it would be a bit messy."

"I think that's probably to do with the fact the house is going on the market. Sophie seemed anxious about her mother's reactions."

"There's something off here. I can't figure out what yet."

They'd left the house and were winding their way back to the city.

"Have they sent a family liaison officer to Megan's family?" Mandy asked.

"Yes. I believe so. We'll need formal identification, though it seems pretty clear the body is that of Megan Pritchard."

"They must be bloody devastated. Your daughter goes off for a reunion weekend and never comes back." Mandy shook her head. "And we're going to have to talk to them, too. Find out a bit more." Further intrusion into a family already bereft. At times she hated this job. Dealing with other people's grief while keeping her own fears and worries at bay.

They passed Cowbridge again on the way back to the city. It was the spot for upmarket shopping with its independent boutiques and gourmet pubs. The Vale was popular because of its share of quaint pubs and country walks. Not that Mandy appreciated either of those. Their trip back to the city was trouble free and by noon they were approaching a well-kept semi, with a blue painted door, in the Llandaff area of the city. They'd parked a little way down the road. The doorbell echoed in the hallway and a female police officer opened the door. Mandy recognised her. DC Helen Probert.

"Helen. Where are they?"

Helen waved to a room at the back of the house. "In there. Mum's a train wreck, Dad's gone to the garden and sister is trying to hold them all together." She kept her voice low, not wanting to be overheard.

Taking a deep breath, Mandy and Josh followed Helen into a pleasant and light room leading through French doors on to a garden. A man was digging a patch under an apple tree as if his life depended on it. The room held a sofa, two easy chairs and a large flat screen television as well as a couple of low side tables. Family photographs hung on the walls. Smiling faces. Happier times. A grey dog, of dubious breed, wandered into the room, sniffed at Mandy's legs and then lay down in front of the open fireplace. Catrin Pritchard and

31

her other daughter, Nia, Megan's younger sister, sat on the sofa together, holding hands.

"Mrs Pritchard, I'm sorry for your loss."

Catrin Pritchard raised reddened eyes to meet Mandy's. "My Megan. Are you sure it's her? Could it not be a mistake?"

This was the worst bit. The dashing of hope. It never got easier. "Someone will have to make a formal identification. However, from the description we were given and where she was found, we are fairly certain that it's your daughter. I'm so sorry."

"What happened? Was it an accident or did somebody do something to her? Has she been, you know, interfered with?" The voice trailed away. Catrin sniffed and started crying again. Nia passed her a tissue and waited. Dark hair and eyes. So like Megan. There was no doubt. Mandy gestured for Helen to make some tea. The panacea for all ills.

"We don't think she was attacked in any way. There will be a post-mortem to establish time and cause of death. We're just trying to find out more about what happened. What can you tell us about Megan? Did she live here?"

Mrs Pritchard shook her head. Nia answered. "No. Not since she left uni. She had a flat in the Bay. There's a spare key here. She left it in case she locked herself out or she was ill or anything. Emergency use only. We didn't go there." She got to her feet and wandered off to search for the key.

"Was there a reason you didn't visit your daughter?"

"She was always busy. She worked so hard, my Megan. She'd come up here to see us at the beginning of every month. Tell us all about the job and that." She sniffed again. "Such a good girl."

"What about her friends? Boyfriends?"

Nia had come back with a keyring. "Oh. Rhys." She put a hand to her mouth. "Has anyone told Rhys?"

"Boyfriend?"

"Yes. He doesn't live in Cardiff though. I think they tended to see each other weekends. He lives in Chepstow. He's got a gardening business based there. Rhys Davies Landscaping. He'd come up to Cardiff some weekends, from what Meg posted on Facebook. She didn't bring him here."

"You didn't see much of your sister then?" Mandy sensed some tension in Nia when she spoke about Megan. More secrets.

"Not a lot. We have, we had," she corrected herself, "different ways of seeing the world."

Mandy thought about it. An interesting comment. What differences did they have? But it wasn't the right time to ask those questions.

"We'll be in touch, Mrs Pritchard. Helen, your liaison officer, is our link. If there's anything you can think of that might help us, then ask her to contact me. I'm sorry to have to intrude at such a time."

Nia followed them out into the hallway. "Here's the address of the flat here." She handed them a piece of paper. "Megan was the golden girl. Did well at university. Landed a good job. Didn't drink or smoke or go to wild parties. An impossible act to follow."

"Didn't drink?"

"No. She was on medication. High anxiety levels. Tried mixing the two and ended up in hospital. After that she never touched the stuff. Unlike her little sister. It's going to take a few shots of something to get me through this. Mum is in meltdown. Dad in denial and I'm holding everyone up." Her face reflected the strain she was feeling and her hands shook a little.

"Speak to Helen. You'll need access to counselling. You need to be strong for your Mam."

Nia's eyes filled and she blinked to stop the tears. She gave Mandy a watery smile.

"Did you get on with your sister?"

"We were siblings. There was always rivalry. You know what I mean."

Oh yes, only too well. Mandy and her twin had shared more than a womb. Despite their closeness there had been competitiveness and challenges. Siblings were like that. She waited for Nia to say more.

"We just went our separate ways. There were six years between us. Mam lost a baby in between. We were never that close but, at the end of the day, she was still my sister." Nia swallowed. "Where did they find her? Can you tell me what you think happened? I'd like to know so I'm prepared." She looked back towards the room where her mother was sitting, gazing into nothingness.

"Megan's body was found in a field in the Vale. She was at a house party and went missing after midnight."

"House party? Who with?"

"Her friends from uni. I'm surprised you didn't know about it. A reunion get together before Megan went to Australia. Do you know when she was planning to do that?"

Nia frowned and shook her head. "Australia? First I've heard of it. I wouldn't know." She hesitated a moment. "We didn't talk that much to each other. Not after she left here."

"Was there a particular reason for that?" It felt intrusive to be asking the question although it could be significant.

Nia just shook her head. "I think Megan had high aspirations. She was determined she was going to get to the top of her field and didn't care who she hurt on the way there. I think she was ashamed of her roots. Ashamed of us." She sniffed and turned away.

As they left the house and walked down the pathway Mandy turned to Josh.

"Well? Thoughts."

"Rift in the family of some sort. Friction between the sisters. Was she going to Australia? I thought Sophie said the purpose of the reunion was to get them all together before Megan emigrated, or was it just a holiday? If she never touched the booze how come Rishi could smell it on her body. And what had made her sick?"

"Exactly. Too many questions. More than an accident do you think? Too many variables on this one. If she never touched the booze because she knew the dangers, why the hell would she do so on a weekend away?"

"You think someone spiked her drink? But they were all friends, weren't they?"

"Were they? A good question, Josh. A bloody good one. We need to find out more. We'll be lucky to get home for food this evening the way this is going."

Taking a peek at Josh's face she grinned. "Don't worry. We'll stop and grab a sandwich before the post-mortem. Or maybe after, if you're squeamish."

Josh's phone rang at that point. He listened and a glimmer of satisfaction crossed his face.

"Saved by the bell. Rishi. He can't do the PM this afternoon. Seems there's a problem at the mortuary. He says he'll do it early tomorrow morning if you want to pop along. He sounded a bit flat."

"Ah, well. That's because he now has to spend the afternoon with his bloody mother-in-law. He calls her Mrs Crocodile."

"They don't get on then?"

"Apparently she spends all her time telling her daughter that Rishi isn't good enough for her. This is despite the fact they've been married ten years and have two gorgeous little girls."

"She sounds just like my mother-in-law. Interfering cow."

Josh spat the words and Mandy could see his hands were forming fists. Oops. A raw point. Time to change the subject.

"Little trip down the Bay? Pick up a sarnie and a drink from Tesco? Stop that rumbling gut of yours, at least. Then we'll pay a nice little visit to Megan's flat. There may be some clues there about her life. Something we can ask the others, perhaps."

They stopped at the supermarket before parking outside Nautica, a block of luxury flats overlooking Cardiff Bay and across to Penarth Marina. The concierge looked surprised when they showed their badges but indicated where they were to go. They'd let him speculate and ask any questions, if they had any, on the way out. Mandy remembered the pristine room at Nythfa and wondered what would greet them inside. One thing for certain, Megan Pritchard earned more than a detective. The apartments were in a good position with stunning views, within walking distance to all the eateries and entertainment, yet a little quieter than some of the other blocks.

They entered the apartment on the third floor and surveyed the surroundings. A diffuser in the hallway gave a faint fragrance of magnolia and the place was sizeable by modern standards. They could see a generous living room to the left with French doors leading to a balcony stretching its length and corner windows to make the most of the views. Mandy whistled.

"How much do you reckon, Josh? Just short of 300k?" Despite the size of the room, it was sparsely furnished. A sofa, coffee table, bean bag, small dining table and two chairs which could have doubled as a patio set on the balcony.

"Did she buy or rent? The sister didn't say. I suppose we need to ask. Not exactly tidy, was she?" Josh asked.

Mandy didn't respond to Josh's comment, thinking of the mess Joy had left behind when she'd swanned off to Greece the year before, leaving her in charge of Tabitha. Josh was right about this place. Pristine it was not. Clothes were scattered on the sofa and the back of the chairs. Carrier bags and magazines littered the coffee table. An empty mug and the remote control for the large screen television sat on the floor beside the sofa.

The kitchen was in a similar state. Stale food in the fridge, dirty plates in the sink and spillage on the top of the ceramic hob. Two other rooms. The first a bedroom; bed unmade, dirty clothes on the floor, en-suite bathroom smelling damp and mouldy. The second a study with desk and chair, piles of scrunched up paper around it and another mug which had left a ring stain on the top of the desk. A laptop had been left open although switched off.

"Better bag that. It may tell us something about her state of mind." Mandy sighed. "I suppose we have three options here. Either it was an accident, or she deliberately took the mix of drink and drugs because she was depressed or overanxious. Third option, someone spiked her drink. Whatever, it's all pretty bloody awful. Waste of a life. What age was she? Thirty-two? Far too young to die."

Josh grunted. "Well, if she really didn't drink, and there's no evidence of anything here, it's either suicide or a deliberate act by one of her friends. Why would anyone do that? And how could she not know she was drinking alcohol?"

"If she drank something strongly flavoured, like Coke or ginger beer, I suppose vodka could be added without her noticing until she felt the effects. But we're speculating here. We'll see what Rishi has to tell us tomorrow. And we'll need to speak again to those four young women." She took another peek out through the window and sighed. Bet Josh's rented flat didn't have a view like this one. It certainly beat the row of terraced roofs she could see from her house in Brithdir Street and the tiny, neglected garden. "If we drop the laptop off with the tech boys, I think we can call it a day. I want to spend some time with my niece, and you look as if you need a nap. Until we get some further information we need to tread softly."

"Right, boss."

"And don't eat anything too fatty tonight or have a gut full of beer. The smell of dead bodies is not a pleasant one."

Josh grimaced at the thought. Mandy remembered his first PM when she'd been with him and he'd been sick in the corridor. Who knew what tomorrow might bring? Whatever, they had to find out what happened to Megan.

* * *

Josh opened the door to his flat, if it could be called that. One room and a bathroom. Not room even to swing the proverbial cat.

"Studio apartment, stunning and modern," the agent had said, stepping aside to let Josh see the space. He'd taken it as it was clean, affordable, on top of the mortgage on the house, and convenient. He reasoned with himself that it wasn't forever, signing up for three months. Short term leases were unusual the agent told him, and the landlord was very amenable so he could extend on a rolling monthly basis if he wanted. At the time, three months seemed reasonable. He'd be back with Lisa by then he'd thought, and he couldn't have gone on sofa-surfing. A week with his brother Jack, two toddlers and Gemma giving him the evil eye every time he came through the door, followed by two weeks with his mate Karl who played loud music at all hours had been enough. He needed somewhere to have peace and quiet. Somewhere to think. No nosy neighbours. Anonymity guaranteed.

Josh put his keys on the work surface. It was modern alright. All shades of grey just like his life. Just as untidy as Megan's flat had been except it didn't have the space, or the view. Two small windows with a view of the carpark and street. It stank of the curry he'd had last night, and his bedding needed to be changed too. The bed settee was left open with the tangled sheets and pillows evidence of his disrupted night's sleep. His cell. That's what it felt like.

His brother Jack had warned him before he'd got married. "She's a spender that one. High maintenance. Just watch it. Keep hold of the purse strings, mate."

Jack had been right of course. First the house in Rhiwbina which needed so much work the already crippling mortgage had to be extended. Then Lisa had a bout of depression and was off sick for months. The worst was when she was made redundant after a restructuring. He'd begged her to find a job, any job, to help with the debts, but she'd refused.

"I can't just do any job. How would that look on my CV? I need to get something decent. You can see that, can't you Josh?"

The strain was ripping them apart. Lisa couldn't understand that the job wasn't nine to five and he was grateful for any overtime going. Now, five months after their split, with a mortgage, rent on the flat and living expenses, the debt was growing. It felt like a sack of potatoes on his head all the time. He hoped that the boss was right, and this case wasn't accidental. At least then there would be overtime.

When he thought about Mandy Wilde it was with respect. The DI was a good detective, working on instinct as much as anything else. She didn't always play by the rule book though and that had led to a few dicey situations in the year or so he'd been working with her. She was tough, but fair, kept herself to herself much of the time and had worked hard to get where she was. A certain amount of prejudice still simmered under the surface of the force. However, she'd bulldozed her way through, determined to get to the top. It was as if she regarded barriers as something to be broken down rather than navigated. No wonder the Super wanted to keep her in check. Ross Withers was old school, near retirement, and liked everything and everybody to keep to strict protocols.

It was going to be interesting to see how this latest case panned out. It was a strange one. There was nothing to suggest foul play and yet there were things that just didn't stack up. He'd spoken to the four young women and they were all intelligent, all with the same story. Megan had gone out. They were worried when she didn't come back. Rang the police and distressed that she was dead. If Megan Pritchard was in the habit of getting hammered on a Saturday night, then the alcohol induced vomit wouldn't be unusual. The fact she never touched the stuff was the problem.

Josh surveyed the mess in the flat. He should tidy up. Tiredness hit him as he flopped down on the bed settee. Just a ten-minute nap. Then he'd sort it all out. He was asleep within seconds.

CHAPTER FIVE

MONDAY

Monday mornings were always crap but to start the week with a post-mortem wasn't great. Mandy hadn't slept well, waking at three o'clock with a dream of her twin standing on a cliff edge ready to jump off. She'd woken in a sweat and had to go downstairs to get a drink.

It was never really dark in the city and she was grateful for that. She imagined that Nythfa was swathed in darkness in the night. Why hadn't Megan stayed on the road? She took the glass of water upstairs and tried to read. Despite thinking sleep was impossible, Mandy must have dozed as the alarm dragged her out of bed at six thirty.

Now, less than a couple of hours later, she was in the car again with Josh making their way through Cardiff to the morgue in Llandough hospital. The hospital was on the top of a hill and, as they were early, Mandy drove around searching for a parking place. Building work always seemed to be going on and the sound of drilling and machinery disturbed the peace of the countryside around.

"Nowhere to bloody park at this place, ever," Mandy sighed. Then, on her second circuit, at the back of the building she noticed someone reversing. She zipped into the empty space and grinned at Josh.

"A good sign. Now let's see what our esteemed colleague has to say."

The mortuary was at the back of the building, out of sight. It wouldn't do to make patients and their visitors aware of death.

Hospitals always made Mandy uncomfortable. Too many memories associated with her sister. Trips to A&E. Bad times. Better if she forgot all that.

Josh sniffed as they entered the building. Mandy turned to him, a glint in her eye.

"I always think the smell in hospitals in the morning is quite disgusting. It's that mixture of disinfectant, fried bacon and shit. Gets you every time." She took a small blue jar out of her pocket and passed it to him.

"What's this?"

"A trick the paramedics use. Vicks vapour rub. Put a bit under your nose before we go in. Helps to cover the stench."

Josh swallowed and paled a little, then did as he was told before passing the jar back to Mandy.

"Ready?"

He nodded and they entered the mortuary. Mandy knew that the smell could be overpowering at first, but they'd soon get used to it. Too long in there and it would cling and she'd feel as though she was travelling in a cloud of death all day. Rishi was waiting for them.

"Well, Rishi. Did you have a good afternoon with the old mother-in-law?" Mandy tried not to laugh as Rishi rolled his eyes.

"That woman. I have dreams of having her here on the slab. She causes nothing but disharmony. Yesterday, she was telling my girls that when they came to be married, she'd find them husbands who would do something good with their lives. 'Something better than being a glorified butcher,' were her exact words. My wife thought it was funny. I did not. I gave her one of my stares." He demonstrated and Mandy resisted the urge to laugh. Rishi was a sweetie, and his stare wouldn't have intimidated a child, never mind a mature woman with strong opinions.

"Oh hell. Not much fun then. Maybe next time you could ask her to read one of your scientific papers and give her opinion on it." They had more serious business to attend to. "So, Megan Pritchard. Time of death? How do you think she died?"

"Time of death, taking temperatures into account last night, between midnight and one in the morning. Cause of death was asphyxiation. Basically, she choked on her vomit. I've sent samples for toxicology and stressed that we need a quick result," he shrugged, "it could take all week. They say they're busy."

Mandy raised an eyebrow. "They're always bloody busy. You said you could smell alcohol in the vomit. She'd been drinking. Do you know what?"

"From the stomach contents I'd say Coke and something else. By the way, she'd eaten a quiche, salad and cake as well."

"What about that medication? She had pain relief tablets in her bag and something else. You should have had the sample. Hang on. I made a note of the name."

She took her phone out of her pocket and scrolled down to the photograph she'd taken of the medication in Megan's wash bag.

Rishi exhaled.

"Yes, I've examined it. That's an antipsychotic. She should never be mixing alcohol with drugs of that sort. She'd know that if she'd read the contraindications. It can cause drowsiness, confusion and in some cases, hallucinations."

"Yes. Her sister told us that's why she didn't drink. I don't like it. Why? All the signs say accident, but my gut tells me something else. The jigsaw pieces don't quite fit."

Although Mandy had got used to the smell in the mortuary, she could see that Josh's colour was changing from white to green. Time to make a retreat. As they were leaving, she remembered something.

"That earring. You said it wasn't hers. Any chance of evidence on it? DNA? Fingerprint?"

"No. The rain and mud would have washed away any evidence. All I can say is that it hadn't been in the ground too long otherwise the mud would have caked around it."

"Hmmm. What about her phone? Did she have anything in her pockets?"

"No. Not even a tissue. And the Rolex; that was a fake. She probably bought it abroad. They do good deals in places like Istanbul. You can't tell the difference unless you know what you're looking for."

"Which is?"

Rishi lifted the watch from a tray on the trolley next to the body.

"There are several ways to check. I used the magnifying glass and the small crown above the 6 o'clock is faulty. See?" He passed the watch and magnifier to Mandy. She squinted through it until she could get the symbol in focus."

"That's tiny. Barely visible."

"Indeed. But you can see how it doesn't match the more visible etching at the top. The cyclops is also shoddy."

"Now you've got me."

"Over the date there is a magnifying glass. You will see this one is not smooth. And finally, the serial number is imprecise. The workmanship is poor."

"Well, Rishi, I didn't know you were such an expert in jewellery. Remind me to take you with me shopping if I ever want to buy a Rolex."

He beamed at them, pleased to have imparted something that could be useful.

"Let me know as soon as those lab tests come back, won't you? Push them a bit." said Mandy. "At the moment, we don't know what we're dealing with. Accident or something else."

"Well, there's no signs of a struggle or defence wounds. No sexual assault. It seems as though she stumbled, fell and then was sick. The mix of drink and drugs would have made her unstable, physically and mentally. If she went out alone in the dark it's possible that she just became disorientated, neurotic, maybe hallucinating. Poor girl."

With a nod of thanks Mandy and Josh left Rishi to get on with his report.

"We haven't got her phone yet, have we? SOCOs didn't report it."

"No. Nothing on the body or in the field apparently."

"Organise a more extensive search of the area," Mandy said. "The house, surroundings, road and where she was found. She must have had a phone. And rustle up her phone records. Actually, do that for all of them. It won't do any harm for us to check up on what's been going on before this goes any further. Now, let's get back to the station and see if anything else has happened.

* * *

When they got back to the station the desk sergeant acknowledged them and spoke to Mandy.

"Superintendent Withers is asking for you."

Josh grimaced. "Oops. Now what have you been up to? Not another warning about not following procedure, I hope."

"Oh hell. Withering has it in for me. Doesn't like women in the CID, does he?"

"Especially ones that talk back at him. You need to be careful, boss."

"I'll use my natural charm."

She winked at Josh, and they went up the stairs to the open plan office. Mandy went to the ladies and tried to comb her hair into a presentable state. She washed her hands and face in the hope she didn't smell too badly of the mortuary. Then again, why the hell should she bother? She'd heard that old Withering, as she called him, was fond of the ladies although not those in his team. Oh well, sod the old bastard. She was a bloody good detective and if she didn't always do things strictly by the book, perhaps the book needed to be rewritten. With a final straightening of her top and trousers she headed to the Super's office.

"Sir. You wanted to see me?"

"Close the door, Wilde."

Oh shit. That wasn't good. She tried to think through the last week. Had she stepped too close to the line at any point? Schooling her face to remain impassive, she met the Superintendent's eyes.

"You're working on the Pritchard case." Statement. Not a question. Direct. To the point.

"Yes, sir."

"Preliminary thoughts?"

Mandy tried not to frown. Why was Withers interested in the case?

"Things are unclear, sir."

"What do you mean? An accident, wasn't it? Any signs of injury to indicate anything else. What about the PM? What's the verdict?"

Bugger. It was like being interrogated by Internal Affairs or something. Mandy took a deep breath. She was still standing and towering over Withers, so she could see his bald spot, though it didn't make her feel any happier. In fact, she was feeling distinctly damp under her armpits.

"It appears Megan Pritchard died by choking on her own vomit. There was alcohol in the vomit."

He nodded, a slight smirk on his face. "Good. Good. Death by misadventure. Case closed."

"Well…"

"Well what?" The smirk was gone replaced by a frown.

"Megan Pritchard didn't drink. She was on anti-psychotic drugs, which she knew interacted negatively with alcohol."

"And? What are you getting at, Wilde?"

Mandy swallowed. "Well, if she never drank because she knew of the side effects of the medication, why do so now? And," she was warming to her theme, "why, if she left the house around midnight, did the others not sound the alarm until five in the morning? It just doesn't add up. Sir."

"Well, I suppose there are questions to be answered. I want a softly, softly approach on this one. I know your enthusiasm has led you to use some unorthodox methods in the past," He glared at her before carrying on, "but I have personal reasons why I should like this to go smoothly and with as little fuss as possible. Diane Grant rang me. She is the widow of a friend of mine. David died in the last year. In fact, Sophie is my goddaughter. They've had quite a time of it since David's death. They don't need any more hassle. Understood?"

"Perfectly, sir. Kitten paws on this one. What about the press?"

"Keep the press out of it. No one needs to know anything at this time, do they? If the press get hold of it, they'll make it into something else."

Good. Press involvement often complicated things.

"Take Jones and that new girl, what's her name, Olivia something, with you on this one. She's keen to move to CID. Fast tracked. Give her a taster. Look after her."

"Oh, I think Josh and I can..." She caught the expression on Withers' face and paused. "Yes, sir. We'll involve Constable Wyglendacz. I'm sure she'll be a great help."

If Withers noticed the sarcasm in her voice, he made no comment, just waved a hand in dismissal.

Olivia was a nice girl. Too nice. She'd probably blow a gasket when she heard some of the words Mandy used when she got angry or frustrated. Plus, as far as she knew, Olivia liked everything to be black or white and Mandy worked in several shades of grey when it came to detective work.

Could be worse. At least he hadn't taken her off the case and given it to someone else. Every cloud. A bubble of laughter fizzed inside her. She couldn't wait to see Josh's face when she told him that goody-two-shoes Wyglendacz was going to be in the team. They'd already crossed paths over the coffee machine. She was still grinning when she got to the office. Helen, the liaison officer, was there, so that was good. Interesting core team to have working with her although, if it turned out to be a homicide, they'd need a few more bodies to help with the legwork.

"Josh. The Super has asked us to include Constable Wyglendacz. She's going to be part of the investigating team. Ask her to join us in the briefing room, would you, please? A little recap I think before we decide on next steps."

Josh's mouth opened and formed a silent "what?" before he got to his feet and went off in search of Olivia. Mandy and Helen made their way to the briefing room with Josh on their heels and a flushed Olivia following him, notebook and pen in hand. Mandy suppressed a smile. She'd soon lose that enthusiasm when she'd seen a few of the things they had to deal with in the CID.

CHAPTER SIX

When the door closed behind her, Mandy surveyed her crew. A skeleton team for a simple investigation. Withers had made it obvious what he thought the outcome should be so it wouldn't be long before he was itching for a result. Perching on the edge of a desk, Mandy addressed them.

"Okay, folks. Let's see where we are on this one. Just so you are aware, Sophie Grant, one of the young ladies at Nythfa, and whose mother owns the house, happens to be the Super's god-daughter."

Josh whistled. "No pressure then."

"We'll do what we can to find out what happened. Meanwhile, let's recap what we've got so far and see where we go next. Helen. The family. Have they made the formal identification yet?"

"Yes. We just missed you at the mortuary. Rishi said you'd left a short time before we got there. The three of them came in. The mother almost had to be carried out. Dad appeared… well, sort of empty too. Tragic."

"And the sister, Nia?"

"She's been holding them together. I gather Mum and Dad worshipped Megan. Clever girl. Always did well in school. Great job. Nice flat, so on. That's what they keep telling me. They're still in shock."

"They've seen it? The flat, I mean. Been there? Thought she didn't have them there. That's what they said, isn't it?" Mandy thought of that untidy place. Soulless. Despite the superb view it had no warmth or personality. For all her expensive clothes and jewellery there was something missing from Megan's life.

"I had the impression she'd shown them photographs of the interior or perhaps told them about it. I don't think they'd visited."

"Hmm. Odd. You'd think she'd want to show it off, wouldn't you? Fancy place in a prime spot. Although we've seen it and sparse is probably the word to use."

Josh was of the same opinion. "Is there anything of hers left in her Mam's house?"

"No sign apart from all the photographs. Megan's achievements in glorious technicolour adorning the walls. I gather she took everything she wanted with her after she moved out. She'd shared a room with Nia and there's nothing of hers there now."

A glance at Josh showed he was thinking the same thing. There was no evidence in the flat of Megan's early days. No photographs of family or friends, favourite books, school memorabilia, soft toys. It was as if she ditched her early life.

"Anything else, Helen? Anything we need to be aware of?"

"Well," she said with a slight frown on her face, "I'm concerned about Nia. She's a bit tearful at times. I get the feeling there's something she wants to say but can't. A couple of times she opened her mouth and then changed her mind, walked off, made a cup of tea or something."

Another nod. "Stay close. See if you can get her to open up about Megan and her friends. Any disputes. What she was like as a child. Anything at all. You never know what little gems could drop out." Mandy turned her head and attention towards the new member of the team. "Olivia. What are you doing? Why are you scribbling in that notebook?"

DC Wyglendacz looked up from her notes. Startled blue eyes over the top of her glasses. "I'm making notes, Ma'am. The main points. Plan of action. That sort…" Her voice faded as she became aware of three pairs of eyes gazing at her.

Mandy closed her eyes, bent her head towards the floor and made a silent count to ten before she opened them again and glared at Olivia.

"If I need you to do that, I'll make it very clear. For now, just listen to get up to speed and see if you can contribute to our thoughts and ideas. Got it?"

"Yes, ma'am."

"And don't call me ma'am." Her voice was more strident than she intended, and she could see Helen and Josh exchange a look as Olivia made a gulping sound. Mandy could have kicked herself. Must remember to be nice. The Super will know if you aren't. Remember, you were like that once. No. Never as acquiescent. Always bolshie.

"So, to recap. We have a death which I think is suspicious, but there's no real evidence. The Super wants it sorted double-quick which means we need to find out what happened at that party on Saturday night. Josh, can you have a search through Facebook, see if there's anything there and the boyfriend, Rhys, has he been told of Megan's death?"

"Yes, boss. Local boys called with him."

"We'll want to talk to him at some point.' Mandy addressed Olivia, "So, next steps, if you want to make notes. Background for Megan, Rhys Davies and those four young women. See what we can find out about Megan's state of mind. That sort of thing. I don't think she did it deliberately, although we need to cover every corner and our backs." She stood, ready for action. "Wyglendacz, with me. We're going to talk to Sophie and Siobhan. Maybe they'll open up a bit more if there's someone younger and prettier than Josh here." She gave Josh a conspiratorial smile as she said it. Wouldn't do to upset anyone. "It just might make them a bit more relaxed."

Olivia leapt to her feet, her eyes alight with anticipation and, Mandy surmised from the slight tremble, apprehension. "Yes, ma'am, ahh…"

"Boss will do. Let's get cracking. We need to get a timeline as priority. Just watch and listen. Make notes." The girl could prove to be useful. She could write up a basic report from her notes. Let's hope they found something helpful. A clue was needed if they were to solve this case before Ross Withers started to breathe smoke and flames down the back of her neck.

* * *

Lisvane. One of the most prestigious areas of the city with some homes in the region of a million plus. The Grant home was at the head of the close with ample parking space. As Mandy drew her Juke in between the garage and the front door she noticed a blue mini to one side. She'd seen the car at Nythfa. Sophie's. So, they hadn't wasted much time collecting it.

She was about to ring the doorbell when, through the glass porch, she saw a figure approaching. It had to be Sophie Grant's mother. Immaculately groomed with a patterned shift dress in what resembled silk, her hair sleek and styled in a chin length bob and with full make-up, she was every inch the rich sophisticate. Mandy showed her badge and introduced Olivia.

Diane Grant invited them in with a slight inclination of her wrist. "Wyglendacz. An unusual name. Polish?"

Olivia said, "Yes. My Bampi. He came here after the war, he..."

She was about to say more when Mandy silenced her with a look. This was business not small talk. Besides she'd seen that shadow of distaste cross Diane Grant's face when she heard Olivia's Valley's accent. The woman was a snob. No doubt about that.

Diane's smile was polite. A gesture. Somehow the calmness of the woman irritated Mandy. She could imagine Withers salivating over her. Her husband had some serious money judging from this house and the other one in the Vale. Like Nythfa, it was a picture of elegance. It was similar to the photographs from House Beautiful that Mandy had seen in the dentist's waiting room. Pale blues, smoky greys and silvery whites were the landscape for bolder contrasts in the paintings on the walls. The wood block floors gleamed. It felt more like a show house than a place where you could kick off your shoes and relax.

"The girls are in the conservatory. Do come through." They followed Diane's ramrod straight back as she led them down a wide hallway through the open plan kitchen to the conservatory. The view outside showed a garden as neat and well organised as the house. Bet every blade of grass stands to attention, thought Mandy. A million miles away from her straggly bit of lawn and overgrown flower bed.

"Perhaps you'd like a cup of tea, or coffee?" They could smell fresh-brewed coffee and Mandy was reminded of the advice given to prospective home sellers to have bread baking or coffee brewing to encourage house sales. This house didn't need that. Not if you had the money, that is. It was pristine, almost as if no one lived in it most of the time.

"That's very kind of you but no thanks. We just need to get some information from Sophie and Siobhan and then we'll leave you in peace. Is there somewhere we could speak privately? Perhaps to Sophie first?"

Another faint social smile. "Of course. Such an unfortunate accident. The girls are quite shaken by it all. I do hope it won't take long or upset them anymore."

She was going to be difficult, that was obvious. Mandy didn't care. A little upset was nothing in comparison to the destruction to the Pritchard family. "We just need to establish a timeline and talk about Megan, so we can get a clearer picture of what happened. The facts are a little sketchy and we need to have everything clear for the coroner. I'm sure you understand."

"Of course. You can use the small lounge. Sophie will take you." She turned to the young women sitting

57

in the conservatory. "Darlings, the inspector wishes to talk to you. Just routine. In the little lounge, Sophie."

Sophie pulled the sleeves of her loose cardigan down over her hands and chewed the inside of her cheek. She led the way to the room. The small lounge was the size of the ground floor of Mandy's house and furnished with cream leather sofas, low side tables and a large television attached to the wall. No cables so it must have been wired into the wall itself. Another expensive option but then it was obvious that there was no shortage of money in this family. Sophie sat on one sofa with Mandy and Olivia on the other. The young woman was a bundle of nerves, pulling at her fingernails and blinking, so unsure of herself. Mandy wondered if she was always like that or as the result of having a domineering mother. Easy questions to start.

"How are you feeling today, Sophie?"

Sophie swallowed before a whispered, "Okay, I suppose."

"It hasn't been easy for you. Your father died last year, and I believe you were living in London until a couple of months ago."

"Yes. That's right."

Mandy was all sympathy. "That's quite a bit of change in a short time. Now this."

"Yes. It's been hard."

God it was like pulling teeth. The girl had problems. Anorexia by her appearance or perhaps just depression. How to get her to relax and open up?

"Did you like living in London? I thought I might join the Met in a couple of years, like." Mandy was startled by Olivia's voice. She'd told her to listen and make notes. However, it seemed to have some effect as Sophie relaxed a little and turned to address the DC.

"London isn't all it's cracked up to be. I was glad to get out and come back to Cardiff. Only problem is finding a job. I had a high paid job as an accountant in a big firm. I haven't been able to get anything here, yet. I was just settling back into Cardiff life."

"So, why come back?" Mandy was curious. Why would you leave a job without another job to go to if you were earning big bucks?

"I…" She hesitated. "…Things happened. There was an intruder in my flat one night. It was a few months after Dad died and I was pretty low anyway. It… it unnerved me. I packed my bags and came back."

That's why she appeared to be a bundle of nerves. Enough to make anyone dash for safety. It must have scared her half to death. And she didn't say home. Back to Cardiff. Not back home. Was that significant?

"We're trying to establish a timeline for the weekend. Whose idea was the reunion?"

"Megan's. She said she'd had enough of Wales, and she was thinking of going to Australia for a year to work and see how that panned out. Said she wanted to meet up with her old pals before she went and for me to organise it. I didn't quite believe it. She was up for promotion. If she'd got the job it was based in London, not Sydney."

"Her family knew nothing about the Australia plan. If she wanted a reunion, why didn't she organise it herself? Apart from Siobhan you all live locally now."

Sophie looked down at her hands, twisted the sleeve of her cardigan again and then exhaled and let her shoulders drop.

"It was a show of power. She wanted me to jump to attention. Do as she asked. She liked playing that sort of game. She always had to be the centre of attention. She's doing it now, even when she's dead, isn't she?" The words were spoken in a quiet voice but there was a bitterness and an edge to them.

So, not such great friends after all. Interesting. "But, knowing she was manipulating you, you still agreed?" asked Mandy.

"I was desperate for a job and she said she might be able to help. Put a good word in. That sort of thing." Sophie was staring at the carpet, not meeting their eyes.

More questions formed in Mandy's head. However, she needed time to reflect, think this through. For now, she needed times and facts.

"Can you talk us through the weekend, please? From Friday onwards until Megan's body was found."

"I picked up Siobhan from the ferry at Pembroke dock about one o'clock. We stopped on the way back and did some shopping for food and drinks. I think we got to Nythfa about four or half-past." She tilted her head while she thought. The others arrived between five and six. Bethan first, then the others. Aisha doesn't drive so Megan picked her up on the way. We had a meal, a few drinks, watched a movie and went to bed about midnight."

Mandy indicated for her to continue. Olivia was scribbling away in her notebook, while Sophie seemed oblivious.

"The next day we went for a hike across the fields and then had a pub lunch in Sigingstone. We were all pretty shattered when we got back so just lazed about a bit. We'd all brought food with us but after the pub lunch we weren't that hungry. The meal was a bit of a hotchpotch of what we had in the house."

Another examination of her hands. The skin beside Sophie's thumb was bleeding and she put it into her mouth to stop the flow, grimacing as she tasted the blood.

"It was all okay. We drank quite a bit. Aisha went to bed with a headache. Megan seemed in an odd mood. She was ranting on about being watched and she was going to see who was out there, spying on us. We didn't take much notice when she went outside, to be honest."

She looked to the left of Mandy and frowned a little as if trying to remember. "She, well, the thing is Megan could be two people. Sometimes she'd be lovely. Clever and funny and then the next minute a horrible piranha of a person you'd prefer not to know. She'd been difficult all evening and I think we were glad she'd gone out."

"Difficult?"

"It started off okay. Then she started being quite horrible to us. She said awful things. We were all losers. No guts. Then she thought there was someone outside. She went out and we were relieved at first."

"There was a lot of rain. Didn't you find it odd that she stayed out? Why didn't anyone go and search for her?"

Sophie flushed a little and she gazed at the floor again. "We drank a lot. We were all pretty wasted, except Aisha. She was in bed and she doesn't drink anyway."

"And Megan didn't drink either, did she, so why do you think she was so agitated?"

"I don't know." A slight shrug. "I do feel awful about it. Someone should have gone after her, but we never thought she was going to end up dead. Well, you don't do you?" She looked straight at Mandy with tear filled eyes.

"We'll need you to make a formal statement and sign it as soon as possible. Today would be best. Do you feel up to that? Just the facts. Times and who was where and when. Got it?"

Sophie swallowed and asked, "Is that it? Are you done?"

"For now. Thank you. Can you ask Siobhan to come and have a chat with us?"

They watched as she almost stumbled out of the room. Mandy raised an eyebrow at Olivia.

"Are we getting the full story do you think?"

Olivia shook her head. "Nah. Something missing for def, boss."

* * *

Sophie was trembling as she left the room. She stood and leaned against the wall for a moment before taking a deep breath and going back to the conservatory. Siobhan was talking non-stop, asking about plants and who did the garden and wasn't it lovely to have all that space. She seemed almost relieved to be leaving Diane's company to be interrogated by the police. As soon she'd left, Diane turned to her daughter.

"Well. What did they want to know?"

"What you'd expect. Times. Who did what and when? The usual stuff I suppose. I have to make a formal statement today. I suppose I'll have to go to the station for that."

Diane fingered the string of pearls at her throat. "Really? Is that necessary? Can't you do it while the officers are here?"

"I don't think so. I expect they'll tell us before they leave. They must go through these formalities you know. They're not just doing it to annoy you and give the neighbours something to gossip about."

A slight flare of the nostrils was the only sign that Diane was less than pleased. Sophie knew she had hit on the real reason her mother was bothered by the police presence. Her place in society was the only thing Diane treasured above everything, even her daughter.

"When is that young woman leaving? I know you told her she could stay here. You should have asked me first. She's very wearing. That constant prattling and that accent."

"God, mother. You're such a snob. Siobhan is very clever. She got a first-class degree." Sophie tried to keep her voice low in case she was overheard, although the walls were so thick, she was sure the police couldn't hear her hissed words. "What does it matter how she speaks? She's a nice person. You've made her as welcome as a nun in a brothel. I'm sure she'll be off as soon as she can. Then you'll only have me to get rid of, won't you?"

Sophie could feel the heat in her cheeks. Diane opened her mouth but said nothing, an expression of surprise and hurt in her eyes. Before she could betray herself by crying, Sophie turned and left, hoping she didn't bump into the police officers on the way to her bedroom. Once there she shut the door and sank to the floor with her back to it.

What a mess. What a bloody awful mess.

CHAPTER SEVEN

Siobhan O'Hare was less frazzled than Sophie although still wary as she entered the room. Mandy wondered if she was itching to get out of the country. If she went to Ireland, they'd have no jurisdiction to interview her there. Better get this case sorted, one way or the other.

"You've managed to rearrange your ferry?"

"Yes. No bother. It was only as a foot passenger so not that dear though I'm running on a tight budget. I nearly didn't come on the trip. If I'd known what a heap of crap it was going to be, I'd have stayed at home. But I'd better not let Mrs Grant hear me say that. She's a bit of a matriarch. Bit like me own Ma with tight corsets."

Despite the seriousness of the situation Mandy wanted to laugh. Siobhan seemed pretty straight with them, although, as she well knew, appearances could be deceptive. She'd come across villains who would look you straight in the eye and lie, so she'd learnt, the hard way, not to trust anyone in an investigation.

"Sophie has given us a sort of timeline. We'll need you to make a formal statement but just trying to get things in place. She picked you up from the ferry, you stopped for lunch on the way and got to Nythfa about four thirty. Is that right?"

"Aye. About that. I think she wanted to get there earlier. I was so hungry my belly thought my throat was cut, so we stopped and had lunch on the way. We grabbed some shopping too. Food and booze. Mainly booze."

Out of the corner of her eye Mandy could see Olivia frowning as she made notes. Siobhan's accent wasn't that broad, but she supposed Olivia's ear was unattuned.

"Then Bethan arrived and Megan with Aisha not long after that," said Mandy.

Siobhan bobbed her head. "That's right. Aisha was a bit quiet. Then she's not exactly the noisy one in the group anyway." She laughed and it sounded half hearted, an attempt at levity that seemed out of place in the circumstances and in the suppressed quiet of the house.

"Was this reunion planned long ago? Sophie said it was a sort of leaving do as Megan was planning to go to Australia."

"Couple of months, I suppose." Siobhan shrugged. "I wish she had gone to Australia. Better than on a slab in the mortuary."

"Why were you hesitant about coming?"

There was a brief silence as Siobhan considered what to say. "I've kept in touch with Sophie since I went back to Ireland. Not the others. I wasn't sure whether I fancied meeting up. We graduated at the same time, but Megan, Sophie and Aisha all got these high-powered jobs, and I was struggling, still am financially. I'm a writer, well, I do journalism freelance but I'm halfway through my first novel, and the tax breaks in Ireland are better."

"I thought you were all on the same course."

"No. We met in halls. Meg, Sophie and Aisha were all doing accountancy, I did English and Bethan was doing business studies. There were six of us in the same block. The other girl dropped out after the first term. Can't even remember her name. Very quiet. Didn't mix much."

"You've been friends since then? Ten years."

"Aye. It was alright. We pretty much stayed together through uni. After that, sure I suppose life took over. Sophie went to London a year later and we were all trying to earn a living. We'd meet up on high days and holidays, but it's been about five years since we had a night out together, all five of us, that is. I'd see the others now and again for a meal or a drink. Sometimes just two of us. Then last year I moved back to Ireland and, apart from on Facetime, I haven't seen anyone since."

Mandy waited to see if there was any more. Sometimes silence worked better than questions and she had the feeling Siobhan was the chatty sort. It didn't take long.

"Megan is, I mean was, a funny sort. She'd be your best friend one day and then she'd stab you in the back the next."

"What do you mean? How was she that weekend? With you and the others?"

Siobhan closed her mouth and chewed her bottom lip. It was obvious there was something she didn't want to divulge.

"Same as usual. You never knew what was going to happen next. She was okay with me, considering, but I think something must have happened on the way to the house with Aisha."

"What makes you say that?"

"I overheard Aisha asking Bethan if she could have a lift back on Sunday as she didn't want to be in the car with Megan."

Mandy felt the tingle of excitement. Bingo. Bloody bingo. She knew something was going on under it all. Wonder if Olivia got that one in her little notebook.

"Bethan was grand with that and probably glad after Megan had been fat-shaming her all weekend."

"Fat-shaming?"

"Och, sure you know what I mean. Sly remarks about how some people didn't know when they'd had enough to eat. How hard it was for some people to stick to a diet. Never directed at Bethan though we all knew that's who she was aiming at. I mean Bethan is the only one who's bigger than a size twelve. Bethan took no notice, but I could have slapped Megan. She could be such a bitch." As if realising what she'd said Siobhan put her hand over her mouth, eyes wide in panic.

"Oh Jesus. I didn't mean to speak ill of the dead. I'm sorry."

Mandy shrugged her shoulders. "We're trying to find out as much as possible about what went on that weekend so that's helpful. What would you say about Megan's state of mind that evening? Before she went out. Can you give us a picture?"

"We were all knackered after we'd been for a walk and pub lunch. We showered, had a cup of tea and sat around. About seven or so, we started to drink."

"What were you drinking?"

"Oh, God help us. Now you're asking. Aisha doesn't drink alcohol, and neither does, I mean, did Megan. And Aisha had a migraine, so she went to bed before we'd eaten. The rest of us... sure, it started with the bubbly, then a couple of bottles with the meal and someone had brought vodka, so we had some of that with cake, I think. Things got a bit fuzzy around the edges."

"Did you notice Megan leaving?"

"Yes. About midnight, I think. She started shouting weird things. Someone was outside. They were trying to kill us all. We had to get out. We had to leave. She tried to pull Sophie to her feet and then gave up. She went out and we just sat there waiting for her to come back."

"Did you not think to go after her? Stop her? It started to rain after that. She didn't have a coat. Did no one care enough to do that?"

As she watched Mandy could see a flood of red rise from Siobhan's chest up her neck and turn her face crimson.

"I think we were all too wasted. It wasn't until a couple of hours later that we sort of straightened up enough to realise she hadn't come back, and we needed to do something."

"Then you waited another two hours and more before phoning the police to report her missing."

Tears began to well in Siobhan's eyes. "There's no bloody signal at the house and we weren't in any fit state to drive. Any of us. Bethan had her head down the toilet. Sophie was almost comatose, and I had the headache from hell. When Aisha came down the stairs to get a glass of water about four or half past, we had been outside to see if we could see Megan. There was nothing. Bethan was the most sober of us after being sick. She drove to the pub with Sophie because she knew there'd be a signal there."

"What did you think had happened?"

"We didn't know. We thought maybe she'd walked to the village and phoned a cab to go home or rung someone. As I said she could be a bit unpredictable. We were going up the walls, especially Sophie, as Bethan had been sick on the floor and she was garbling on about her Ma and the mess and, well, it was chaos."

"After the police had been informed what did you all do then?"

"We sat around for a bit and then Sophie said we'd better clean up everywhere as the estate agent was coming on Monday morning again. Something about more photographs. So that's what we did. Cleaned it all up."

"Who tidied up Megan's room?"

"Sophie. I think."

"Did anyone come across Megan's phone."

Siobhan shook her head. "Was it not with her? Or in her handbag? There was no signal at that place which is why we couldn't ring anyone earlier."

"Okay, thanks Ms O'Hare. When is your ferry back to Rosslare?"

"Oh, not for another wee while. I cancelled the booking. I'm going to stay with another friend for a few days before I go back. I hadn't planned to, but now I'm here sure I suppose I might as well take the good of it."

"Okay. Please leave the address of where you'll be staying with us before you leave Cardiff. Oh, and did you lose an earring by any chance? A little gold stud?"

"No. I don't have pierced ears. Couldn't bear the pain of it. I'm a wimp. Sounds like the one Aisha lost. You could ask her."

Mandy bowed her head in agreement. Oh, she'd be certain to ask Aisha how her earring just happened to be lying near the body of her friend.

* * *

Siobhan heaved a sigh of relief when she left the room. She stood for a moment gathering her thoughts again. Jesus that big detective was scary. Black eyes that bored right through to your soul. And the guilt trip. As if it was their fault Megan was a diva. Well, no one was to know what was going to happen when she went out that night. Yes, she felt guilty but then Megan hadn't been exactly the best friend in the world. Truth was she'd felt a sense of relief when Sophie had told her about Megan's proposed trip to Oz. That's what had persuaded her to travel over for the weekend. God, she wished she'd stayed at home away from all this mess.

Mrs Grant appeared and was about to say something when the detectives came out of the room. Siobhan made a quick getaway upstairs to her room. She could hear the mumbled voices and the footsteps across the hall. The front door closed and more footsteps receding. Ma Grant had gone back to the kitchen then. Good. Although Sophie had said she was welcome to stay, Siobhan knew when she wasn't wanted. Sure, you could cut the air with a knife in that house. Sophie had never said much about home, and they'd always met out in the town so her only experience of meeting Mrs Grant had been graduation day. That seemed a lifetime ago. Diane had been with her husband then and much more relaxed if still a bit up herself.

Where the hell was Sophie? A soft knock on Sophie's door didn't produce an answer, so Siobhan went back to her own room and lay on the bed, staring at the ceiling. It just goes to show you, she thought, wealth and privilege doesn't always bring happiness. This was one of the most unhappy houses she'd ever been in. She'd no intention of spending any more time here than necessary and being questioned by Diane Grant again. It was bad enough that inspector grilling her as if she knew there was something more. Well, she hadn't told any lies. And if they didn't ask her the right questions that wasn't her fault, was it?

She got out her phone and pressed connect. She wasn't welcome here, but she knew where she would be welcomed with open arms.

"Hi. It's me. Can I come and stay with you for a few days?"

Tick. Escape route planned. Now to tell Sophie she wasn't prepared to stay and be a buffer between her and her domineering mother.

CHAPTER EIGHT

On the way to Pontprennau, where Aisha lived, Mandy said little. She was turning over things in her head. Siobhan, for all her apparent openness was hiding something. What was it she'd said? Something about the weekend not being too bad considering. Considering what? Olivia was subdued. What were her impressions of Sophie and Siobhan?

"Well? Any thoughts?" Mandy squinted at Olivia who appeared surprised at being asked her opinion. That was the trouble with some bloody people in the police force. See a little woman and think she had two brains cells that worked alternate Sundays. She'd have to give Olivia some lessons in assertiveness. Maybe she needed to be a little less brusque with her.

"Well…"

"Out with it." Balls. That sounded a bit gruff. Keep a measured tone. Don't scare the girl.

"I think they're both hiding something, but I don't know what, I don't. Sophie is obviously cowed by her mam. I mean, that woman makes the ice queen look like a fluffy bunny. And Siobhan, for all her nattering, isn't giving us everything either, is she? I don't understand why, if Megan could be so difficult, they're still friends. Who needs friends like that? I don't."

The girl had brains then. She'd make a good detective. Instinctive. Listening not just to the spoken words, also thinking about what wasn't said. What lay underneath. Bloody good show.

"Exactly my thoughts. Now, let's see if Aisha recognises the earring we found near the body. We want to find out what happened in that car on the Friday evening too. Megan Pritchard wasn't the golden girl her mother believed she was. Then parents don't know everything about their children, do they?"

They'd gone through the lanes from Lisvane to Pontprennau. It was a rabbit warren of streets with a variety of house styles. Aisha's was a modest, two bedroomed terrace and, judging from the "To Let" signs, in an area where the population changed on a regular basis.

The house appeared well maintained with a small grass area at the front by a parking bay and a pot of petunias by the front door. The striped cat that was sleeping on the grass scarpered when they stopped the car. Aisha seemed unsurprised to see them and welcomed them into the house. The door opened into the tiny hall with a compact kitchen to the right and a modest lounge straight ahead. A quick peek showed that Aisha had been preparing food. Something delicious and spicy. That's why she wasn't surprised to see them. The kitchen had a clear view of the road. She'd already spotted the car before opening the door.

The lounge, with the stairs leading upstairs was painted in neutral colours. Not exactly magnolia, but something similar. The back garden was laid to grass with a teal-coloured bistro set on the tiny area of decking. Everything was neat and tidy. Aisha sat on a tub chair by the open patio doors. They could hear the whirr of a lawnmower and the smell of fresh mown grass wafted into the room. Aisha closed the door and the noise was muted. She gestured for them to sit on the two-seater green velvet sofa tucked under the stairs. Mandy sank into it, hoping she wouldn't hit her head when she stood up again. Olivia perched on the edge with her notebook ready.

"Thank you for seeing us. You aren't working today?" Obvious. An easy opener. Get the buggers relaxed first then go in for the tougher questions.

Aisha shook her head. "I rang in sick. Explained to my boss what had happened. I just needed some time to sort of get my head together." Her voice was well-modulated, calm with just a faint Essex twang at times.

"I understand. It's been quite a shock for everyone concerned. We're just trying to fit the pieces together. Get a picture of Megan and a timeline so that we can find out what happened over the weekend. Would you say you were good friends with Megan Pritchard?"

"Well, we'd been through uni together. We worked in the same field, in the same company, but in different areas. We weren't best friends or anything like that. I don't think Megan had many close friends."

Curious. Megan was a successful young woman. Good job with career prospects. A flat in a prestigious area of the Bay. No shortage of money yet lacking in some way. "Oh. Why is that?"

"She was very competitive. Saw everyone else as a threat to her success. She could be very, how can I put it, challenging at times. She didn't let people get too close."

"That's interesting. You had a lift to the house with her, so you were in touch on a regular basis?"

"Yes. Our offices were near each other. In the same building. We'd sometimes see each other when passing or have lunch together once in a while."

"How often would that be?"

Aisha shrugged. "Not that often. Every six months or so."

Strange. If they were friends, even if not bosom pals, you'd expect them to meet more often, especially as they had a common work interest.

"How would you describe Megan? Apart from competitive. Anything else?" Mandy fixed Aisha with her crow's eyes, watching.

"I'd say she was a typical Gemini. All sweetness and light and good fun some of the time, but she had a darker side too."

Mandy exchanged glances with Olivia. That's what the others had said too. Megan Pritchard was definitely not the golden girl her parents thought she was.

"Can you tell us about your journey with Megan on the Friday evening. Was she in good spirits?"

Aisha stiffened and shifted in her chair before she answered.

"She was... a little agitated. Sort of, I don't know how to describe it. Tense. Driving a bit too fast for my liking. I don't drive. I had lessons but I was too nervous. I'm a nervous passenger too."

"Is that why you asked Bethan for a lift back on Sunday? Did you feel uncomfortable with Megan's driving?"

"How?" Aisha's reaction was swift, a slight tension in her neck, although she recovered quickly. "Oh, you've spoken to Siobhan. She overheard me."

It wasn't an answer, but Mandy let it pass. There were other things to ask. She took out a photograph of the gold stud. Passing it to Aisha she asked, "Do you recognise this earring?"

Aisha's face lit up. "Oh. You found it. It's mine. My grandmother bought those earrings for me when I graduated. She passed away last year so I was devastated when one went missing. Where did you find it? Was it in the house?"

Mandy scrutinised Aisha's face. Her relief at finding the earring seemed genuine. How would she react when she knew where they'd found it?

"It was in the field where we found Megan Pritchard's body. Quite close to the body, in fact."

The reaction was immediate. Aisha's eyes opened wider and an expression of horror spread over her face. She dropped the photograph; her mouth fell open and she covered it with one hand while taking shuddering breaths.

"No. How?"

"That's what we'd like to know. Rather strange place to find it, I'm sure you agree?"

Shaking now, Aisha said, "I... I noticed the earring was missing on Saturday afternoon. I searched the house for it and Sophie said we'd probably find it when we were cleaning. I don't know how it got there." She gazed into space and frowned a little as if trying to recall something.

"We'd gone for a walk over the fields. There are several pathways in that area with open access. At one point it started to rain a little and I pulled up my hood." She stopped and took a deep breath. "The string caught in my hair and the earring must have come out at the same time. I can't believe you found it there. That's so awful. I don't think, now, I'll ever be able to wear them again. Not knowing that." Her voice trailed away.

"We'll be able to return it to you when our investigation is complete."

An expression of puzzlement spread over Aisha's face. She tilted her head to one side. "But I thought... Why are you investigating? Wasn't it an accident?"

Mandy wasn't prepared to divulge her suspicions at this point. "We have to file a report for the coroner so the more information we can compile the better. What was Megan drinking? Any alcohol?"

"No. She didn't drink. Only Coke. She liked to take photos of the others when they'd had a few and post them on Facebook with rude comments. Thankfully I don't drink so wasn't a target. That's what I mean about how she could be like two people in one. Upset people. Sometimes the photos were the sort you wouldn't want your mother to see."

"Or your employer I expect. Thank you, Ms Matharu. We'll be in touch, and you'll have to make a formal statement."

As they left Pontprennau Olivia said, "She didn't tell us much about the journey, did she, boss? She did seem shocked that her earring was close to the body. Do you think she found Megan before that bloke did? From what Siobhan said Aisha was the only one sober."

"And in bed with a migraine. I get those and believe me; a migraine lays you out like you've been hit by Joe Calzaghe. Still, she's hiding something."

Olivia shrugged. "Could be that she's gay. I don't suppose that would go down well with her family or community."

"Gay? How do you know that?"

"Takes one to know one." She smiled. "Well, that's not strictly how I guessed. There was a magazine open on the floor beside the sofa with a cross beside an advert for a gay club I know about in London."

"Interesting."

Olivia Wyglendacz was clever alright, but Mandy wasn't relaxed with her in case she was reporting back to old Withering. This investigation was getting no-where fast. What they had was a lack of hard evidence. Motive? They were all friends. You should be able to trust your friends although not one of them yet gave the impression that they could trust Megan. Perhaps Bethan Rees would give them something more substantial to fit in the jigsaw puzzle.

* * *

Aisha Matharu watched the car turn the corner away from her house. She'd go back to work tomorrow. Staying at home was an indulgence. Her earring near the body. The very thought of it made a shudder run through her body. That detective was clever. She had thought it odd that she didn't spend more time with Megan when they worked in the same building. How could she explain that? That she didn't want to get too close to someone who would steal her ideas and present them as her own? The first time that had happened Aisha hadn't believed it. Her friend, Megan, had milked her for ideas then presented them to the board as her own. After that, Aisha was wary. Kept her plans to herself. Except her application for the job in London. Bigger firm. Bigger salary. And the chance to be herself instead of living this half-life.

Megan had applied for the same job and bagged it, triumphant. Even that victory hadn't stopped her cutting comments. Maybe now, Aisha thought, she'd have a chance for that job, escape to the big city and some anonymity. She didn't want to tell anyone what had happened in the car on the way to Nythfa. What had been said and the underlying threat in Megan's words. Aisha had determined that after the weekend she was going to cut all links with Megan. She'd keep in touch with the others, of course. Maybe she'd even be able to persuade Sophie to apply for Megan's job. Sophie needed to get away from that mother of hers. That woman had to know everything about everybody, and she lacked empathy. Poor Sophie must be going through hell.

The earring was a problem. In the same field as the body. That wasn't good. It was suspicious. She could tell that DI Wilde thought it was important. That one had eyes that bored right through you and the other one with her was more like a punk than a policewoman. Or officer. That's what they called them these days. Police officers. None of this sexist stuff. Her mobile phone buzzed. Sophie.

"Hi. Yes. They've just been. Lots of questions. No, I didn't tell them about London or that I knew the Australia trip was another of her fantasies."

A mumbling on the other end. Aisha flicked a strand of hair off her forehead as she listened. Sophie sounded fraught, agitated. But Aisha had her own worries.

"And Sophie, they found my earring near her body. I'm not sure they believed me when I said I'd lost it earlier in the day. I'm worried. I don't know what they're searching for. It has to be an accident. None of us saw it happen. What else could it be?

* * *

Back at Central station Josh was wading through Facebook. Megan's Facebook pages had few restrictions and she had posted copious photographs. Mainly selfies he noticed, or where there were a lot of people in the background, so it appeared as though she was always with someone and not by herself despite the loneliness that echoed in that apartment of hers. In the last year there were a couple with Sophie, one with Aisha and several with a bloke she labelled as Rhys. The boyfriend. There was something not quite right about those and he couldn't quite put his finger on what it was. Maybe Helen could give him some feminine insight. Megan's parents said they wanted to be left alone, thank you very much, so Helen was back in the office sifting through Megan's LinkedIn profile.

"Hey, Helen. Got a minute? Have a look at these. Tell me what you think."

Helen came over to his desk and stood behind Josh. She was a bit older than him, almost forty he guessed, married to a solicitor and had two boys. She exuded a sense of calm. He'd never seen Helen in a flap which is why she'd been chosen as liaison. As she bent over Josh caught a hint of her perfume. Givenchy Amarige. The same as Lisa wore. Swallowing his feeling of loss, he scrolled through the photographs. Several with Rhys. The only one he seemed to appear relaxed in was the group graduation photo with the girls. Ten years ago. Megan had posted it quite recently with the caption. "Almost ten years ago. Who can believe that?" In that photograph Rhys was on the end of the line with his arm round Siobhan.

Helen frowned. "He's not exactly giving Megan the look of love, is he? More as if he's captured. Not a happy bunny."

"That's what I thought. The boss needs to see these. Maybe we should talk to Rhys Davies and see if he has anything useful to tell us."

"A little trip to Chepstow then. That's where he lives, isn't it? I thought the local boys had been and spoken to him?" Helen asked.

"Just to inform him about Megan's death. If we want to know more about her life, we'll need to speak to him." Josh chewed the end of a pencil as he thought about it.

"The boss doesn't think it was an accident then?" Helen asked.

"Megan Pritchard never drank. You heard what the sister said. Scary episode before uni mixing the booze and meds. She knew the dangers."

"Suicide?"

"You've been with the family. What do you think? Is it a possible? What were the vibes?"

Helen considered the question for a moment. "She was the treasured daughter. They were very proud of her. Top of the class all through school. Outstanding results. 100 percent in some of her maths exams. That sort of thing. I felt sorry for Nia, in her shadow all the time. She left school at sixteen and worked in an office for a couple of years before deciding to go and do her A levels. Turns out Nia's just as clever as her sister but in science. She's applied to go to university to study biochemistry."

"Was she jealous of Megan?"

"I think she was when she was younger. They didn't see much of each other once Megan left home. I got the feeling there'd been a rift of some sort, though she was genuinely shocked and upset at her sister's death. As you would be."

"Yeah. Don't know why I'm asking. She wasn't even at Nythfa over the weekend." Josh frowned at the screen as if the answer was going to appear if he concentrated enough.

"Don't you think it's odd the family knew nothing about this Australia thing? If you were going to the other side of the world, you think you'd tell them, wouldn't you?"

"Unless the reason you were going was to get away from your family. Either that or Sophie Grant is lying."

Mandy arrived back with Olivia and overheard the comments.

"Check with Megan's firm. What were relations like with Aisha? General background. What they knew about the Australia plan. That sounds bloody dodgy to me. I'm not convinced we're getting the full picture yet." She frowned. "Bethan Rees is the last on the list so let's see what she has to tell us now, shall we? Josh?"

She waved for Josh to follow her out. She was tired but if there was something odd about Megan Pritchard's death she'd plough on until she found it.

Seeing the determined set of Mandy's mouth and her steady march out of the office, Josh was reminded of a tortoise he'd owned. Herman. They used to make an obstacle course for him in the garden. Nothing got in his way. If Herman couldn't move it or go around, he'd go over the top. DI Mandy Wilde was just like that tortoise.

CHAPTER NINE

Bethan Rees. The last one in Nythfa that weekend. Down to the Bay again. She'd moved in with her boyfriend for a couple of days they'd been told. They'd have a quick word with her and then home. The trouble with this job was the hours. They could go for weeks with humdrum things going on and then boom. Something would blow the normality away like an elephant landing on a whoopee cushion. Just the thought of that image made Mandy smile. When Tabitha was little, she was fascinated by elephants and Mandy used to make up all sorts of adventures for Jeremiah the imaginary elephant. Jeremiah. The same name as the grandfather from across the seas that she'd never known.

Mandy sighed as she remembered those happier days. Josh took it as a signal to break the silence with a question.

"Why did you want to join the police? If you don't mind me asking, boss?"

"The question I ask myself every day. I could ask you the same thing. You've got a degree in what? Some ology? There must have been more attractive options."

"Yeah, well, I suppose I thought I could save the world or something. It seemed more exciting than a nine to five in some anonymous office."

"Now, with Lisa on your back you've changed your mind."

Josh's sigh told her more than a reply. She wondered if his heart was in the job anymore or if he was considering giving into his wife's pressure and leaving CID.

"I had a skim through Megan's Facebook page. Loads of photographs."

"And. Anything? Clues? What does it tell us?"

"There's something odd with the boyfriend."

"Odd? What do you mean?" She glanced at him with as they rounded a corner.

"It's difficult. Helen reckons he's not comfortable in the photographs. I thought they were a bit dodgy, but I needed a woman's view to make sure."

"Well, that's good. I'm so glad you think we women are useful for something." Mandy's eyes flashed at him. He should have more faith in his own ability. She must remember to give him a boost now and again. What did the training programme say? "Always ensure that people working under your supervision feel valued. Teamwork is the essence of good police detection." It was true. The right team got the best results.

The flat where Bethan was staying was close to where Megan had her luxury place, though a more modest block than Nautica. They pressed for entry and made their way up the stairs. Bethan was waiting for them, door open. She greeted them as if they were old friends, not police officers making enquiries after a friend's death, nodding for them to follow her along a narrow passage. That led to the main room; a lounge with kitchen corner all in soft pastel shades. It was all a bit tired and lacking any soul. More a man cave than anything else. Mandy thought it could have been anywhere, a room in any of the anonymous blocks surrounding them. A man was sitting at a desk in the corner by the window, but he stood when he saw them enter.

"This is Luke. My boyfriend. He works in IT so he's at home most of the time doing stuff online. I live in a flat in Fairwater. We're hoping to buy somewhere together." She beamed at Luke who said nothing just made a little bow and left them alone. There was a delicious smell of baking.

"Something smells good." Josh's stomach rumbled as he said it and Bethan laughed.

"Chocolate and walnut cake. New recipe. Baking relaxes me." Mandy was surprised at how upbeat she seemed, then people responded to death in different ways. She could be in denial.

Bethan didn't ask them to sit down but Mandy sat anyway. The springs in the sofa had gone. It was uncomfortable. Josh sat beside her leaving Bethan to perch on the chair vacated by Luke.

"This is quite close to Megan's flat. She lived in the Bay too. Did you see her often?"

The smile left Bethan's face. A little frown, as if remembering that Megan had died. "No. We'd bump into each other now and again but, as I told you, I don't live in the Bay. I just needed to be with someone close for a couple of days, after what happened." A tightening of her lip as she glanced away for a moment. Interesting that she chose to be with the boyfriend rather than family. Mandy was intrigued.

"We're just trying to speak to everyone today to get a picture, a timeline. You've been friends since uni?"

"Since primary school, actually."

That was a surprise. They hadn't been aware of that. Why the hell hadn't anyone found out that little nugget of information? Josh made a note. Something to follow up on later.

"So, long standing friends who didn't see each other very often?" Mandy raised an eyebrow. She waited, aware of Josh beside her, tensed. "Were you aware why Megan didn't drink?" As best friends she should know. Didn't friends confide in each other? Darkest secrets and all that?

Bethan pouted a little and shook her head. "She didn't like the taste, I suppose, and she liked taking photos of people in compromising situations when they were pissed. A sort of way of eliminating the competition."

"What do you mean?"

"She was always driven. Even as a little girl. Wanted to be first in everything. Then at uni. When it came to getting jobs and she found out that your employer might check out your Facebook page. Well," she shrugged, "a way of coming out top. Golden girl. No dancing on the table or moonies out of windows for her. No way. Squeaky clean."

"And was she?"

"What?"

"Golden girl. Everybody's friend. Squeaky clean. She could just be presenting that façade. A secret drinker."

Bethan snorted. "We went back a long way, Megan and me. She could get right up your nose at times. She'd do something to really piss you off and then she'd call full of apologies. She wanted her bosses, people who mattered to her career to think she was perfect. I don't think she had many real friends. Our Mums are friends too, so I suppose we stuck together out of habit." It was a strange thing to say. Mandy thought about how some people did stay together, like in a marriage, because they couldn't be bothered with the disruption to their lives.

"What did you think when she left the house in a state on Saturday night. Did you think about following her?"

"I wasn't feeling too good. Head down the bog. Sophie and Siobhan said she'd gone out. I didn't think about it too much, at first."

"And Aisha?"

"In bed with a headache. Aisha's the quiet one. I think it was all a bit too much for her."

"So, no one was fit to raise the alarm." Mandy stared at Bethan who flushed and turned away. Upset? Ashamed? Guilty? All three? Good. Let her stew. Josh was fidgeting and Mandy caught his eye. Josh coughed and Bethan turned towards him.

"Em, we were told that Megan had a habit of saying rude things to you, about your weight. Is that true? Did it upset you?"

Another snort of humourless laughter. "Megan has been fat-shaming me since we were in reception class. I've always been a big girl. At one stage I tried dieting but then I realised that I was never going to be a stick insect," she paused, "so I came to terms with it. In fact, I work part-time as a plus model. Now, I'm proud of my body and the pay is good. I've got a website for my modelling. Bethan on Fire, it's called. You should check it out."

Josh blushed at her flirtatious look. Good on you, Mandy wanted to say. Bethan was what the renaissance painters would have called voluptuous and appeared to be well-toned. She seemed well-adjusted. And she knew Megan better than the others.

"Thank you, Ms Rees. We're beginning to put together a profile of your friend. Her boyfriend, Rhys Davies graduated at the same time. What can you tell me about Mr Davies?"

"He's the reason Siobhan went back to Ireland. Well, him and Megan, that is."

Now, that was useful. Gossip. Always a gem in these sorts of investigations. Mandy kept her face as impassive as possible.

"I don't quite follow."

"Rhys went out with Siobhan all through uni. Well, from second year on. Inseparable. It seemed inevitable they'd get married. Then about eighteen months ago – boom. The big split." Bethan moved her arms apart to demonstrate. "Siobhan heads back to Ireland. Leaves the job she has in the university library. Says she's going to write the novel she's always planned and it's cheaper to live in Ireland. Big smokescreen."

"Why?"

"Turns out Megan bumped into Rhys one night. Got him so drunk he could hardly walk and took him back to her place. She told everyone they'd slept together. Rhys couldn't remember anything except waking in bed the next morning stark naked and with a crashing headache. Megan took photos of him and posted on Facebook. If you look at her Facebook profile, it's full of pictures of them together."

"So, Siobhan thought they had sex. He'd betrayed her." Mandy said.

Bethan shrugged her shoulders. "Who knows? It broke Siobhan's heart. I'm surprised she came over for the reunion. If it was me, I don't think I could forgive and forget that sort of betrayal. Siobhan is a pussy cat."

As they left the block of flats Mandy was elated. "Well, do you think we've got a motive here? Could Siobhan have spiked Megan's drink? Revenge for seducing her boyfriend?"

"Why wait so long? Surely, she would have been angry at the time, but her life has moved on?"

"Haven't you heard the saying that revenge is best served cold? Maybe she's been waiting for such an occasion to get her revenge. We need to speak to Rhys. Tomorrow."

* * *

Luke came out of the bedroom when he heard the door close and all went quiet. Bethan was sitting on the sofa staring into space.

"Cake smells good."

"Umm. Hope so. Lashings of chocolate in it."

"What was all that about? Fuzz wanted to talk about Megan?"

"Yeah. I'll have to go in and make a formal statement about Saturday night."

"You tell them about...?"

"No. I answered their questions. It was an accident. I told you. An unfortunate accident. I don't want to talk about it anymore. It's all too depressing."

"Okay, babes. I'll have a coffee with a slice of that cake when it's ready. I've stuff to do." Luke returned to the computer and carried on working.

Bethan sat for a minute or two. This was real then. Megan was dead. That shouldn't have happened. Not to a healthy thirty-two-year-old. She thought about some of the things Megan had said to her. Meant to raise a laugh. That's why she liked the other girls. They didn't laugh. They didn't find Megan's bitchy comments funny. She'd told those police officers that she was immune to Megan's comments, but it wasn't really true. Megan had been the cause of her bulimia when she was in her teens. It had been a struggle to get over that. It had made her stronger, more confident and Luke's obsession with her had been the icing on the cake. He'd made her see that she was beautiful. Loved. That was something Megan wasn't able to spoil.

She shivered. Same age. Just goes to show. Nobody knows when their ticket's up.

* * *

By the time she got home Mandy felt drained of energy and enthusiasm. She had no evidence of anything. Each of Megan's so-called friends had a motive to dislike her. Enough to kill? There wasn't any evidence despite her gut feeling that things were not right. She'd always found instinct had served her well in the past and this mystery niggled away at her like a weevil gnawing through biscuits.

Tabitha was at the dining table doing her homework. She was such a good kid and clever too. Mandy encouraged her studies, helped when she could, although some of it was unfamiliar. Wouldn't it be wonderful if Tabs got into university? How proud she'd be then. First one in the family. It hadn't been an option for her and Joy. No money. No support. Joy had gone from one dead end job to another and so had Mandy for a while until she'd seen an advert for recruitment for the South Wales Police. Joy had thought it hysterical.

"You're never going to be a pig? That's frigging hilarious." The ridicule had just made her more determined. It was with some pride when Miranda Wilde first put on the uniform and stepped out into the streets of Cardiff. It had been hard slog getting into the CID and to inspector level. A lot of life, such as long-term relationships, had fallen to the wayside. When Joy had cleared off and she became guardian to Tabitha, that had filled a gap. But when Tabitha went to uni in a couple of years or so, what then? Mandy didn't want to think about it. She shook the thoughts away. Priority. Food.

"Fancy omelettes?"

Tabitha looked up and smiled. "Yummy. With cheese and onion?"

"And red pepper and salad? I think there may even be something naughty in the freezer like ice-cream to have with that melon. It smells so ripe I thought that cat, Satan, had been in and left a puddle."

"Double yummy. I'm nearly finished this essay, so I'll clear my stuff off the table and get the cutlery."

"Teamwork. Super Niece to the rescue." Mandy punched the air. They both laughed. How lovely it was to come home to someone so sweet. She could do with more of that in her life. A contrast to all the crap she had to deal with in work. It had been an interesting day but one of those times when she felt as though she was climbing a sand dune and no hope of reaching the top.

CHAPTER NINE

TUESDAY

"Just who is responsible for this?" Withers threw the South Wales Echo down on Mandy's desk. Megan's death had made the front page. There it was all in print. Undeniable.

Local Girl Found Dead in a Ditch

The body of Megan Pritchard, 32, from Llandaff, was found in a field in the Vale of Glamorgan in the early hours of Sunday morning. The body was discovered by Raymond Charles, a retired army major, who was enjoying an early morning walk with his dog. Mr Charles said he went home and called the police. He could see, even from a distance, that the young lady was dead.

Ms Pritchard had attended a party at a private house close to where her body was recovered. Our investigations point to the country home of the Grant family. The house, architect designed for the Cardiff businessman, David Grant, is to be sold following his tragic death last year. Mrs Grant was unavailable for comment.

A spokesperson said that police are making inquiries, but it would appear that this was a tragic accident, and our sympathies lie with Megan's parents and her sister, Nia.

Mandy could feel the colour drain from her face as she read through. Withers was breathing down her neck and he wanted to put the blame on someone. Well, it sure as hell wasn't going to land on her patch. No bloody way.

"So, who's this spokesperson? Which idiot spoke to the press? Eh? I told you to keep this one quiet. I've already had Diane Grant on the phone to me. Can't you be trusted?"

Gritting her teeth and clenching her fists by her sides, Mandy struggled to maintain a calm exterior even though her heart was beating overtime and she was aware of everyone's eyes on them. There was a hush in the room. A collective sense of everyone holding their breaths as they waited.

"No one in my team would breathe a word of this, sir. I suggest you put the blame on Mr Charles whose photograph is there beside the field. As for a spokesperson, you know as well as I do, that the press makes things up. This has nothing to do with me, or my team. Sir."

She watched as Withers stood, nostrils flared, glaring down at her with a vehemence that was palpable. Then, picking up the paper again, he growled at her. "I want this investigation sorted. I don't want a step out of line. I'll release a bland statement to the press. Get them off our backs. They'll be watching now, so you'd better do it right. Got it?"

"Sir."

Mandy stood up and eye-balled him. The only way to deal with Withers was to be on the offensive. Any show of weakness and he'd chew her up and spit her out like a piece of rotten meat. He stood glaring at her, then turned on his heel and marched back to his office. Mandy muttered, "bastard", under her breath. She didn't think anyone noticed until Olivia caught her eye. An ally then, not an enemy. The office hum started again, and Mandy spoke to Josh.

"Where did you say Rhys Davies lived? A little trip to Chepstow?"

Olivia was disappointed when Mandy asked her to chase up forensics on the items from Megan's washbag and her computer, but she figured the girl would be thorough in her checks.

"And Olivia, follow up on the missing phone, will you? Ask the local boys to go in and do another search of the house and surroundings. See what turns up. It has to be somewhere. We should have the telephone records. Chase that as well. See what's been happening in the last week or so."

Driving soothed Mandy's frayed nerves. The Super was the devil when he got angry, and she didn't think he should have shouted at her in front of everyone in the office. She had an idle thought about bringing a grievance against him. No. The best way to get her own back would be to prove that she was right. It was homicide, not accidental. Josh didn't mention the fracas in the office, spending most of the journey on his phone. What the hell he found to do with it all the time was another mystery.

"What's the address?" asked Mandy as they headed out of the city on the M4.

"Bulwark. It's off to the right before you go into the town. I checked that he'd be at home today. Pretended to be a client so he wouldn't have an excuse. The local boys said he wasn't very forthcoming. I suppose as they were delivering bad news, it stands to reason he wouldn't be chatty."

"Naughty. You're beginning to pick up some of my bad habits. You want to watch out or old Withering will have your balls on a platter if you step out of line. I'm already on his radar. Not that anyone would have noticed." She grinned, more relaxed now she was on the road and out of the office.

The traffic had slowed.

"I thought they were going to do something about these bloody Brynglas tunnels. This is frigging ridiculous. We could have been there by now." She tapped the steering wheel. "I had a quick scan of Megan's profile. Those photographs on Facebook didn't exactly spell someone madly in love, did they? Of course, some people don't like having photographs taken. Maybe Mr Davies will enlighten us. Bit off I thought. Dumping your long-term girl for her friend. No wonder Siobhan ran away."

Bulwark was a mixture of what had once been council property and other houses built in the seventies and later. Rhys Davies lived in a terraced ex-local authority house in a cul-de-sac. Mandy parked and they stepped down from the road to the front door and rang the bell. The door was opened by a woman. Mandy tried not to appear surprised although she could hear Josh's sharp intake of breath.

"Siobhan. We didn't expect to see you. This is a nice surprise." Mandy beamed as if she'd just met up with a long, lost friend.

"Oh. I didn't know. I wasn't expecting you. Rhys said he had a client coming."

"DS Jones and his idea of a joke. May we come in or do you want the neighbours to listen to what we have to say?"

"Sorry. Come on in. Rhys is in the kitchen."

The hall was small. Stairs to the left and a door into the main room to the right. It was a bright room with windows at both ends and long enough to take a sofa, a recliner, television on a stand and a small table and four chairs at the far end. Some sort of vaporiser was working so there was a hint of jasmine above the more obvious smell of fried food and something else Mandy couldn't quite identify. There was a mirror over a wooden fireplace with electric fire insert and pieces of paper with drawings on scattered in various piles on the floor. A hissing sound from the kitchen indicated the kettle was boiling. Would they be offered anything? Another man cave. It didn't seem as if a woman lived here at all, despite Siobhan's presence. Rhys emerged from a door to the left. The kitchen. Dishevelled and caught unawares, he glanced with curious eyes from them to Siobhan. She had wrapped her arms around herself.

"It's the police. They're here to talk about Megan." Her voice was a whisper as Mandy and Josh waved their identification.

Without waiting to be asked, Mandy sat down on the sofa. Siobhan sat on the easy chair and Rhys pulled up one of the dining chairs. Josh stood by the window, gazing out at the rockery and the neighbour who was wheeling a baby in a pushchair up and down the pavement in an attempt to stop it crying.

"What you want?" Rhys's voice held a hint of distaste, almost aggression. No chance of a cup of tea then.

Mandy surveyed Siobhan, silent and watchful, a multitude of questions forming. Get them talking. See what emerges. Despite his seeming indifference she knew Josh was alert, ready to note attitudes as well as whatever Rhys had to say.

"You know why we're here. Megan Pritchard was found dead on Sunday morning. You were all at university together. You and Megan, Siobhan, Bethan, Aisha and Sophie." It was a statement, but Rhys treated it like a question.

"Yep. Ten years ago." Silence. Nothing more forthcoming. It was obvious Rhys didn't want to talk. Okay, let's go in heavy. See what happens.

"And at that time, in fact until about eighteen months ago you and Siobhan here were an item. Right? So, what happened? We'd like to know."

Even though she knew the answers Mandy was interested to hear what Rhys had to say about it. Siobhan gasped and she turned towards Rhys. Her eyes were almost pleading. What was she trying to convey to him? What message?

"I don't know what that's got to do with anything."

He really was on the defensive. What did he have to hide?

"We're covering all bases, talking to everyone about Megan. Trying to establish what happened and why. It seems she was a complicated character. Her sister, Nia, told us that you were her boyfriend."

Rhys sneered at that remark and Mandy raised an eyebrow. "If that's not true then perhaps you'd like to tell us about your relationship with Siobhan. And, of course, Megan."

With a sigh Rhys complied. "We met in the first year. I saw Siobhan in the union bar, asked her out and that was it. We just clicked. Soul mates. That's how I got to know the rest of them. They lived together in halls and then student houses."

"You didn't live with them?"

"No. Too many women in one place is not a good mix." It seemed an odd thing to say and Mandy wanted to know more.

"What do you mean by that?"

"There was always a bit of friction there. Nothing serious, just things like whose turn it was to do the washing up. Who'd borrowed something without asking. Normal stuff, I suppose. I've got three sisters. I'm used to the girl fights. I didn't want to be in there with them." He half-laughed.

A nod from Mandy. Yes, too many women together could be a problem. "Okay. So, you and Siobhan were inseparable until about eighteen months ago and then one day she just decided to go and live back in Ireland. How's that?"

Siobhan opened her mouth as if to say something, but Mandy shook her head. She wanted to hear his version.

"That bitch Megan set me up." His jaw was stiff set, so the words came out almost in a hiss. Full of venom.

Another pause and the air so heavy it felt like a thunderstorm was due. Rhys gave Siobhan a look of tenderness, an apology, before he said any more. He was different, less aggressive as he gazed at her. The bond between them was obvious.

"Megan could be gorgeous. You know, sort of flirty. It meant nothing as she knew Siobhan and I were together. It was all a bit of a laugh. She had loads of boyfriends although nobody long-term. She'd dump them after a couple of months. Flighty."

He was looking down at his hands, clasped together on his knee.

"Well, one night, I was out with the boys. Stag do. Megan was out too. We bumped into one another. Literally. I was on my way to the bar and she was on her way back from the loo. She was in flirty mood and I'd had a few. All quite harmless. She bought me a couple of drinks and we were chatting about this and that. I couldn't find the boys. They'd moved on. I was pretty pissed by that time. I said I was going to go home but when I got outside my legs were like rubber bands. Couldn't stand. Megan said her place was nearby and why didn't I go back with her. She'd make me some black coffee and ring Siobhan to let her know where I was."

"She didn't." Siobhan interrupted, "If she had I'd have gone over. Things would have been different."

Another regretful look from Rhys.

"No. Instead the bitch set me up. I don't know what she'd given me in the bar. By the time I got to her flat I was almost out of it. I remember going through the door. I must have passed out soon after. Next thing I know the sun is shining in my face and Megan's there in a little nightie thing. I'm in her bed naked with no idea how I'd got there." He shuddered. "She'd taken photographs and put them on Facebook. I made her delete them, but it was too late. Siobhan saw them and refused to believe that I hadn't slept with Megan."

Turning to Siobhan, Mandy asked, "So why did you agree to go to a weekend house party when you knew Megan was going to be there? Wasn't that painful for you? Especially as Megan was still supposed to be with Rhys, according to her family."

Siobhan opened her mouth to reply. Rhys interrupted. "But I wasn't. I haven't been. Ever. Another of Megan's fantasy scenarios. When Siobhan went back to Ireland, Megan came to me and said she'd always fancied me. Now Siobhan was out of the way we could be together. I think she was nuts."

"Megan's Facebook page is full of photos of you two together. How come?" Josh looked straight at Rhys as he asked the question.

"She stalked me. She was always turning up at places where I posted I was going to be. I stopped using Facebook. If you check my pages, there's nothing new. In the end I told Megan if she carried on following me, I'd get a restraining order."

"I'll do that," said Josh, nodding. He didn't admit he'd already checked Facebook. Nothing on Rhys's page for at least a year although he'd been tagged in other people's pages. He had a separate account for his business.

"After a few months I followed Siobhan over to Ireland and begged her to believe me. It's taken a while but we're back together again. I'm going to sell up and move the business over there. Plenty of land and people wanting their gardens landscaped." He stretched out a hand and Siobhan took it with an expression of such tenderness Mandy felt embarrassed at the intrusion.

"From what you say, Mr Davies, you're not heartbroken Megan Pritchard is dead."

"I'm sorry for her family and it's a tragedy to die so young. After what she did to Siobhan and myself, well, I can't say I'm going to be awake at night weeping."

"And you, Siobhan. You didn't tell us this when we spoke to you. Any reason why not?"

Siobhan tucked a stray hair behind her ear and met Mandy's eyes. "Rhys and I kept our reconciliation secret. Sure, I haven't told any of the others yet. I'll admit I hated Megan's guts after that night. I didn't want to see her again but when Rhys and I got back together," she smiled at him and squeezed his hand. "Och, I just felt sorry for her. Anything she said about Rhys I knew was a lie, so I didn't give a damn. In fact, it was all okay until Saturday night when she went a bit off the wall."

"And nobody cared enough about her." Mandy left it there. They seemed to be telling the truth and they certainly appeared to be in love. Secrets and lies. Lies and secrets. Megan Pritchard was quite a complex personality. Two days in and nothing except a gut feeling that Megan's death was more than an accident. There were too many empty boxes. Too many unsolved questions.

"Just as a matter of interest where were you on Saturday night, Rhys?"

"In a house over in Tutshill, Gloucester Road. I do a bit of DJ work on weekends. There was a birthday party. I was there until about three in the morning." He scrambled on the floor for a scrap of paper and handed it to Josh. "This is the number. You can check."

"We'll do that." Josh made a note of the number and handed the paper back. "You can be certain of that."

* * *

When they'd left, Siobhan put her head in her hands. Rhys wrapped his arms around her.

"It's alright. Don't worry. They can't pin anything on me. Just as well I had the diffuser going though."

"I knew they'd find out. I should have told them. Sure, now they're going to think I'm trying to cover up something. Why didn't I tell them? It's not a crime. God, I need to go out and shower my head. I can't think straight now. What the hell next?" Siobhan had got to her feet and was pacing the room

"You're wound up. It's a good idea. Clearing heads with a good walk on the bridge. Don't fret anymore, love. Megan's death had nothing to do with either of us so just relax a bit."

"Those detectives. They don't think it was an accident, do they? The questions they're asking. Wondering where you were on Saturday night. Do they think someone killed her? What's going on in that big one's head? It's scary. I wish to God I hadn't come over for that reunion party. You know I don't even think Megan was planning on going to Australia. I think it was some sort of trap. One of her fairy tales to make her the centre of attention."

"I know I shouldn't have said she was a bitch, but really she was trouble. Why the hell did you want to expose yourself to all that again? I can't understand it."

With a sniff, Siobhan turned away from Rhys. "I thought maybe she'd say she was sorry. That she'd acknowledge in some way that what she did to you was wrong." Rhys snorted at that, but Siobhan continued. "I think, you know, she might have been working towards that. Your name wasn't mentioned all weekend. Even when we talked about the good times, we had in uni. That was weird, then, sure, they knew..."

"... and they didn't want to upset anything. Bet Megan staged it all. Maybe she was going to make a big scene over it on Sunday. That would be her style."

"We'll never know. She did come into the kitchen when I was making a cuppa on Saturday morning. She gave me a hug, just out of the blue. She could be lovely, you know. I thought she was going to say she was sorry at that point, when Aisha came in. Och, maybe that's just wishful thinking."

Rhys stroked her hair. "Maybe. Let's hope she was sorry. I'm sorry she's dead. That's a tragedy you wouldn't wish on any family. Still, I'm glad she's out of our lives and we don't have that shadow to live under." He drew he close again and kissed the top of her head. "And let's hope those police officers didn't cotton on to why the diffuser was running. Now, come on. Walk. Let's clear, no, what do you say, shower your head." He said it with a mock Irish accent and Siobhan laughed. No matter how awful things were, she had Rhys to lean on. She knew that now. He'd proved his love for her, hadn't he?

CHAPTER ELEVEN

As they walked along the path to Mandy's car, they were both digesting and thinking about the scene they'd just witnessed.

"What you think, Josh? Motive? Could Siobhan have spiked Megan's drink? Revenge?"

Josh was busy on his phone, so he didn't respond straightaway. That irritated Mandy. She fumed while he prodded and pressed keys and then read the screen, oblivious to her impatience.

"Rhys is in the clear. I texted the number he gave us, and his alibi is solid."

"Check the number. It could be just a mate of his."

"You've got a devious mind, boss. I'll check it out when we get back. Right now, I think it's lunchtime and I'm hungry. Is there a pub near here? With a beer garden?"

"Why a beer garden? It's a nice day but still a bit windy."

"I need a fag." Mandy glanced sideways and noticed how tense Josh seemed. Come to think of it he'd been a bit on edge on the way down too. She'd been too absorbed in thoughts of the case to notice.

"Thought you'd given up."

"I had." He grunted. "We had our first counselling session last night."

Ah, that was it. Trying to fix his marriage. Stress of that on top of work stress. Living in what was little more than a kennel. She waited. Didn't ask the question.

"It didn't go well."

"Oh."

"Apparently I am oblivious to her needs. Causing emotional distress because I'm never at home. Long hours working. Uncommunicative. Difficult. Choose whatever adjective you like to describe a useless husband. By the time Lisa had finished saying her bit, I felt as though I'd been kicked in the balls so often, I was paralysed."

"Did you say anything to defend yourself?" Mandy curbed her tongue at that point although her thoughts ran on. Like how his wife's spending and idealised view of reality didn't coincide with the life and salary of a police officer?

"What could I say after that? I mumbled that I was in a stressful job. She knew what I did before we got married. The counsellor said we'd made a good start. Sure as hell didn't feel like it. That's why I need a fag."

Mandy pulled into the car park of the Two Rivers. She gave Josh a twenty-pound note.

"I want to ring in to see if forensics have come up with anything yet. I'll have a pint of soda and lime and the soup of the day. Get yourself something to eat. No beer. You're not going back stinking of booze and fags. We're working."

Josh hesitated and rubbed his nose for a second before heading off to the bar while Mandy made her way to the beer garden. The morning had been cool, now the warmth of the sun was pleasant, and she was glad of a chance to stop and recap what they'd learnt that morning. The hum of traffic could be heard, children's laughter and a waft of warm air from the kitchen carried cooking smells. Her stomach grumbled in response. That bowl of soup would be welcome. She wandered over to one of the picnic style benches and took out her phone. A movement behind alerted her to Josh's return and then an arm snaked around her waist and a rough stubble rubbed against her neck.

"Hey babe. Haven't seen you for a while. Did ya miss me?"

Mandy swung around grabbed the man and twisted his arm behind his back before he had time to do more than growl, "What the fuck?"

"What the hell do you think you're doing, dickhead?"

A startled face twisted around to look at her. He was shorter than her, muscled with a tattoo of a dragon on his forearm. Shaved head and casual clothes and smelling of strong aftershave or something heavy like that, despite the stubble.

"You're not Joy. Lemme go, bitch."

Josh appeared and was as bemused as some of the other customers. Lucky for them it was mid-week and quiet so only a couple of smokers were witness to the fracas.

"What's going on?" asked Josh.

Mandy released the man and he stood up adjusting himself and shaking his shoulders. "Made a mistake, didna? No need to get all the aggro though. I should give you a slap."

"I wouldn't do that if I were you." Mandy took out her warrant card and waved it at him. For a moment alarm showed on his face.

"Didn't mean it, did I? Mistaken identity. Sorry. Whatever."

"Sit down. Tell me about Joy."

He hesitated, eyes moving from Mandy to Josh and back again before perching himself edge of the bench. Mandy sat down too. He glared at Mandy through narrowed eyes.

"Looks just like you, Joy does. Bit darker 'suppose. Could be your twin. Made a mistake."

"So where does Joy live? When did you last see her? What do you know about her?"

"Why? She done summat wrong? I ain't seen her for weeks. End of April. Naw, beginning May. Just before the bank holiday. Down the Coach and Horses, she was."

"End of April?" Mandy's head was working overtime. Joy had last been in touch with them to say she was back in the UK in March. She'd been here, in Chepstow in April or May. So where was she now?

"Where did you meet Joy?"

"Bus. On way back from London. Sat beside her. She said she was going to Cardiff but got off wi' me in Chepstow. Seen her a couple times since."

Mandy thought about the way he'd greeted her before she'd twisted his arm. That sort of familiarity didn't come from a casual encounter on a bus. He wasn't telling the truth, or not all of it.

"I think there's more to it. How close were you?" She glared at him and he glared back. No reply. Time to get evil.

"That's fine Mr?"

"Mickey Mouse."

Josh snorted with laughter. "You'll have to do better than that, mate."

"Perhaps Mr Mouse would like to accompany us to the station so we can charge him with assaulting a police officer." Mandy was beginning to lose patience and her left eye was twitching.

"Hey. Okay. No need to get nasty. It was a mistake. Said I'm sorry. I dunno where Joy is. We had a couple of nights together. Then she says she's gotta go. Get her head together. Saw her once after that. Swear."

Mandy still didn't believe him, but she was in the middle of an investigation. No time to go off on a tangent. Recalling the scene in the station with Withers this morning she couldn't pursue this now. Bugger. It would have to wait.

"Give me your real name and address and we'll let you go, for now. If you see Joy again you tell her that her family is searching for her. Right? Got it?" She stared at him in what she hoped was a menacing way. He stared back and shrugged, unconcerned it seemed.

"Yeah. Got it. You're nearly as crazy a bitch as her." He spat on the grass and one lip curled in disdain. Mandy ignored it and got to her feet, pretending a nonchalance she didn't feel.

Josh took down the guy's particulars while she paced up and down. Where the hell was Joy now? Still in the area or moved on? Why wasn't she coming home to her daughter? Should she tell Tabitha about this? Bollocks. As if life wasn't complicated enough. The guy moved off with a quick peep over his shoulder to make sure they weren't following. The waitress came out with their food which provided a distraction. Mandy's appetite had all but disappeared, although she knew she needed to eat something. She brooded while Josh attacked his meal with relish. He was always hungry, or so it seemed. Being separated from his wife seemed to have increased his need for sustenance, not diminished it.

CHAPTER TWELVE

Josh didn't ask any questions, but Mandy felt she needed to offer him an explanation.

"Joy's my sister. We haven't seen her for a year. Last time we heard from her was March. It seems she doesn't want us to know where she is."

"Wow, boss. I didn't know you had a sister."

"More than that. Identical twins." Josh's mouth dropped open and Mandy had to laugh at him. "Didn't think there could be two of me, did you?"

"Well, it's just that I never thought about it. It explains that guy's reactions. He must have been freaked out." Josh laughed. "He was coming on to you, wasn't he?"

"Ha bloody ha. You might never have thought I had a sister, but I've thought of little else except her for the last year. Joy upped and left. On holiday for a week in Greece was the story. Could I look after Tabs for her? That's my niece, Tabitha." Mandy had spotted Josh's confused expression. "So, off she goes. Next thing she's got a job over there in a bar or something. Mam said, "Oh, proper Shirley Valentine, isn't she?" and didn't worry. Neither did I, at first. Joy's always been a bit on the feral side."

Josh was frowning now, no doubt wondering what she was going on about. "Sorry, Josh. Before your time. Shirley Valentine is a film about a woman who goes on holiday to Greece and meets a man so stays there. We all thought she'd be home for Christmas. Tabs was full of it. Really excited. Three days before a parcel and card arrives. She's coming back after Christmas. March was the last we heard. She was on her way back. She didn't make it to Cardiff though. Now I know why or at least, where."

"Sounds as though she's around here somewhere. Do you want to go and ask the local boys?"

"Not today. We've a case to solve and a short time frame to do it. I'm just bloody furious. How can she be so damned selfish? Her daughter is the loveliest kid and she's just abandoned her." Mandy slapped the table with such force the glasses rattled. "I'll come back one day and have another little chat with Mr Mickey Mouse."

"She's still with you? Tabitha, I mean?"

"Yeah. I like it to be honest. This job can be a killer and it's good to have a grounding. Something else to worry about. Otherwise, it sucks the very soul out of you."

"I know what you mean."

Their food was good. Mandy's soup and crusty bread was piping hot and Josh had a mound of pie and chips. Not exactly healthy food. Mandy couldn't help comment.

"Hey. I know it's none of my business but smoking, drinking and eating fatty foods all the time isn't good for you. You want to live long enough to get your pension at least."

"I know that, but I'm no cook. My wife was the health expert. I'm past caring now."

Another bloody problem to lay on her plate. The inquiry seemed to be going in circles. Mandy was sure there was more to find out. Why hadn't Siobhan told her about Rhys? Why did no one seem to care when Megan went wandering off?

"What are your feelings about Siobhan and Rhys? Is she genuine? I mean do you forgive the woman who set up your boyfriend, broke up a long-standing relationship and then stalked him afterwards. If Rhys had been around over the weekend, I'd suspect him. Megan was evil towards him. Would Siobhan take revenge on his behalf? On her own grounds? After all she'd been wronged. Humiliated."

"Don't know, boss. Siobhan strikes me as genuine. She wasn't expecting to see us there, was she? They seemed close, and she doesn't seem the vengeful type. Bit too laid back for that, I'd say."

"What have we got? Anything at all? We need to chase forensics. See if they got anything from the wash bag or in the house that might point to foul play."

"Like what?"

"Balls. I don't know. Anything at all that confirms I'm right. Something went on in that house and they aren't telling us what. We need to keep digging. Let's hope background comes back with something we can use as leverage. Get those four musketeers to open their gobs."

The journey back was quick enough until they got to Cardiff. End of school time so heavy traffic. Mandy thought about Tabitha and her upcoming test. She hoped Kelly wasn't being too much of a distraction. Tabs was a bright girl. She'd do well with her studies, given half a chance. Mandy intended for her to get every opportunity available and things she didn't have when growing up.

* * *

Olivia stood up as soon as she saw Mandy and Josh. "Ma'am. Boss. There's been a development."

"Out with it."

"Well, they found two sets of fingerprints on those pills in Megan Pritchard's washbag, didn't they? Hers and somebody else's."

"So, somebody else knew Megan was on antipsychotics. Who? And will that make a difference to the case? We still haven't got strong motive or evidence of any sort. We can't just go and ask for fingerprints from those four women without a reason. Still, it's something." She sighed. Another clue or just a complication?

"Well, we've got Aisha's fingerprints, haven't we? That's a start." Olivia's head was bobbing up and down. Mandy thought she looked like a puppet.

"Have we? How? Has she got previous?"

Olivia snorted. "No. On the photograph of the earring you showed her."

Bloody hell. Why hadn't she remembered that? Of course, too busy thinking about Joy and whether to tell

Tabitha about the latest development. At least she knew her sister was in the country and still alive. Or was still alive a few weeks ago.

"Nice one, Olivia. Get the photo down to them and ask them to check. Josh, I want you to check Siobhan's movements from about the time of the break-up with Rhys. Oh, and have a butcher's at Bethan's modelling profile. That should liven up your day." She smiled at him and raised her eyebrows. "Where's Helen?"

"Here, boss." Helen came into the office behind Mandy's back. "I've just been speaking to Megan's family. They want to know when they can have the body."

"Have another word with Rishi. See if he's got all the evidence, and samples, he needs in case there's any further investigation. If he says so, then we can release her. Oh, and Helen, do a little digging for me. Speak to Megan's employers. What did they think of her? Did she have close friends in the firm? Anyone make any complaints? That sort of thing."

"Yes, boss."

"And do the same with Sophie Grant. She walked out of a job in London with nowhere to go. I know she's had a tough time of it but check out with the Met about that break-in at her place. See if there's anything there. Oh, and keep it under the radar. We don't need to let the Super know everything."

A knowing look spread across Helen's face. God, did they all know that she'd had more than one run in with Withers.

"Any sign of that missing phone yet?"

"No. Local boys did another search of the house. Clean."

"Did they search the garden and lane?"

"Yes, like you asked. They checked the field where she was found, and the neighbouring fields were searched too. Do you want them to search anywhere else?"

"Then it's either in a ditch somewhere or someone's got it. Did Olivia get the telephone records up? See who she's been talking to. Any threats or anything at all that's amiss. From what we've learnt so far, she could be a nasty piece of work when she wanted. Maybe someone thought she'd gone too far. Let's dig deeper. See what emerges."

The Super emerged from his office and glared at them on his way out. He wanted results and an outcome that pointed towards misadventure would suit him. Well, Mandy wasn't sure he was going to be pleased when she did find something significant. By seven she called it a day and sent them all home. Josh was the last to leave. Not much joy for him in a bedsit. He took his laptop with him. No wonder his wife complained. He was, like a lot of coppers, married to the job but it wasn't always a good bed mate.

As Mandy was leaving the building a figure approached and hailed her.

"DI Wilde. I believe you're the one investigating Megan Pritchard's death. Have you got something for me?"

As he got closer Mandy recognised Tod Blakeney, wannabe reporter with his own blog relating to news around the city.

"No comment. Speak to Superintendent Ross Withers."

"Aw, come on. I'll make it worth your while. I may have some interesting information on the case."

"If you know anything then you are duty bound to report it to the authorities. Otherwise, if I find out you've been withholding information, I'll see you in court."

As she turned away from him, Tod reached out and grabbed her arm. She stopped and through clenched teeth said, "Get your filthy paws off me or I'll have your balls on a platter."

He dropped his hand. "Okay. Sorry. I've heard stuff. Thought you might be a little interested in an exchange of information, like."

It was impossible to hide her dislike of him, but any gem of information could help.

"I'm not saying jack shit and, if you know anything, you'd better spill. Now."

He took a step back and put both hands in the air. "Hey, okay. Seems that there's a rumour there was something going on in that fancy house in the Vale. Nythfa was built on the plot where another house stood for a century."

"Tell me something I don't know."

"It was haunted. The resting place of a witch. Maybe those women had a coven. Bit of Ouija board gone wrong. Something not quite right there."

"Tod. You are talking through your arse. Go home. Find something else to write about. Rats with three heads or something equally fascinating and just as credible."

Fuming, Mandy got into her car. Haunted houses. Witches' covens. He needed his head seeing to.

* * *

Kelly was still with Tabitha when she got home. She could hear them giggling from the hallway. The television was on, its flickering light reflecting on the pale walls and the music background drowning the click as she opened the front door. When she entered the main room, they were sitting, heads together, huddled over something on a mobile phone. Alerted by Mandy's footstep on the wooden floor, Kelly glanced up and then put her phone in her pocket. Mandy raised an eyebrow and Kelly met her gaze with guileless blue eyes. So, something she didn't want to share with her best friend's aunty. Oh well. That was part of growing up. She'd giggled with Joy over the dirty pages in their Mam's novels and ogled the blokes in the Littlewoods catalogue. Normal curiosity.

"Well, what have you two been up to? Have you had something to eat?"

"Umm. We went to Lidl and got the shopping and a couple of slices of pizza. I got some cooked chicken drumsticks in case you were late. What happened?" Tabitha stopped when Mandy shook her head. She didn't want to talk in front of Kelly. Besides talking about some of the cases she was involved in would give anyone nightmares, never mind an impressionable fifteen-year-old.

She was grateful to Kelly for keeping Tabitha company but then she suspected Kelly enjoyed getting out of her own over-crowded house. With three brothers it must be good to escape now and again. Kelly beamed and Mandy thought how different she was from her niece. More streetwise. Just fifteen and beginning to be more than aware of her sexuality with tight low-fitting tops and short skirts. Full make-up too. Too heavy for such a pretty girl. Black lined eyes, baby pink lipstick and cloying perfume. Tabitha didn't seem to be following suit so that was a relief. How do you deal with teenage girls? When she thought about some of the things she'd got up to with Joy. Well, she hoped she wouldn't have that sort of behaviour from her niece. She smiled at the memories.

"What are you smiling about?" Tabitha had noticed.

"Just remembering some of the things your Mam and I did when we were fifteen."

"Oh, do tell." Kelly's eyes were sparkling in anticipation.

"There's nothing too awful." Mandy laughed. "Well, nothing I'm going to tell you, anyway. Joy used to pinch Mam's cigarettes and we'd go down the park."

"You don't smoke." Tabitha frowned. "My Mam did." Mandy noticed the use of past tense. Did Tabs think her mother was dead or was it just because she was talking about the past? One day they'd have to have a frank discussion about that. Today wasn't the time.

"No. I don't, and I didn't then, but Joy did. One day she persuaded me to try one. I took a huge drag, coughed so much I was sick over my new skirt. Joy thought it was hilarious. Mam made me wash it myself by hand and then do all the ironing to boot. I think that's why I hate ironing." She turned towards the kitchen.

"Now, I'm going to make a cuppa. Do either of you want anything?"

"I think I'd better be getting home, ta. Would it be alright if Tabitha came over one night and stayed at ours? Maybe Thursday?" Kelly's blue eyes were wide-open and questioning.

"That should be fine. Any night? Why Thursday?"

"We've a test Friday morning and we thought we could revise together. If that's okay." Her eyes met Tabitha's and Mandy thought she saw something pass between them. A warning? A message of some sort? What were they up to? Probably meeting boys. That's what she was doing at that age. What should she do? God parenting was hard. Like walking on the edge of a skyscraper in bare feet with no safety harness.

"Well, I'm probably going to be tied up with this case over the next week and possibly more. Tabs is likely to be having a lot of time alone. Why don't you come here and stay over? I'm sure you'd be glad of the peace and quiet and your Mam might enjoy having one less under her feet."

Kelly's mouth opened and closed for a moment. Mandy had to suppress a giggle. She was right. They were up to something and trying to have a cover story.

Kelly shrugged. "Suppose. I can ask Mam. It's just that school is a bit closer from our house. More revision time in the morning."

Despite herself Mandy laughed. That Kelly was a minx but if they were together, it was probably going to be alright. Safer at least.

"Good point. We'll think on it."

Tabitha went to the door with her friend and there followed more whispering and giggling. When she came back and sat on the sofa, she was a bit flushed. Some conspiracy between them. Certain of that, Mandy questioned her niece.

"So, what's the deal with Kelly? She's got a boyfriend or something? Wants a cover story for being out late?"

The expression of astonishment in Tabitha's eyes was enough proof. Should she do something about it? A hard call.

"Well, just be careful, okay. Don't let Kelly draw you into her little schemes if you don't feel happy about it. Make up your own mind. I trust you to be sensible."

Tabitha didn't speak and the hint of anxiety was back in her eyes. Mandy felt a real killjoy, but she saw too much in her job to be flippant about things and Tabitha was too naïve at times, believing the best of everyone. Maybe by Thursday they'd have changed their minds about whatever the plan was. She wondered what Kelly was going to tell her parents. Should she check up on that?

Mandy made popcorn and they sat together and watched a comedy film. It was good to have a home life that was restful. She thought of Josh in his lonely flat and felt a wave of pity. When they'd sorted this mystery death out, she'd invite him over one evening and cook. She suspected he was living on takeaway meals and beer and it wasn't good for him. He needed to get his life sorted.

It was a pleasant and relaxing evening. As the tension left her body, Mandy was grateful for that. God knows what mayhem the rest of the week would bring.

CHAPTER THIRTEEN

WEDNESDAY

Despite her scepticism Mandy thought it was worth checking out the history of the house. After all, some people were susceptible to suggestion and maybe they had been doing those sorts of silly games and it had unnerved them. It didn't explain the alcohol although it could relate to the reluctance of those professional women to divulge whatever it was they were hiding. She Googled Nythfa, not really expecting anything to turn up and was amazed when the first thing was a picture of the house and a potted history dated two years previously.

Nythfa – a restoration of renown

This stunning architect designed house has just been completed. It is to be the new country home of David Grant, local businessman and entrepreneur.

A building has stood here for over two centuries. At first it was reputed to be a resting place for smugglers on their way from the coast to Cowbridge. A shelter, no more than a hut, hidden in the dip.

Then in the early twentieth century a more substantial building was erected.

John Jones settled with his family but when all his animals, and then, his wife died, he left, believing the place to be cursed. He sold it to Emrys Hughes in 1920. However, the house burnt down in a mysterious fire before Hughes could move in.

The ruin remained, crumbling and overgrown, with rumours of ghosts and strange sounds haunting the area until two years ago, when David Grant saw the plot. He decided it was the perfect place to build his dream home ready for his retirement. Let us hope the curse of Nythfa does not spoil those plans and the ghosts have been laid to rest.

The curse of Nythfa. Mandy thought for a moment about it. David Grant died before he could live there and now a young woman's death was connected to the place. Coincidence. Nothing more. Who wrote that claptrap? What a load of bull. Suppose that's what Tod was getting at. Waste of time. The only thing Mandy had experienced in that house was envy. To have all that space. The downside was it was in the middle of nowhere. She shivered. Nightmare to think of living there. City dwelling, noise and pollution was the way to go.

With the team engaged in various tasks Mandy sat down with a sheet of paper and started making a mind map of what they knew or suspected. Four friends. Or were they? She'd already uncovered secrets that impacted on the relationships. She thought about Tod and his witches' coven. She didn't believe for one moment anything like that was going on, yet those young women had time to get their stories to line up while they waited for the police to arrive. For God's sake they'd cleaned the bloody house. Who does that when your friend is missing? Nuts. What had they found out so far in this investigation?

She started with Megan Pritchard and drew a circle in the middle of the page. Until they had some feedback from her line-manager and the people she worked with they only had what the others and her family had said. The family. The golden girl in their eyes. Bright. Beautiful. Done well for herself. Worked hard to climb the career ladder. And that flat. Expensive place to live although it was pretty comfortless. Was that significant? Did her anxiety prevent her from anything? Was she depressed? Why did she tell her friends she was going to Australia? None of them believed it anyway.

"Boss, bit of info from Megan's firm." Josh interrupted her train of thought. "She was ambitious, capable and had just landed a plum job in London. Two of the staff from the firm were shortlisted. Megan pipped the other one at the post. Guess who that other one was?"

"Aisha Matharu."

Josh frowned, disappointed that she'd outwitted him.

"Did you know before?"

"No Josh, although I don't know anyone else from that firm who was at Nythfa over the weekend, do I?

Makes sense. It's not exactly top-notch detective work." Josh flushed and she wished she'd kept that thought to herself. "I wonder if that means Aisha will get the job. Not much of a motive for homicide. Anything else? Gossip? Little gems of wisdom?" Mandy was tempted to cross her fingers. Anything, however small, could make a difference in the direction of this investigation.

"She was well liked although no close friends in the department. She did her job, kept everybody happy, from cleaners up to the big boss, was a team player when she had to be, but regarded as a bit of a go-getter. Always telling everyone about her successes."

"And this Australia thing?"

He shook his head. "Doesn't seem as if that was anything except an excuse for a get together. She'd got the job in London after all."

There was nothing, so far, to suggest there was any truth in that Australia story. Her friends said she could be a bit of a drama queen and two-faced at times, but they still met up with her. Why? Did she have some hold over them? The more Mandy thought about it the more confused she became. Megan was an enigma. A complicated character whose death was also a mystery.

In fact, the more she thought about it all, the more convinced Mandy became that it wasn't an accident. Nia had told them that Megan never drank after an incident in the past when she'd had a psychotic episode following mixing alcohol and her medication. Perhaps they should talk to her doctor or psychiatrist. It could give some insight into her past. What had happened. Why she needed such strong medication and if she suffered from delusions as well as anxiety. Without reasonable suspicion of foul play, and possibly a warrant, Mandy doubted if any information would be forthcoming. Patient confidentiality and all that.

Then there was the place she'd been found. That didn't make sense either. Why go on a walk through a field in the dark? Why not stick to the road?

Mandy checked out the floorplan of the house. She marked out who was where and at what times from the information they'd been given. She noted whose bedroom was nearest Megan's. Entrances and exits. The front door wasn't the only way out. She wondered if it would be possible for someone to go out unseen. Or to enter unseen. If someone else could have been present in the house at the time. Someone who threatened Megan, perhaps.

That was probably a step too far. Any car approaching would be seen at night so unless someone was on foot, they'd be spotted. Besides, nobody mentioned anything unusual, although she was convinced that they were all hiding something. So, back to the question. Could someone have left the house unseen by the others? Both Bethan and Aisha were alone at the time Megan ran out, but she could have been followed. Chased by one or other. No sign of attack. Maybe the terror she expressed was real to her. So, why across fields?

Only one way to find out. She sent a quick text to Tabitha, trying to quell the feelings of guilt as she did so.

'Back late. Vegetable lasagne in the freezer. Don't wait up.'

Then she cast her eyes over the team. Josh? No. He said he wanted to talk to Lisa later, didn't he? Another case of being made to feel he's in the wrong with his wife calling all the shots. Helen had family commitments, an ailing mother and two children, so she couldn't ask her at short notice.

"Olivia. Have you got plans for this evening?"

Olivia stared at her through round glasses. "Just a bath and Netflix. I'm watching this lush..."

"Great. You can come with me. We're going on a little adventure this evening. How's your sense of direction?"

"Eh, pretty good. I was in the scouts, I was. We did..."

"Even better. We're going to have another look at Megan's flat first. Talk to the concierge. You can bat your eyelashes at him. Then we're off to the Vale this evening. I'm going to see if I can unlock one of the mysteries in this damned puzzle. Josh, text if you find out anything useful. I'll be out of signal range until about ten tonight. Come on, Olivia. Stuff to do."

Olivia blinked, grabbed her notebook, shoved it into her bag and, with her jacket half on and half off, trotted out after Mandy who was already striding down the corridor.

"Where to are we going tonight then?" asked Olivia.

"Nythfa, if I can find it again, and the field where Megan Pritchard's body was found. I want to know why she was wandering around fields in the dark. Why she didn't stick to the road. Before then, a closer look at the apartment. See if we've missed anything. Okay?"

Olivia almost jiggled. She was full of enthusiasm. Mandy recalled being as eager when she'd started in CID. Cases like this one, where nothing seemed to fit, were both frustrating and exciting. Pitting her wits against the odds and seeing what happened.

The same concierge was on duty in the foyer. Mandy flashed her badge again before they went upstairs. Questions later.

"Nice view," said Olivia when they entered the apartment. She wandered over to the window. Down below they could see people wandering around in shorts and tops, even though the temperature was below seventeen. What was the matter with people? A bit of sun and they thought they were in the Med. "What we looking for, boss?"

"I'm not sure. Evidence of a life, I suppose. What do you see? What does this tell you about Megan Pritchard?"

Olivia squinted through her specs and wandered around the room taking note of everything on display, not touching anything.

"She's messy. Doesn't have visitors. Not much in the way of reading for pleasure or home entertainment, there isn't. It feels sort of lonely. Does that sound daft?"

"No. That's what we felt too when I came here with Josh. Like the trappings of a successful life were all a front and on her home turf there's nothing."

"No photos. You'd think she'd have one of her family or something now, wouldn't you? Left it all with her Mam, did she?"

Mandy shook her head. "That's the other odd thing. She took all her stuff when she moved out, but we didn't see any of it here. Still, we didn't search too far, so you and I are going to do it more thoroughly. Backs of wardrobes and cupboards, under the bed. You know the drill. I did wonder about sending forensics in to check for fingerprints. That's probably a waste of resources. Whatever happened to her, didn't happen here."

Donning latex gloves, they set about searching through each room in turn. A few receipts from the supermarket revealed that she preferred fruit and vegetables to cake and sweets. No alcohol on any of them so, if she had ever entertained at the apartment, she would only have offered her guests soft drinks. The kitchen cupboard had a few cans of Coke, tins of beans and stale cheese biscuits. In the fridge a lonely piece of brie sat beside a pot of Greek yogurt and a bag of soggy salad.

The study had a bookcase, but the only books were about accountancy and management. No novels or poetry.

"She was a go-getter, wasn't she? Look at these, boss." Olivia read out the list of titles. "How to get Ahead by Beating the Competition. Be the Best; to Hell with the Rest. Stepping Up to the Next Level. Tells you she put the job first."

"Everyone says that she was highly competitive. Cut-throat by the sounds of it. If one of the others had been found dead in a field, I'd suspect Megan."

The desk drawer had a couple of notebooks and a diary. Unusual for a modern woman. Everything was online these days. Mandy flicked through. A few initials here and there. Pedicure. Hair. Manicure. Massage. High maintenance woman.

The bathroom cupboard had more of the anti-psychotic drugs, painkillers and an assortment of expensive toiletries and cosmetics.

"Wow. Chanel, Mac, Bobby Brown. She knew how to pamper herself, didn't she now?" Olivia was amazed. On her constable's salary she would opt for cheaper brands. It was luxury that seemed to jar with the almost austere surroundings of the apartment.

It was the same in the bedroom. The wardrobe had fewer clothes than Mandy had stuffed into her wardrobe. Each item with a designer label. The exterior girl. All show to cover up what? Did she feel inadequate? Under stress all the time? Could that have been the root of her anxiety?

Olivia was rooting about in the bedside table. "Well, she didn't spend all her time alone, she didn't."

Grinning at Mandy, she waved a box of condoms in the air. "Right at the back of the drawer. Pack of twelve with seven left. So, she saw a bit of action, at least."

"With Rhys do you think?" asked Mandy. "Was he two-timing Siobhan even while he was persuading her to get back with him?" Mandy thought about it for a moment, but she remembered the looks the pair had exchanged and the Facebook photos of Rhys showed him more caught than complicit. "I don't think so somehow. It may not be relevant. Maybe the concierge would have some ideas."

She thought about the scowl he'd given her on the way in and figured Olivia might be able to elicit a more open response from him than she would. Mandy's brash approach didn't always work, and she didn't do flirting.

"I'm going to bag those up and some other bits. Go and flash your teeth at the concierge. Show him the photo of Rhys on Facebook. See if he recognises him. Try to get a bit of gossip out of him. Any visitors. You know the sort of thing. I'll have a poke around in the chest of drawers and meet you downstairs in about ten minutes or so."

"Sure. No probs." Olivia bounced out of the flat with a last glance at the view.

Mandy took the bagged items and put them on the worktop in the living area. A seagull perched on the balcony and stared at her with its beady eyes. She stared back and then went back to the bedroom. The chest of drawers provided nothing except a selection of good quality underwear, some of it a bit racy, most Marks and Spencer.

The wardrobe had a drawer at the bottom and that was the last place to check. God knows what she expected to find but sometimes little things led to avenues yet unexplored and she needed to find something. An old handbag, stuffed with photographs was shoved right to the back. Mandy took it out and flicked through. They were school photographs showing Megan at various stages of her life. A chubby infant and youngster, right up until secondary school where a dramatic change took place. She was almost gaunt in one photograph and then in the next more rounded. Mandy wondered if that's when the anxiety had set in, resulted in an eating disorder. The haggard look on that face reminded her of Sophie Grant. Had Megan's ghosts come back to haunt her? Perhaps Megan had drunk the alcohol deliberately, to gain attention.

* * *

Olivia stood by the concierge and gave him her loveliest smile. Get him relaxed. Get him talking. He was late fifties she reckoned, bit like her uncle Joe, thickset with one cauliflower ear. Bet he was a good player in his day. His uniform stretched across a waistline that indicated a more sedentary pace of life now.

"Gosh. Do you get bored being here all day? It's a lovely view but I'd get a bit fed up, I think."

"Oh, it's interesting enough at times. Deliveries. Checking up on people. Delivering a service." His accent indicated he was local. "Sometimes we have visitors who come and want to know about the history of the Bay. That's what I like. I've lived here all my life. Know Cardiff both old and new. Years ago, this was all the docks. Tiger Bay. Now look at it. High rises and luxury hotels. Who'd have believed it?"

With a murmur of agreement, Olivia said, "Bet you see some cases, heh? After the rugby like? You played?" Establish a rapport. Rule One when interviewing. Olivia tried to remember the rest of the rules.

"Indeed. All good fun. We see quite a few visitors when there's a game at the stadium. Some of these flats are rented out." He gave Olivia a quizzical look.

"You're with the police. Investigating that death I suppose. I saw that photograph in the paper. Poor young woman."

"You knew her, or at least you'll have seen her."

"Oh yes. Always very well-dressed. Pleasant enough when she had a parcel to collect from the office. Some of the residents can be a bit stand-offish. Miss Pritchard wasn't one of those."

"Did she get many visitors?"

"Not that I saw."

"Men?" Olivia scrolled through Facebook and brought up the picture of Rhys Davies. "Ever seen this guy with her?"

He took a pair of spectacles out of his inner pocket and peered at the photograph. Olivia flicked through to show him others so that he had a wider idea of Rhys, his build, dress sense, that sort of thing. He shook his head.

"No. Definitely not. She did bring a gentleman back with her from time to time but, ah, not the same gentleman. If you get my drift."

"No regular guy?"

"No. And not many others that I saw. And we see quite a lot going on, you know." He paused, allowing her to make her own assumptions. "Miss Pritchard, she was quiet now. Never gave any bother and nothing dodgy about her."

"Thanks for your help. If there's anything you remember then let us know, won't you?"

Mandy came down the stairs at that point and Olivia gave her a discreet thumbs up. They had all the information they were likely to have from Megan's apartment, so it was time to move on.

Olivia smiled and gave a friendly wave to the concierge as they left.

"Want to grab a bite before we head out to the Vale?" asked Mandy. "I'll just put these things in the boot. We can grab something from Tesco and find a bench or somewhere we can talk without being overheard."

After their supermarket visit, armed with drinks and snacks they headed away from the general crowd and found a bench near the Norwegian church. The wind whipped around them, and the waves were beginning to become choppy but the change in the weather helped their purpose as people didn't linger too long. Looking up at the grey clouds scudding across the sky Mandy hoped it wasn't going to rain. That would make their little evening adventure a bit miserable.

"Anything useful from the concierge?"

"Well, he was totally confident he'd never seen Rhys. Mind, he's only worked there a year."

"And, according to the story Rhys broke up with Siobhan about eighteen months ago. So, it looks as though he's been telling us the truth about Megan, at least."

CHAPTER FOURTEEN

Despite her concerns that they might not be able to find the house again in the dusk, it was easy second time around. They had a set of keys for Nythfa, but it was the surrounding countryside that Mandy was most interested in. As they got out of the car something was hovering in the air around them.

"What the…?" Mandy swiped as something brushed her hair.

"It's only bats," said Olivia. "They do come out at this time of night. Cute little things really."

"Bats, cute? You must be bloody joking. Mice with wings. After blood."

Olivia laughed and the sound echoed around the hollow. It wasn't dark but the place was shrouded in shadows and Mandy had an uncomfortable feeling that perhaps someone was watching. That's what the countryside did for her. Made her neurotic.

They approached the house and a light flicked on, illuminating their steps to the front door. They let themselves in and had a quick scan around. Mandy's eyes crinkled in amusement at Olivia's open-mouthed appraisal of the building.

"Wow. This is something else. Like out of a fancy mag."

Rishi had confirmed that Megan had died in the field, not anywhere else, so they were just seeking evidence. Anything. Mandy didn't know what to expect and the house looked, and smelled, clean. No ghosts or ghouls. The outside bins hadn't been emptied so the rubbish was still there. Bin bags and recycling. Might be something in there worth gathering for the forensic guys.

Mandy left Olivia upstairs with instructions on which direction to look towards. She drove to the field where the body had been found and gazed towards Nythfa. The house was almost hidden, though she thought she could just catch sight of the rooftop and perhaps a faint light from the bedroom window. She hoped Olivia could see through the trees as she held her torch up and signalled. A moment. Nothing. Damn. Try again. Click on. Off. On. Off. On again. Then, at last, an answering signal. Mandy turned in the opposite direction and saw what she needed to see. She got into the car and drove back to the house and Olivia.

"So, what did you see? Beyond my signal, I mean. Could you see it too?"

"Yes, beyond that there was a light, there was. Don't know what though. House? Pub?"

"Pub, I think. Okay. Think. Let's put ourselves in her shoes." Mandy deliberated. "So, it's dark. Darker than it is now. Megan goes out in a distressed state. She gets to the end of the lane. It's the main road, such as it is, and what does she do? She walks a bit then sees something that makes her leave the road. That light? Heads towards it."

Olivia tilted her head to one side and shrugged.

"Is it possible that's what happened?" asked Mandy. "Let's go and find out."

They secured the house again and walked down to where the sign pointed to Nythfa. Although the sun was dropping and it was that time when it's too dark to drive without headlights, it was still not the denseness of midnight. A scream cut through the air.

Mandy reacted in alarm. "Is that a child? Someone's crying."

"Nah. It's a fox. Sounds like someone in pain, don't it? Proper scary if you were out here and didn't know that's what it was. Scared me too first time I heard one. Camping, I was. Thought someone was being attacked or something. Weird sound."

Mandy kept quiet. She was glad Olivia couldn't see her heightened colour. What a fool. The small village where Olivia was brought up was surrounded by countryside, obviously. Made sense she'd know. There were city foxes, of course, but Mandy had never heard that eerie sound before. It sent shivers down her spine. Had Megan heard something when she came out that night? Maybe she followed a sound or was frightened by something else.

"Right, Olivia. Imagine. You're having a psychotic episode. You think there's someone after you so you're running away from them. Desperate to find someone to help. You're confused about where to go. What do you do? Right or left? Which direction?"

"Right." Olivia didn't hesitate, turning to the right and starting to walk that way.

"Why? What made you decide on right?"

"She was right-handed, wasn't she? Makes more sense she'd turn right."

"How do you know that she was right-handed?"

"I saw the photos of the body. The watch was on the left. Left-handed people often put their watches on the right arm, don't they now?"

God, this girl was good. Bright and observant. Now she was beginning to realise why they'd fast-tracked her. Plus, no one, but no one, would expect a five foot nothing with pink hair and Harry Potter glasses to be a deductive genius. Mandy uttered a silent thanks to Withers. He thought he'd saddled her with a clown. He was wrong.

"Good thinking, Olivia. So, she'd probably go with her dominant side. Let's go right and see if your theory holds up."

The new moon was obscured by cloud and darkness had descended with speed. It was difficult to see more than a little way ahead until their eyes became more accustomed to the gloom. High hedges meant they could see little to left or right. The air hung heavy with smells Mandy couldn't identify. Damp earth. Rain in the air. Snuffling sounds and rustling in the hedges. The feeling of being watched. God, she hated the countryside even more in the dark. They turned one corner and then another and Mandy was about to suggest they turn back when a gate to the left offered a gap in the hedgerow. The remains of the police tape clung to the metal gate and the thorns in the hedgerow. This was where Megan Pritchard had been found.

"Over there." Olivia pointed and there, in the distance was a light. Was it the light they'd both seen?

Olivia was excited. "So, she comes out along the road, she does. Gets to here and sees that. Thinks, 'a shortcut', tramps across the field in a state; falls and doesn't get up again; vomits and chokes to death."

"Good theory. It gives us one answer but there's still the other women. Why didn't they go after her? And why delay reporting her missing?"

"Maybe they thought she'd be back. They'd all been drinking, hadn't they? They must have had awful hangovers in the morning."

"Yeah. None of them seemed too clever when we came out on Sunday. I wonder if that's the light of the pub. We'll have a look on the map tomorrow and see if we can locate the possible pathway. If they'd been out walking during the day, she might have thought she knew the way. I don't fancy tramping through here in the dark. Right. Time to get home. Thanks, Olivia. You've been a real help."

Olivia peered at her. "Can I say something? Something personal?"

Mandy took a deep breath. What was coming now? She couldn't see Olivia's face clearly enough, but she had the impression that the girl was blushing. "Go on."

"Well, it's just when Superintendent Withers told me I was going to be on your team I was all excited, like. Then he said he wanted me to report back as he was sure this was an accident and that when you got a bee in your bonnet over things you didn't know when to stop, you didn't." She gulped after the rush of words.

Mandy felt sorry for her and furious too. She bloody knew it. Old Withering sending in spies to keep her in check.

Olivia was still talking, fast, as if she had to get all the words out before they disappeared. "I've seen how you work, and you don't just do things because you've a notion 'bout something it's because you use that gut feeling and you're right here. This doesn't feel right, it really doesn't."

"Carry on."

"From what we know about Megan, she wasn't going to drink alcohol, was she now? So, stands to reason, it does, that somebody spiked her drink. One of her friends. Glad I don't have friends like that. And what's more I think Withers is an arse if he thinks differently."

Now that she'd said her piece, Olivia seemed subdued, as if afraid she'd overstepped the mark.

Mandy said nothing for a moment, too stunned by the outburst. Then she laughed. It sounded louder than normal in the quiet road. A bird, an owl, rose from a tree, wings flapping as it swooped over the fields.

"Olivia. Welcome to my world. And I agree. Withers is an arse. And while we're here let's get the bin bags from the house and take them back for forensics. You never know what might turn up. They were pretty careful to make sure everything was tidied up before we arrived on Sunday. That makes me suspicious as well."

It was with a lighter heart that Mandy drove back to Cardiff. She felt she could trust the girl now and Olivia Wyglendacz had a brain to boot. Bonus. In a couple of years Olivia would be sergeant material. Thinking about that, she wondered how Josh was doing. As if by telepathy, her phone rang. It was sitting in the tray between her and Olivia.

"See who that is, will you please, Olivia."

"It says Josh."

"Wonder what he's found out? Too late for anything more tonight. Early start tomorrow. Time's passing and Withers will be breathing down my neck. With a bit of luck, we've got something to take us out of his sweaty grip."

Culverhouse Cross loomed ahead. The roads were quiet, so they were back to the station by just after ten o'clock. Mandy dropped Olivia at the door of the station and drove home. The lounge lamp was on but no sign of Tabitha. Poor kid. She'd make it up to her once this case, and Tabitha's exams, were over. Maybe she'd take some of that overdue leave and they could go to Tenby for a couple of days to relax. The shadow of her sister still hung over her. That was another thing she needed to follow up. See if she could locate Joy and find out what the hell was going on with her madcap sister.

CHAPTER FIFTEEN

THURSDAY

Time was running away with them and there was still nothing more than this nagging feeling in her gut. They'd checked the map and settled on the theory that Megan had turned off the road into the fields as a shortcut to the pub. Mandy wondered if she'd stayed on the road would the results have been the same. Too many ifs. They needed more.

Then Josh came in and things started to move forward again.

"You told me to let you know if anything turned up. Well, we've spoken to the Met. No break-in reported at Sophie Grant's flat, so that's a lie. On top of that she left her job in a bit of a hurry. Just walked out one day." He paused, a triumphant glint in his eyes. "I've spoken to the firm. They said, 'unusual circumstances' whatever that means."

Great guns. Nothing like a good scandal to get the blood going in the morning. "Do we know why?"

"Nope. They wouldn't say. Confidential. Stuck up cow I spoke to made it clear she wasn't going to talk to me about it. Rabbiting on about needing authorisation. Regular jobsworth."

"I wonder what happened? I think we need to speak to Sophie Grant again. Have Megan's phone records turned up yet? Anything from her computer? Time to get heavy with forensics and give them a push. Plus, they've now got a black bin liner of stuff to sort. Tell them I'll call when I get back from a cosy little chat with Sophie."

Diane Grant raised one perfectly formed eyebrow when she saw them at the door again. There was no false smile or offer of coffee this time. Despite the fact Mandy was six inches taller than her, the cold greeting made her feel like a five-year old summoned to the head teacher's office.

"DI Wilde. To what do we owe the pleasure? If you want to speak to Siobhan she's not here."

"Yes. We know. She's in Chepstow with Rhys. We've already had another conversation with her. We'd like to have a few words with Sophie, if she's at home. There are just a few little blank spots we need to fill. You know what it's like. An itch that has to be scratched."

She doubted if Diane Grant ever scratched an itch. No doubt she'd get someone else to do it for her.

"Sophie's resting. She's very highly strung and this has been quite an ordeal for her. I do hope you don't upset her any further."

"Well, perhaps you wouldn't mind asking her to call into the station when she gets up. Just a few questions. Filling the gaps." Calling her bluff. The last thing this woman would want was her daughter going into a police station again.

Mandy watched as Diane's nostrils flared and her lips drew into a line of disapproval. Realising that the battle was lost, she left them standing in the hallway while she went upstairs, heels clicking as she passed.

"This is some place, isn't it?" Josh was taking it all in.

On the previous visit they'd been ushered through to the back of the house without delay but today, standing in a hallway the size of the entire ground floor of Mandy's house, they could see they were surrounded by wealth. A console table, with a thick cut glass vase held an arrangement of lilies, their scent heavy in the space. Floating down, they could hear mumbled voices before Sophie appeared at the top of the stairs, dressed in jeans with a loose jumper over the top, sleeves pulled down over her hands. She was picking at the ends of the sleeves as she descended.

"The small lounge, darling." A command, despite the endearment. Mrs Grant followed her daughter down then detoured to sit in the room at the front of the house. Mandy and Josh trooped after Sophie who led them to the room they'd been in on Monday, close to the kitchen.

Sophie's eyes flicked from Mandy to Josh and back again. She plucked at her sleeves and waited. Mandy stared and counted to thirty before she spoke. Making people nervous helped loosen tongues.

"We saw Siobhan yesterday. In Chepstow with Rhys. You failed to mention she was back together with him. In fact, I don't recall you mentioning him at all. Is that correct DS Jones?"

Josh made a show of flicking through his notebook, taking his time turning the pages. Mandy watched as the corner of Sophie's eye started to twitch, and her breathing became more rapid. What was this woman hiding?

"I didn't know until, until after, on Monday, after they, after the body and everything." Jumbled words then a deep breath. "Siobhan told me. She'd rung him and arranged to go down there. They'd been keeping it quiet. That they were together again. I'm glad for them. Those two were meant for each other. Megan was never really in the running."

"Did you know that Megan was stalking Rhys? That all those photographs you'll have seen on Facebook were a set-up? Why do you think she'd do that?"

Sophie's eyes had widened, the twitching stopped. "Really? Siobhan didn't say. Megan could be a bit kooky but that's just plain weird. I didn't know that. I mean, I knew that Siobhan had gone to Ireland after she split with Rhys, obviously, and that Megan had been involved. Megan was a bit like that."

"What do you mean, 'a bit like that?'"

"Megan could be a bit of a man magnet, or she liked to think she was. She'd flirt with any man who gave her a second glance. She didn't care who she hurt in the process. She'd made a play for Rhys a few times before. We all knew to keep boyfriends away from her."

Well, that was something. A few days after your friend is found dead, and already you're dishing the dirt. Time to get to the real questions.

"Tell us about your reasons for coming back to Cardiff."

The twitch was back, and Sophie didn't meet Mandy's eyes when she answered. "I had a bit of a bad time. Dad died unexpectedly and I was finding it hard to concentrate. Then someone broke into my flat and that was the final straw. I was afraid. I packed my bags and left."

"Just like that? Without a job?"

"Yes." The word was whispered, almost inaudible.

"So, were you at home when you were burgled?"

"Oh, there wasn't a burglary. Nothing was taken. I was, I mean, it shook me up. It was scary. I felt I couldn't stay there. Mum said I should come home. I'm looking for a new job."

"So, did you report it to the police?"

"No. I expect you've already checked that." A faint glimmer of a smile. "But there was nothing taken, and I wasn't harmed."

Mandy shook her head. "We've checked. You didn't report it. So, what are you covering up, Sophie? Why are you lying to me? What really happened? Why did you suddenly pack your bags and come home to Mummy?"

Sophie swallowed and then heaved a sigh. "It's complicated. You've probably found out already that I just walked out, haven't you? And I had no-where else to go."

"Yes, we know that. We want to hear the story from your viewpoint. What happened? Why did you leave so suddenly? The firm are very tight-lipped about it all."

Hesitant at first, then with growing confidence, Sophie told them her story.

"I loved it in London. Loved the job, the money, the kudos of working for a reputable company. It was brilliant. Straight out of university and already earning big money. I couldn't believe my luck. Then Dad died and things changed. I suppose I was a bit depressed. In shock or whatever."

Mandy waited, willing her to carry on.

"One of the senior partners, Mark, noticed. He asked me how he could help. He was so understanding, such a good listener. It was innocent at first. Then we had a few big projects which meant working late. One night a crowd of us went to the pub, Mark included. I had a bit too much to drink and he came with me to make sure I got home safely. It shouldn't have happened but, well, you can guess. We ended up in bed."

She was blushing now, and her hands were clenching and unclenching.

"So, you had an affair with your boss?" Josh was scribbling away, trying to be unobtrusive while watching Sophie's body language.

"I fell for him, big time. He didn't feel the same. I was just a bit on the side. When I became too clingy, he told me it was over. I begged him. God, what a fool. It was obvious to everyone else what was going on, so it had to stop. He had his reputation to think about. His wife and children too." She swallowed and then gulped a breath of air. Her hands were gripped tightly together now, the knuckles white.

"Mark came round to my flat. Let himself in and told me I had to stop making a fool of myself and him. I was distraught. I threatened to call the police and report him for intrusion. Pathetic. They'd have laughed at me. He had the key I'd given him for God's sake." She wiped away a tear at the corner of her eye. "The next day at work I handed in my notice. Mark said that if I went quietly, I could have a good reference, otherwise they'd make sure I didn't get another job with any reputable firm. I packed my bags and left that day."

"And told your mother a pack of lies so she wouldn't know what had really happened." It was a statement, not a question.

"My mother is a strong woman, but she likes to keep up appearances. If she knew there was the chance of a whiff of scandal, she'd be furious with me. This investigation, the police and reporters, it's killing her. She doesn't tolerate fools and I've been the worst sort of fool."

Sophie shook her head as if trying to rid herself of the memories of that time.

Mandy felt sorry for her. "You were grieving. Probably saw Mark as a father figure in the beginning. Sounds as if he took advantage of his position and your vulnerability. The bottom line is that you lied to us. That makes me doubt if you've told us everything about that night and your relationship with Megan."

Giving Sophie one of her 'tell me more' looks, Mandy waited to see if any more gaps would be filled in this enquiry.

"Megan asked me to arrange the weekend. I don't know what her motives were. The Australia thing was just a cover story for something else. I don't know what. She knew I needed work, there was a job coming up in her firm. I was hoping she'd put in a good word for me. Besides, I haven't seen as much of the others as I'd like. Chances for all of us to be together were few and far between." Sophie shuddered as she took a deep breath. "What happened to her was just awful."

Josh tapped his pen on his notebook and cleared his throat. Mandy looked at him, one eyebrow raised.

"We're still wondering why you didn't follow Megan when she left the house," Josh said. "It was obvious there was something wrong. She was paranoid about someone or something being dangerous. How come no one thought she needed help until it was too late?"

Sophie peered out of the window where the sun reflected on a bird bath. "Megan could be a drama queen at times. She'd tell all sorts of stories and then, when you'd be completely taken in by it, she'd laugh and tell you it was a pack of lies. She thought it was funny. We thought it was one of her jokes. And we'd drunk a lot. Well, not Aisha or Megan. The rest of us made up for them."

"Who was pouring the drinks?" Mandy asked.

"I don't remember. I think we passed the wine around the table."

"And spirits?"

Sophie shrugged her shoulders. "We might have helped ourselves or taken it in turns. We got through a bottle of vodka, and I think there was gin as well. We all had too much."

"And Aisha was in bed the whole evening?"

"She gets the most appalling headaches. Migraine." Sophie explained. "It started about the time we were eating, and she had to take tablets and go to bed to sleep it off."

Mandy exchanged a questioning look with Josh who shook his head. They had enough for the moment.

"Thank you, Ms Grant. That's all for now."

Sophie appeared relieved as they left. Mrs Grant was nowhere to be seen.

When they were outside again Josh asked, "What do you think, boss? Is she telling us the truth?"

"About the reasons for leaving London and setting up the uni weekend? I think so. I also think there's something more she's not telling us."

* * *

Diane Grant waited until the police had left before speaking to her daughter. Sophie could feel her eye twitching again. Had her mother been listening? Was she aware of what had been said?

"What did they want?"

"Just some more questions about Megan."

"Really Sophie, this is beyond. Police at the door. Reporters ringing asking for a statement. All sorts of speculation. I've had to withdraw from the art group for the time being. The questioning looks and whispers is bad enough. It's the pitying glances I can't cope with. You can just imagine what they're saying behind my back. 'Oh, poor Diane. Her husband dies and then her daughter ends up unemployed and in trouble with the police.'"

Sophie closed her eyes and counted to ten. When she opened her eyes again, she scowled at her mother.

"If you cared more about me and less about your precious bloody reputation, I wouldn't have so many problems. I'm a wreck and it's your fault."

"Sophie. That's no way to speak to your mother. Apologise."

"Oh, go to hell."

Sophie turned and ran up the stairs to her bedroom, slamming the door behind her. Why couldn't her mother just give her a hug and make her feel as though she mattered? The world was a horrible place and without her friends she'd be lost.

CHAPTER SIXTEEN

When they got back to the station Superintendent Withers was waiting for them.

"Wilde and Jones. My office. Now."

Oh crap. Now what had she done? With a resigned roll of the eyes Mandy did as she was told, and Josh shuffled in after her. Withers stood behind his desk his eyes narrowed to slits and his mouth a pencil line of distaste.

"I thought I told you that Sophie Grant was my goddaughter, and you were to use a softly approach."

"Sir."

"So why have you been harassing her?"

"Hardly harassing her, sir. We needed to ask some more questions."

"Her mother does not appreciate police officers knocking on her front door. It's a respectable neighbourhood. The family has a reputation to maintain and your presence does not help. Between this intrusion and the cock-up with the press it's bordering on harassment."

"With respect, sir, we discovered that Ms Grant had been, well, less than truthful about her reasons for leaving London."

"And how does that relate to a body in a field? Huh? Tell me now. How does that count? Have you found any evidence that Megan Pritchard's death was anything other than an accident? Huh? Have you?"

Withers had moved closer so they could smell his aftershave. He was almost spitting the words and Mandy could feel Josh flinch as the Super glared at them with his piggy eyes.

"We have suspicions, sir. We believe that Megan's drink was spiked. That would mean one of the four women was involved in her death."

"Suspicions? Suspicions? Have you got any hard evidence? Evidence that will stand up in a court of law. Well? Have you?" He had gone red in the face and Mandy wondered what would happen if he had a heart attack while he was berating them. She wouldn't be in too quick a mode to give first aid. "You have days. Do you hear me? If you haven't uncovered something by the end of the weekend that will convince me there is foul play involved then what you've got, which is not a lot, goes to the coroner. Got it?" He eyeballed both of them one at a time.

"Sir."

"Yes, sir."

Josh almost fell in his haste to get out of the office. Everyone in the outer office had heard most of the shouted conversation. Olivia winked at Mandy. It was cheeky and could be regarded as disrespectful, considering her rank. Mandy took it as a mark of solidarity.

* * *

Ross Withers could feel his blood pressure rising. DI Wilde was a good detective, although she never knew when to let go or how to do things in a way that didn't irritate people. Diane was being overprotective of her daughter in many ways. He had a great deal of empathy with that. Sophie had problems. Anyone could see that. The girl had a haunted expression, ever since she'd come back from London. Terribly thin too. As her godfather he felt responsible for her welfare since her father died. He'd hoped to be able to use that as leverage and get closer to Diane as well. He thought about his chances of forming a closer, more intimate relationship with her. Diane was a strikingly attractive woman. A desirable companion. Since his divorce he'd longed for a bit more female company. The fact she was loaded was a bonus.

This investigation had put that hope right back into a box and, if he couldn't get Wilde to keep a low profile then his chances with Diane would go back down to zero. Maybe he needed to speak to Sophie. See what lay at the root of her problems. He knew Sophie had lied to her mother about the break-in, but he had no idea why. A mysterious death involving a friend was the last thing that young lady needed. He'd do what he could to protect her from too much pressure from Wilde. He remembered her as a child, carefree and always laughing. Life had taken its toll and he'd like to see some sunshine back in Sophie's life. Fulfil his promise to always keep an eye on her welfare. David had been a good friend, supportive and kind and not averse to putting in a good word here and there. He owed it to him, and his widow, to give his support to their only child.

* * *

"Good news, boss. We've got a match on those fingerprints. Both sets of pills in Megan's wash bag had Aisha Matharu's fingerprints on them."

"We're sure they're Aisha's prints?"

Olivia peered through her specs. "She handled the photograph. A match with prints on the pills. We couldn't use that if it went to court but…"

Naughty. Mandy couldn't help being pleased. It was the sort of little trick she liked. They could get legitimate prints later, if necessary. Sometimes the way to the truth was on a circuitous pathway.

"Nice one, Olivia. We know that Megan offered her tablets when she developed the migraine. If she checked out the other blister pack, she'd know that Megan was taking something else. We may be on to something here. Theories, anyone?"

Josh spoke first. "Aisha goes to get the migraine tablets and sees the antipsychotic. She did biochemistry for a year, didn't she? So, she realises what they are and that they'll have an adverse effect when mixed with booze so doctors Megan's drink. Then she goes to bed so there'd be no suspicion on her."

"Motive?"

"Well, with Megan out of the way she was up for a big promotion, wasn't she? And she'd had a row or something with Megan on the way. Maybe she wanted to get her own back." Olivia said, putting her head to one side and narrowing her eyes while she thought about it.

"Is that enough of a motive to kill someone? Maybe we need to think in a different way. What if, let's say, Megan had pissed one of them off so much they wanted her to make a fool of herself. Maybe the intention wasn't that she'd end up dead in a field. Maybe they just hoped for a bit of revenge."

"In that case, they all had motive and opportunity. Who'd do that to a friend?" Josh asked.

"Oh, come on, Josh. You know what happens on stag or hen dos. Pissed up. Couple of dozen drinks in, they decide to get a tattoo, shave off an eyebrow or do something else equally useless and potentially dangerous. They're all hiding something. We just need to dig a bit deeper and a bit faster if time is limited. Back to basics. Double check everything, including bank records for all of them, Rhys included. Go further back on Megan's phone records, up to a year or more. Olivia, go and blink your baby blue eyes at the forensics guy. See if he can prioritise fingerprinting that empty vodka bottle from Nythfa. And let's get Aisha in. See what she's got to tell us about the fingerprints."

* * *

Aisha Matharu seemed tiny as she sat in the interview room at the station. They could have gone to her home or office, but Mandy wanted results. If that meant putting pressure on, then that was fine by her. Fear was the smell of a police station. There was something about being in an interview room that left even the innocent feeling guilty. Like the confessional. Not that Mandy had any time for that either.

They left Aisha sitting for about fifteen minutes, observing her through the two-way window. She glanced around her, fiddled with her hair, played with her phone and then sat twisting her earrings and bangles. When at last Mandy appeared, she seemed relieved if puzzled.

"DI Wilde. I don't understand why I'm here. I just got a call at work asking me to come down to the station. Do you have news? Do you know what happened to Megan now?"

"We haven't had the toxicology report yet, although we think we know what happened."

Mandy sat down opposite and Josh beside her. They said nothing. Aisha turned from one to the other.

"So, why am I here?"

"Tell me about Saturday evening."

"Is this about my earring again? I told you. I lost it. I didn't know where. I don't know how it came to be near the body." A puzzled frown creased Aisha's forehead.

"Yes. You did tell us that. You said that you had a headache and spent most of the evening in bed. You didn't see Megan becoming paranoid or hear her leaving."

"That's right. I took painkillers and fell asleep not long after we'd eaten. About seven perhaps. I knew nothing until the middle of the night when I got up to go to the toilet and have more tablets. Everyone was still up and a bit fraught."

"Where did you get the tablets?" Mandy asked.

"Megan's wash bag. I'd taken paracetamol when we got back from the pub, but it got worse. I tried to eat something even though I was nauseous. Megan said she had headache tablets in her wash bag and to go and have a couple of those as they might help."

"She didn't mind you going into her things?"

Aisha shook her head. "She was busy in the kitchen, I think."

"So, you went to her room and took out the tablets?"

"Yes. There were two blister packs in there. I took the tablets and went to bed. Within about twenty minutes I was out cold. I didn't hear anything."

Another nod. "Can you remember what the other blister pack looked like? Or what the tablets were for?"

She shook her head again. "No. I assumed it was an antibiotic or something. Megan had a sore throat, and she was prone to tonsillitis. I didn't recognise the name. I can't remember."

"You studied biochemistry in your first year, didn't you, before swapping courses? We've checked."

"Yes." Aisha seemed more perplexed now. "What's that got to do with anything?"

"Would you not be aware of the components in anti-psychotic drugs? Like those in Megan's Pritchard's possession. The ones you handled?"

Aisha started as though she'd been slapped by a wet fish. "What? Is that what they were? I had no idea. Why was Megan taking anti-psychotics?" She paused a minute as if recalling something. "And how did you know I handled them? I said I'd taken tablets from her washbag but... have you been using fingerprints? I didn't consent to my prints being taken. She stood up as if to leave, her face set in a determined way. "I think I need a lawyer."

Mandy had a moment of panic, despite her calm exterior. Oh bugger. If she goes and makes a complaint it will be my arse being kicked all the way from here to the dole queue. Calm things down.

"My apologies, Ms Matharu. Please sit down. We were just making a guess that you'd seen those anti-psychotics. Putting two and two together and making five. No one is accusing you of anything. We are trying to get to the truth. Migraines are hell, aren't they?"

Josh shifted in his seat and Mandy could tell he was feeling uncomfortable. The apology seemed to have worked as Aisha sat down although her tight lips and set jaw showed how she was feeling. Somehow, they had to get more out of her without aggravating her any further.

Adopting a conspiratorial tone Mandy leaned forward a little and lowered her voice. "We really need your help to unlock this mystery. We think, and this is confidential you understand, that someone spiked Megan's drink. Mixed with the alcohol it precipitated a psychotic attack and she left Nythfa in a distressed and disorientated state. Now, obviously, as you were in bed asleep, you had no part in what could have been intended as a sort of prank."

Aisha said nothing, a wary glance from Mandy to Josh and then back again showed she was mollified but still not prepared to say anything. Mandy nudged Josh with her knee and he took the lead.

"Megan was quite a difficult person. From what we've found out she could be the most generous and lovely person one minute and then do something hurtful the next. We know she was the cause of the break-up between Siobhan and Rhys. That's not the act of a friend. I'm surprised, after the way she's behaved that any of you were still friends," he said.

"So am I. We've all had what we termed a 'Megan attack'," She made quotation marks in the air as she said the words, "at some point, but she was always so contrite afterwards. We'd been through uni together and that creates a bond, still we weren't bosom buddies or anything. Megan's latest attack on me was pure jealousy. I think that was her motivation for a lot of the things she did. In many ways I felt sorry for her. She had no reason to be jealous of anyone. She had everything. Loving family. Good job. Prospects."

Mandy felt the tension leave her body. Aisha wasn't going to make a formal complaint. Now she knew the suspicion was no longer on her she had relaxed.

"We all had reason to be angry with Megan, though we're all devastated by her death. I'm sure no one would have wanted that to happen," said Aisha. "I'm sorry I was asleep when it happened. The others were pretty out of it when I got up in the night. I don't think any of them went to bed at all. I wish I had been there. Maybe I'd have been able to stop her."

It seemed genuine. What had she to gain from Megan's death anyway? A promotion. Another one with a weak motive. Maybe there was more.

"Was Megan aware that you are gay?"

Aisha reacted as if someone had confronted her with a gun. Her eyes widened and her mouth dropped open.

"How? I'm not. I..." She stopped then and closed her eyes, bending forward and resting her head on her hand, one arm on the table. Mandy and Josh waited. After a minute Aisha straightened again and glanced from one face to another.

"Megan had suspicions. She tried a few times to set me up with some of the blokes in work, but I wouldn't play. Then she mentioned one of the other girls and I hesitated. She knew that in my religion it would be frowned on. It was my secret and, although she had no proof, she used it to hold over me. The London job was my escape plan. That's why she went for it."

Josh and Mandy both took note of that comment.

"Was she blackmailing you?"

"Not really. Well, she never asked for money or anything like that."

"She put pressure on you?" Josh asked.

A sigh from Aisha. "Yes. I knew not to compete with her, or she'd give me a warning, or invite me to lunch so she could taunt me. When I applied for the job in London, she couldn't believe it. She applied too."

"And got it?"

"I almost withdrew from the interview. We travelled down together on the train and the subtle hints she gave made me a wreck. I didn't do as well on interview as I could. She threatened to expose me if I got the job."

What a bitch. The more they found out about Megan the more she disliked her. Yet they were all enthralled by her for some reason. This also gave Aisha a motive for wanting rid of Megan. Like Sophie, Aisha had been manipulated and controlled by Megan Pritchard. No wonder they didn't pursue her into the darkness. Yet, the question remained. Had they done anything to precipitate that bolt into the night? More digging needed. The waters were becoming muddier by the moment.

"Thank you, Ms Matharu. If you remember anything else, then please let us know. My apologies for our misunderstanding. I'm sure you realise that we are trying to do what we can to find the answers as quickly as possible. You've been a tremendous help in building a profile of Megan."

Mandy gave Aisha a smile of approval although there was no answering warmth. It was going to be fingers crossed for a few days in the hope she didn't make a formal complaint. Josh escorted Aisha out of the building, and she could hear him on charm offensive as they went. He knew only too well the thin line she had crossed and was doing his best to smooth things over. Thank God, Withers wasn't about. What a bloody mess this could turn out to be. At least she felt they had made some progress. Motives for resentment but who hated Megan Pritchard enough to harm her? Which of her friends would be mad enough to do that?

* * *

As she listened to DS Jones talking platitudes on the way out of the police station Aisha was thinking hard. If, as they had said, they suspected someone of deliberately spiking Megan's drink then all that confidential stuff was nonsense. They were trying to rattle her. They had her earring near the body and her fingerprints on those tablets. All circumstantial evidence. Except they'd also investigated her background. Knew about the biochemistry course she'd dropped out of. She'd been asleep when Megan went AWOL, although no one could verify that. The others were so out of it anyone could have wandered through the house and poisoned the lot of them. Had any of the others mentioned how they were so far gone that they couldn't go after Megan? Bet they hadn't.

The next thing Aisha thought about was her friends. Should she ring around? Warn them that they were all suspects in what, a homicide? And now she'd told the police her story they would think that she had a motive. She shuddered at the thought. Then she thought about work. Was this going to impact on her job? Megan getting that job in London had been a blow, now though, as second choice, it would be hers. With Megan gone, everyone would see just how capable, innovative and hardworking Ms Aisha Matharu could be. Yes, Megan's death was awful, but it also presented an opportunity. And, if she escaped to London there would be more anonymity. She'd be able to live her life the way she wanted without the fear that someone would condemn her for her sexual preferences.

CHAPTER SEVENTEEN

Josh came back in and whistled. "Close call, boss. I don't think she's going to make a complaint. Still," he shrugged his shoulders, "you never know."

"Bloody hell. She's sharp, isn't she? And she knows her rights. Heads down and hope we don't have to ask her any more questions. Although she's got motive for wanting Megan out of the way. She was being controlled. Just like Sophie. If we do need to speak to her again, I'm going to send you, Josh. You had the old charm going there. I could see that." Mandy's eyes gleamed at him and Josh shifted, rolling his shoulders. He didn't like being teased, and she needed him on her side just in case there was an inquiry.

"Right team. Back to business. We have sweet F A except some circumstantial stuff and gut feelings that this is more than an accident. Sophie and Aisha were both being manipulated to a degree by Megan. She'd put a strain on Siobhan's relationship and was a total bitch to her best friend, Bethan. Not much on the motive side really, is it? Where's Helen?"

"I think she was going to Megan's flat with Nia today to collect her personal things." Olivia said. "It seems the flat was rented and the rent was due now. They've explained to the landlord but obviously he wants it cleared out. Costing him money when it's empty."

"So, it was rented then. Well, that's useful to know. Megan wanted the lifestyle on the other hand she didn't have the money to buy. Or maybe she was going to move away. Leave everything."

"Well, she's done that and no mistake." Josh said.

"Hmmm. Lovely flat with no personality. Expensive clothes, shoes, jewellery. All the outer trappings of wealth but a place that was devoid of anything other than what was provided. What does that tell us?"

"She was after a rich man, I bet. Bit of a gold-digger?" Olivia chewed the end of a pen and raised her eyebrows above the rims of her glasses.

"Then why all the stalking of Rhys? What was the point in that? He lives in a little ex-local authority terraced house in Chepstow. Not exactly the high life, is it?"

Josh coughed. "Actually, I did a bit of digging when we got back. His business is booming. He's taken on extra staff, established a network in Ireland as well and is set to grow. So far, the company is recording a one hundred and fifty percent rise year by year. If he has a firm base in Ireland on top of that he could be worth quite a bit in five years or less. Lucky bugger."

"Maybe we should all become garden designers or whatever it is he styles himself. Do you think Megan would have known this?"

Josh shrugged. "Maybe. The information isn't that hard to find and there was an article on him in one of the Cardiff magazines not long ago. 'Young and nearly minted'."

"I missed that, then I haven't got much time for magazines." Not much time for anything these days.

"Lisa brought it back from the hairdressers. I was just flicking through when I saw it. An article about the up-and-coming stars of local business in south-east Wales. I remembered after we met him. His face was familiar."

"Pity you didn't mention it at the time. He's not exactly living the high life, is he? I mean a terrace in Bulwark. Tidy enough though not if he's loaded, or on the way to it."

The smile of satisfaction was wiped from Josh's face. "I didn't remember until we got back and then it slipped my mind. Other things to think about." Josh was staring at the floor with that 'little boy in a sulk' face he had now and again when things didn't go as he expected. Mandy could understand how frustrated his wife must get with him at times. Although he needed to have a bit of a boost. No time to slack.

"Good work, Josh. That gives us a possible motive other than to ruin Siobhan's love life. Maybe Megan was delusional as well. Find out about any other side effects of those tablets she was taking. Maybe, after a time they have a negative effect or something. Hell's bells, I'm clutching at straws here. Anything else to throw into the cooking pot?"

"They were hoping to get Megan's phone records, they were. Should we check the social media of the others? See if there's anything there?" Olivia asked.

"Yes. I did ask someone in the tech department to do that, but they said they were busy and it could be a few days. Maybe things were not all sweetness and light. Olivia, have a nosey at Siobhan O'Hare's profile in particular. She's the one with the most motive from where we're sitting. A friend who seduces the love of your life isn't really a friend, is she? I'm not totally convinced she could forgive and forget. Maybe that's my evil mind. If a friend did that to me, I think I'd want to beat her senseless."

Scanning Josh and Olivia's faces, Mandy had to laugh. They were staring at her, open mouthed. "I wouldn't do it, of course. I'd be more likely to beat him black and blue for being such a fucking prick."

Olivia gasped, put her hand to her mouth and started to laugh. "What's so funny, Olivia?"

"Nothing really, except I feel better now. They all told me I wouldn't be a proper part of the team, I wouldn't, until you felt comfortable enough to swear your head off. It's great. I really feel I belong now."

Mandy didn't know what to say. She'd changed her mind about Olivia and could see the girl's potential. Josh appeared to be a bit sheepish, so she presumed he'd been the one dispensing advice and wisdom about Mandy's filthy tongue. Oh well. She could have worse habits.

"Josh. What about Bethan Rees? She said she worked as a plus size model. See if you can find out anything more about that. Should be a nice job for you as long as you like big girls. I think we all need to go and light a few candles or do whatever we can to move things on. We need a lead of some sort. A break. Let's hope forensics come up trumps. What about toxicology? Anything there?"

"Not yet? I'll give Rishi a ring first, shall I?"

Mandy agreed. "Please. We don't have time on our side."

Something was digging away at the back of Mandy's mind. There was something she'd forgotten. Something said that had raised a thought at the time then, with everything else going on, had disappeared as fast as next door's cat after he shat in her garden. Best to start at the beginning. Go through all the interviews again and see if anything rang a bell.

* * *

Olivia hummed to herself. She'd been a bit scared of the boss in the beginning. Well, she was so tall and with that wild hair that had a life of its own. She resembled a mad professor or as if she'd had an electric shock. Aside from that, there was so much to be learned. The boss was driven to uncover the truth, despite Withers and his dire warnings to them. The whole office had stopped and listened when he'd started shouting. All grateful they weren't on the receiving end. He hadn't liked it either when she'd been called in to report to him.

"Well. What have you got to tell me? Is this investigation just a wild goose chase? Is Wilde just wasting police time? What's she been up to?" The "she" had been spat. It was obvious that he didn't like her.

"There's nothing, sir. I do think there's reasonable doubt in this case. I'm inclined to agree with DI Wilde that there's something not quite right here. All little things, I suppose, but it could have been malicious and not misadventure."

It wasn't what he wanted to hear so he grunted and narrowed his eyes at her.

"Don't get caught up in her web. She's too fond of doing things her way. One step out of line and I want to know. Got it?"

"Yes, sir. Of course."

Smiling to herself, Olivia thought about those fingerprints. He wouldn't approve, would he? Was she going to tell him? Not a hope. She was going to keep working and help solve this and Withers could puff and blow as much as he liked.

* * *

The house was dark when Mandy got home. Of course, Thursday. Tabs was staying over at Kelly's. There were boys involved in some way, however she trusted Tabitha to be sensible. More so than Kelly. That young lady was a bit too worldly wise at times. A nice kid, though, for all that and she had supported Tabitha through some rough times. Nice to have a best friend. Her best friend had always been Joy until things started to go adrift. She'd thought about that incident in Chepstow. Why would Joy not want to get in touch with her family? Was she in trouble of some sort? Isn't that when you would turn to family?

It felt too quiet in the house despite the muffled sounds of a television next door. Mandy switched on the lights and went out to the kitchen to make something to eat. Her stomach rumbled. She'd had breakfast but lunch? That business with Aisha had turned her stomach into knots. She should have brazened it out more. Instead of which there was now a possible complaint about unfair practice or whatever heading her way. Plus, she'd indicated that they suspected foul play of some sort. Better hope Aisha didn't warn the others.

The kitchen floor gleamed and she suspected Tabitha had done a bit of cleaning before going out. Everything had that fresh smell about it. Febreze or some other cleaning fluid. Although she preferred to use eco products the reality was that cleaning with white vinegar and baking soda just made things smell like a fish and chip shop. It was lovely that Tabitha had tidied and cleaned, although also a bit of a concern. When she couldn't concentrate on her schoolwork, she'd do some housework. Distraction she said. A way to be in control. Did Joy realise what her continued silence was doing to her daughter, to all of them?

Mandy made some scrambled eggs on toast and a mug of tea and wandered into the lounge again, slumping on the sofa to eat. She always made a point of sitting at the table with Tabitha. A reminder of her childhood when the family always sat down together. She ate and then put the television on, flicking through the channels and then switching off again. There was still that niggle in the back of her mind. What had they missed? What didn't add up? Tomorrow she'd chase up toxicology. Have a chat with Rishi. See if there was anything else. Facts. Evidence.

She sent a quick text to Tabitha. No reply. That was unusual. When her phone rang a few minutes later

Mandy felt a little jump of anticipation. Josh. Maybe there was news. Something to move things along. Josh sounded weary.

"Hey, boss."

"Josh. Anything?"

"Nothing to do with the case but," a slight hesitation, "I'd appreciate a word sometime."

Mandy's heart sank. Bloody hell. He was going to complain about the way she worked. The incident with Aisha. Covering her tracks with old Withering.

"It's… well… the job."

What was coming next? Mandy waited for him to carry on.

"I'm thinking I'm going to apply for something nine to five. Lisa says it's the hours I keep that's been the problem. When there's a big case on, she says she doesn't see me. That's no good. And if, or when, we have kids it'll be no good having an absent father."

Mandy's heart sank. She got on with Josh. He didn't question her methods, well, not very often, and she knew he had her back when the going got tough. She'd met Lisa before they got married and could tell there was going to be friction in the marriage. Lisa was high maintenance. Except you can't go telling someone they've made the wrong choice at their engagement party, now can you?

"Is that what you discussed? With the counsellor, I mean. Not that it's any of my business. Sorry."

"Sort of."

Mandy frowned. What the hell did that mean? He didn't seem very sure of things. She wished he'd spoken to her in the office where she'd have been able to see the body language clues as well as hearing the words.

"What do you mean?"

"We talked about what we wanted. Took it in turns. Lisa said she wanted children but in a stable and loving home. Both parents playing equal roles. That sort of thing."

"And?" What was he trying to say? Bloody Lisa.

"Well. I've been thinking. Doesn't that mean she wants me to be there more?"

Mandy rolled her eyes and sighed. God, he could be so dense. Maybe it was all men. Emotionally inept at times.

"Did you suggest changing jobs to see if that suited Lisa?" Then, taking a breath first and hoping she wasn't going to upset anything, "And what do you want, Josh?"

"That's the trouble. I don't know what I want. I like the job. The variety. The challenge. Being a copper is all I've ever wanted to do. I can't imagine sitting behind a desk all day. Sounds boring as hell."

Counselling had been a great success then. A couple at odds and no solution offered by either. Bloody great stuff. A sergeant with his head up his arse and a superintendent breathing hellfire and spit down her neck with the clock ticking to find the key to the mystery.

"We'll have a chat tomorrow, Josh. Or when we get a chance. It's something you need to work out for yourself though I'm happy to listen. Just don't pack it all in before going through the options. It's early days with the counselling." And we need to sort this bloody case.

"Yeah. Sure. Ta. Thanks, boss."

Closing her eyes for a moment Mandy felt her shoulders slump. More problems. She opened her eyes again and stared at the picture above the open fireplace. Tenby harbour. Little boats. Some days she felt as though she'd like to get into a boat and just sail away. Anywhere. It was one of those days.

CHAPTER EIGHTEEN

FRIDAY

The Oasis ringtone dragged her out of sleep before six on Friday morning. Mandy yawned as she grabbed her phone from the bedside table. Not another body, she hoped. One at a time was enough to deal with.

"DI Wilde."

"It's Sergeant Williams, Pontypridd police here. We've two girls here who have given your number to contact. One says she's your niece, Tabitha Wilde and Miss Kelly Williams."

"What?" Pontypridd. What the hell?

"Tabitha and Kelly in Pontypridd? Are they alright? What's happened? Why are they there?" Mandy felt a wave of nausea. Her head was swimming too. She couldn't think straight or form her words properly. Is this how parents felt when their child went missing?

"Well, now that's a bit of a story. Are you able to come and identify these girls?"

Identify. Oh my God. Her heart had stopped. No. It hadn't. It was still there. Beating much too fast.

"What do you mean identify?"

"You're a police officer. You know what I mean. You need to come and see them and tell me they are who they say they are. We can't have young girls going off without making sure now, can we?"

"I'm sorry. I thought... I've been dealing with a suspicious death. My mind's blown. I'll be there in half an hour."

"No speeding now." He laughed but Mandy felt far from laughter. What the fuck? Not now. Not a family crisis when she was dealing with such a difficult case. Bloody awful timing, then wasn't it always the same? Trouble never travelled alone her mother always said. How true.

She'd need to ring Josh. Tell him her movements and what had happened. It would do him good to take charge for a day. Maybe it would put the notion of quitting out of his head. Despite his grumbles, and didn't they all grumble, he enjoyed the challenge, the variety. No time to get bored. Frustrated. Exhausted. But never bored.

It took a minute or two for him to answer and she could tell he'd been fast asleep.

"Yeah? Wassup?"

"Josh, I need you to cover for me. There's been a bit of a crisis. My niece and her friend have been picked up on the road near Ponty. I've got to go up there now."

"What? At Ponty. What happened?"

"I'm not sure, so I don't know how long I'm going to be. Have you checked Megan's emails at all?"

"Er, a bit." No, he hadn't, had he? Too wrapped up with that counselling stuff.

"Go through and see if there's anything that strikes you as odd. Emails between Megan and Sophie in particular. I've got a feeling."

A yawn. "Okay, boss. I'm on it."

"And Josh. If Withers comes searching for me make up some bullshit to put him off the scent. I don't want him to know I'm scrutinizing his precious goddaughter."

"Got it. Will do."

Pulling on her clothes Mandy's mind was working overtime. What had happened to Tabitha and Kelly? How did they even get to Pontypridd? She swilled out her mouth with a minty mouthwash, no time for brushing, grabbed her bag and car keys and was on the road within ten minutes. Early morning and the traffic flow would be heading into Cardiff, not out, so she could make it there in twenty minutes up the A470. There were few cars on the road and the morning was dry although grey clouds swirled above Castell Coch, and the temperature had dropped.

The road wrapped around the mountain and it was as if, once past that part of the road, under the castle, the weather system changed. A slight mist descended and a fine drizzle. Mandy's mood had not changed. She was feeling a range of emotions tumbling through her head. Fear was uppermost in her mind. Until she saw Tabitha and Kelly unharmed, she couldn't stop that gnawing in her gut. Her responsibilities to her niece were just as important as those of the job and sometimes she forgot that. This was what? A wake-up call? Isn't that what they called it when you began to see more clearly what was really important in life? Maybe Josh was right in trying to save his marriage. Maybe she should think about a partner. Death was a cold bed partner.

She made the police station in fifteen minutes, waved her badge for entry, and, almost shaking in her attempt to stop panic overtaking her, asked about the girls.

"DI Wilde, is it?" the sergeant said. "Come through. They're in the back."

"What happened? Can you tell me anything?"

He shrugged his shoulders. "Patrol car picked them up trying to walk to Treforest in the middle of the night. They said they was trying to get to the train station there. Something about a stolen bag and tickets. I dunno, really. Best ask Nick. He's the one brought them in. He'll be coming in again soon. They've just picked up a drunk creating a fuss down the train station." He pointed ahead. "They're down by there. Last door on the right."

The building was quiet enough. The hum of computers, clink of a mug somewhere and a few voices reverberating. Calming sounds, muffled in comparison to the blood rushing through Mandy's ears. The sergeant opened the door to a small room smelling of stale milk and ripe socks. There they were, Tabitha and Kelly, huddled together on a couple of plastic chairs and appearing as tired and stressed as Mandy felt, all Bambi eyed and pale as dishwater.

Tabitha threw herself at Mandy, tears and snot mixing together as she tried to speak. Kelly had black streaks down her cheeks and her hair was all tangled. It looked and smelled as if she'd been sick.

Mandy hugged Tabitha tight, closing her eyes and making a silent thank you to a deity she didn't believe in. She kissed the top of her niece's head, rocking her a little. Kelly watched, biting her upper lip, eyes red-rimmed and hands clasped between her knees. When

Tabitha had calmed down a little Mandy drew her over to the chairs again and sat down beside the girls.

"Are you alright, Kelly? Somebody want to tell me what happened? How come you're here?"

Kelly bent her head, swallowed and in a voice that would have made a church mouse seem as loud as a fireworks' display, she said, "It's all my fault. Don't get cross with Tabs. She just came to make sure I was alright."

Patience required. Not something Mandy regarded as one of her virtues, although she made an effort to present a façade of calmness.

"Let's start at the beginning, shall we?"

Kelly nodded again before she started to speak. She was hesitant at first and didn't meet Mandy's eyes, as a steady flush of red made its way up her neck and over her face. Shame? Guilt? Mandy suspected it was a mixture of things.

"I've been messaging this bloke, Gary, for a few weeks. On the internet. He suggested I come up on the train and meet him for a chat. I wasn't too keen at first, so Tabs said she'd come to make sure I had some company."

Tabitha agreed with her, blinking too fast with what Mandy assumed was nerves. "I thought it was a bit dodgy and Kelly's my best friend. I just wanted to help. That's what you do for friends, isn't it?"

Kelly smiled at Tabitha and stretched her hand out. "We arranged to meet in this wine bar. I said I didn't have ID and he told me it didn't matter. If anyone asked, I was to say I was with Gary. I'd seen his picture and he seemed nice and, well, proper fit, you know."

Mandy struggled to keep a bland expression on her face. She wanted to shake Kelly for being so stupid and putting both girls in danger. And for nearly giving her a heart attack thinking her niece was injured, or worse.

"Anyway, when we got there, I didn't see Gary. Not the boy in the photo," she sniffed, "so I phoned him on the number he'd given me. I case I get lost, like." She peeped at Mandy, unsure. "There was this old bloke at the back, must've been about thirty, and he answered. He spotted me and Tabs and called us over. People were gawping at us then, so we just did as he said. We should have left then. I… I know that now but at the time we didn't know what to do." An inflection made it sound like a question. As if Mandy had an answer.

Tabitha joined in at that point. "I thought he'd be cross or something at me being there. Then he said he'd a mate that would like to meet me and wasn't it lovely that Kelly had brought a friend. He called over this other bloke." She shuddered at the memory. Kelly took up the tale again.

"We were sort of stuck. They wanted to buy us a drink. I said we'd just had one and it was okay just to chat. He was creepy and said some stuff that was a bit, you know?" Her voice tailed off. Mandy gritted her teeth. She'd like to catch this Gary and mangle his balls in a cheese press.

"We waited a bit and then I said I needed the loo and Tabitha came with me. There was a back door, so we did a runner."

"So why didn't you get the train home then?"

"We'd missed the train, so we thought we'd be able to get a Coke or something somewhere else while we waited for the next one. When we tried a couple of other places, they wouldn't let us in. Then there was a group of lads who said we could go in with them to have a drink. They seemed okay, friendly like, so I said yes. Tabs didn't want to. I made her."

Tabitha's head was bent towards the floor. No eye contact. She'd learnt a lesson if nothing else. Mandy knew she'd need to talk to her alone about what had happened. Not now. For the moment it was enough that both girls had a fright.

"I didn't drink anything." Tabitha's voice was low, not a protest just a statement, letting Mandy have more insight into the situation.

"They must have put something in my drink 'cause I felt a bit sick. I asked Tabs to come to the loo with me, but I forgot my bag. It had my purse and phone in it. When we got back to the table the lads had left. My bag was still there. It wasn't until later we knew they'd pinched my purse. My Mam's going to kill me."

More noisy crying and sniffing followed. Through sobs and hiccoughs, she managed to carry on.

"I felt, really, really sick and when we got outside, I felt worse. My head was throbbing and my legs were all jelly. Tabs had to hold on to me. We found a wall and I sat down for a while. I think I must've passed out. I don't remember."

Tabitha said nothing. She was chewing her fingernails. Mandy caught her eye and raised an eyebrow.

"Yeah, she sort of slumped against me. I didn't know what to do. I asked a couple of people to help but they just thought she was pissed or on drugs or something.

I don't know." She shrugged. "Nobody would stop. When she began to come round a bit, I sort of dragged her to the station. We'd missed the last train by then."

"Why didn't you ring me? I'd have come to get you. What were the two of you thinking?" It was hard not to shout at them. She could have shaken both of them or banged their heads together.

"My battery was dead. Kelly had dropped hers when we came out of the wine bar, and it wasn't working. We hung around the station for a while. The next train wasn't until after five in the morning and that's when we found out that Kelly's purse was gone. She'd put the tickets in there for safe keeping. I hadn't taken much money with me either."

"No phone. No money. No tickets." Mandy whistled. Thank God the patrol car had picked them up. Anything could have happened.

The words came tumbling out. "It wasn't very nice around the station after dark so we walked around for a bit, 'cos we didn't know what to do. Kelly was still all over the place and slurring her words, so we thought if the police found us, she'd be arrested or something. And it wasn't her fault." Tabitha stuck her lip out and it reminded Mandy of when she was two and didn't want to do something. Petulant. Kelly was back on track with the explanation.

"By the time my head had cleared it was well dark and we didn't know how we'd get back to Cardiff. I didn't want to hitch."

Thank God for that. Mandy was almost faint as a range of emotions flooded through her. Relief, anger, frustration all mixed up and a special tenderness towards her beautiful niece. Kelly was a bit shame-faced now aware that, as well as being her best friend's aunt, Mandy was a police officer.

"There's no ticket barrier at Treforest. So," a pause, "I thought if we got down there it would be quiet like, and we could get the train. Maybe get off at Cathays, being as we didn't have tickets. And, well, the police stopped us on the way."

"And if you got on and off at unmanned stations, you'd avoid paying the fare? Train fare evasion on top of everything else." Mandy let that sink in for a minute. "Have you told all this to the police officers who rescued you?"

Kelly and Tabitha nodded together.

"Where does your Mam think you are now Kelly? And do you really have a test in school this morning?"

"I told her I was staying at Tabs. That's what we planned. Tabs said you were always back really late when you were on a case so you wouldn't know if we were in late. We thought we'd be back and in bed before you got in." She blinked away a tear. "The test is at ten o'clock this morning."

Tabitha's eyes were full of guilt and panic. Mandy could see that she knew there would be a reckoning at some point. That wasn't the priority now.

"Mam's going to kill me." Kelly's voice was almost a wail.

"I doubt that when she finds out you've been the victim of grooming, larceny and doping in one evening. I think she'll be very worried, a bit cross and you are likely to be grounded for some time." Turning to Tabitha, "Both of you. Now, I need to go and speak to someone to see about getting you two to school in time for that test."

Stupid. Stupid. Stupid. How could Kelly be so naive? There'd be follow-ups from all this. The police would need to find out all about Gary and his little grooming business and the lads were also in for the magistrate's court. If they found them. Still, that was in Pontypridd's hands. Right now, she needed to get the girls home.

After a quick chat with the sergeant about next steps, and giving the details he needed, she bundled the girls into the car and headed back down the A470. They were silent as the car snaked down the dual carriageway. Mandy was thinking about Megan. She needed to speak to the parents again. The traffic was beginning to thicken as they approached the suburbs. She turned off at the Mason's Arms and went a more roundabout way back to Brithdir Street. It was almost eight o'clock by the time they were all back in the safety of her house.

"Right, you two, wash and into school uniforms now. I'm going to drop you off at school. Later, Kelly, I'm going to take you home. And talk to your Mam and Dad when they're home. They need to know what's been going on."

Kelly's eyes widened but she said nothing. It wasn't the start to the morning Mandy had planned although now she knew what had been niggling her about Megan Pritchard's death.

CHAPTER NINETEEN

Josh rang just after she'd dropped the girls at school. Mandy had a quiet word with the teacher about what had happened and arranged to pick them both up later. Kelly's parents were going to go apeshit so it would help if she was there to explain. Somehow, she didn't think Kelly would give them the whole picture. It would help them to be more alert in the future if they knew the facts.

"Hey, boss. There is something in the emails as you said. It's not very obvious but Olivia thought it was a bit dodgy."

"And? I don't know what it is unless you tell me. Maybe you think I've developed telepathy or you're going to use owl service or smoke signals. Put Olivia on." She'd done it again. Put Josh down. She hadn't meant to. It already felt as though it should be the end of the day. Tiredness and worry were biting into her.

She could hear him say, "She wants to speak to you," and could imagine him pulling a face. The wicked witch is in a mood. Olivia sounded a bit apprehensive too.

"Hi. It's nothing much now, it seems Sophie bought that ring for Megan. She says, 'Thanks for the bit of Welsh gold. I knew you'd see things my way.' So, I mean who buys their friend a Clogau ring unless they're rolling in it?"

"Or they're being blackmailed? Thanks, Olivia. Well spotted. Have another scan through and see if there's anything else on the others, will you? We want other evidence that Megan was manipulating any of them. No matter how subtle. Read between the lines. I'm going to have a little chat with the family. Oh, and tell Josh, I'm sorry for biting his head off."

Mrs Pritchard opened the door. She didn't seem surprised to see Mandy. She shuffled into the room where they'd spoken before. The dog was still there, almost as if nothing had changed since Mandy had left.

"When can I have my little girl back? We need to lay her to rest. She'll be lonely in that mortuary. We're going to put her with her Nan and Gramps."

Catrin wasn't crying now but had the demeanour of a sleepwalker, not quite in tune with the world. Undoubtedly due to whatever the doctor had given her to keep her calm. Mandy swallowed the lump in her throat. How would she have felt if anything awful had happened to Tabitha? She didn't want to think about that or how intrusive this visit to Megan's family must seem to them. Except it was necessary. Things she wanted to find out. Things that could help get to the truth.

"We hope to be able to release Megan's body very soon, Mrs Pritchard. We're just waiting for some results from the lab. Then we'll be able to let you have her home to make arrangements for the funeral. I'm so sorry. It's been a dreadful time for you."

Mrs Pritchard swayed a little as she sat with her arms wrapped around her body. No sign of her husband. Helen said he'd taken it very hard and kept out of the house as much as possible. He couldn't bear to talk about his dead daughter, spending his time in the garden or down at the allotment. Denial and distraction. People grieved in their own ways and in the police force, they found it best to let people find what worked for them. Some reacted in hysterics, some in anger and others seemed like the life had been sucked out of them, like Catrin Pritchard.

Mandy sat on the sofa beside her and asked, "Can you tell me about Megan as a child? What was she like? Did she have many friends at school? Any problems?"

Mrs Pritchard shook her head. "Oh no. Megan was always the centre of attention. She had loads of friends. She was a little live wire. The teachers loved her as she was so bright and well behaved. An angel in the classroom but so full of it when she got out." A softness crossed her face as she reminisced. "She was invited to all the birthday parties. Even when she went to secondary school there were always lots of friends. Boys and girls. Full of life she was, my Megan."

"No rows, squabbles? You know what teenage girls are like. Always falling out one week and best friends the next. Egging each other on to do daft things."

As if considering the question Mrs Pritchard stared at a crack in the plasterwork near the fireplace. "Not that I can remember."

"Bethan was her best friend."

"Oh, those two were thick as thieves since primary school. Like sisters when they were small."

"And later?"

"Same through school and university. Our Megan was always talking about how she was going to get to the top. Bethan worshipped her. Always trying to please our Megan."

And they'd maintained that friendship through all those years. Even though Megan teased Bethan about her weight. Wasn't that what Tabitha had said? "That's what you do for friends." So, Bethan was the support system for Megan just as Tabitha had been for Kelly.

"What about her sister, Nia? Any fuss there?"

"Well, you know what siblings are like. Little squabbles now and again. There's a few years between them. I lost a baby in between. A little boy. Oliver. Still born."

It didn't answer the question, but Mandy pressed on.

"Do you have any photographs of when they were young? That's a nice one there on the table. What age was Megan then?"

"About ten I think."

"Pretty. Chubby cheeks."

"Oh, she was bonny. Solid they'd say. All the weight dropped off by the time she got to her teens."

"And the anxiety? When did that start?"

"About the same time. She got very nervy about things. Anxious all the time. Everything got to her. I took her to the doctor, and they put her on pills." She sighed and gazed into space. "It took a while before they found something that worked though. And all that time she'd be eating and then not eating. Happy one day. Down the next. Always loving. A bit of a worry at the time, but it passed. A good girl."

Mandy listened, her mind working. She was beginning to get more of a picture of Megan now. A troubled child and teenager. Anxiety so severe she was still taking medication years later. But then who hadn't found adolescence difficult? That's when Joy had started to be difficult too. Hormones had a lot to do with it.

"I'm sorry to have to ask this next question. Megan was wearing some expensive jewellery when we found her. A Clogau ring as well as diamond studs. Did she buy those herself or do you know who might have given them to her?"

Mrs Pritchard turned sad eyes towards Mandy. Vacant. It felt as if everything was in slow mode as she thought about her answer.

"Which ring? Was it a sapphire? That was my Mam's engagement ring. Too small for my fingers." She looked down and twisted her wedding and engagement rings around her fingers. Swollen and knotted with arthritis.

"No, not a sapphire. This was a Clogau ring. Rose gold. The design was Tree of Life. Leaves on a gold band."

Mrs Pritchard appeared to be totally blank, and Mandy realised that the poor woman was finding it hard enough just to be alive without all the probing.

"Maybe Nia would know. Is she at uni today?"

"Nia?" Another blank stare.

"Your daughter, Nia. Is she here?"

"I don't know. I don't think so. What day is it? Is it Friday?"

"Yes."

"Friday." A sigh.

Mandy stood up, ready to leave.

"She said she was meeting a friend, I think. If it's Friday that is. You will let me know when I can have my baby home, won't you?" She got to her feet and grabbed Mandy's arm, gripping it with a surprising fierceness and shaking her head as she stared through drugged up eyes.

Mandy patted her hands and loosened Mrs Pritchard's grip on her arm. "Yes. As soon as possible. I'm truly sorry. We are doing our best to find out what happened."

She let herself out of the house and sat in the car for a moment regaining some sense of equilibrium while she planned the next steps. Time to get back to the station, check over what they had so far. Precious bloody little. There had to be something to give them a lead. Maybe she was wrong. Maybe it was just an unfortunate accident. No. The pieces didn't quite fit.

As she drove down past Llandaff Village, she spotted Nia and recognised her companion. That was something she hadn't expected. Nia was with Bethan Rees and the two of them were deep in conversation. Were Nia and Bethan friends? There was an age difference though Bethan said she'd known Megan since primary school. It wasn't inconceivable that Nia would be in touch with her sister's oldest friend. Did that mean that she shared information about Megan's anxiety with Bethan? Or did Bethan already know? It seemed very possible. In fact, it seemed very likely.

CHAPTER TWENTY

"We need to speak to Sophie Grant again. There are things that don't add up. Those emails sound quite sinister to me, now I've read the whole sequence. Megan had some sort of hold over Sophie. That's for sure."

"Should we get her in, boss?" Josh asked.

"And risk Withers seeing her here. No way. We need to get her on her own. Which means when the dragon lady is out."

Olivia was staring at the screen of her computer. "Maybe she goes to bridge or something? There are all sorts of events in the village." She reeled off a list of activities.

"Golf. She plays golf. I saw shoes in the kitchen and I'm pretty sure they didn't belong to Sophie. Now, do a bit of a recce and find out which club she belongs to and if they have a ladies' afternoon. She might well be occupied elsewhere this afternoon. I've a feeling Sophie will be a lot more forthcoming when her mother isn't hanging over her like a bird of prey."

Within twenty minutes Olivia uttered a "Yeeees," and punched the air. "She's playing at Llanishen Golf Club this morning. Some ladies' match followed by lunch. She's the captain so has to be there. That's why her name came up. If you go now, you should catch Sophie if she's at home."

"Josh. Give Sophie a bell. Tell her we're on our way and we'd like a quiet word. Let's hope she'll open up a bit. Bring those email printouts and meet me downstairs in five. I need to be somewhere else by lunch-time."

While Mandy waited for Josh she tossed over things in her head. Sophie would have had some inheritance from her father but to spend in excess of four hundred pounds on a ring for a friend. Is that how the other half lived?

On the way to Lisvane, Mandy turned to Josh.

"What do you think? Blackmail would give Sophie a motive. We have only her word that Megan wanted this reunion. Why now? What do we know about these relationships?"

Josh puffed. "We don't know if Sophie gave her the ring out of affection. Maybe they were having a relationship? We know Megan was stalking Rhys, although she could have been bisexual. From the tone of those emails though there seems to be an underlying threat. Also, we know that Megan rang Sophie five times the day before the reunion."

"That's a lot. But we don't know what was said, do we? Could just have been things like, 'Is everybody still coming? What food and drink shall I bring? I've got details of the hike for Saturday.' We can only guess."

"Unless Sophie tells us. If we can get her to talk. She's been holding things back all the time."

"Yeah, we need her to be honest." There was no disagreement there. "I may need to do a bit of creative talking here."

"Oh God. Not like you did with Aisha, please. That nearly went tits up. I had to tell her it was standard procedure to test people with leading questions and half-truths."

"See, I knew you'd understand." Mandy glanced at him as she pulled up outside the house. The neighbour was in the garden, so Mandy waved and beamed at her. No doubt she'd report to the neighbourhood gossip machine. Sophie was waiting and opened the door as they came up the pathway. She was pale and drawn and her eyes were shadowed. She took them into the kitchen at the back of the house and they sat around the table. Sun glinted in through the window and a blackbird was singing its heart out in the garden. She glanced from Mandy to Josh and back again.

"What did you want to see me about?"

"Why do you think Siobhan went to stay with Rhys?"

The question was unexpected, and Sophie gave a mirthless laugh.

"My mother wasn't exactly the most hospitable hostess. You'll have seen for yourself what a snob she is. I think she just wanted her out and Siobhan was glad to go. I wish I could escape too."

They didn't respond to that, though Mandy surmised that was a good summing up of the situation. If she'd been staying here with the ice queen, she'd have been glad to escape.

"How long have you had anorexia?"

"What? I haven't." She sighed. "It's not anorexia. Not really. It's just stress. When I get upset or feel under pressure I can't eat. Everything tastes like cardboard."

"Like now. Since you've been back home or before?"

"Since just before. It was all that fuss over...'

"Your boss. The affair. Losing your job. Must have been pretty awful."

Sophie's eyes filled and she turned away from meeting Mandy's gaze. She was vulnerable. A victim of her own fears, a domineering mother and open to being controlled.

"Why are you asking me all these questions? What has any of this got to do with Megan's accident? I don't understand."

Sophie was twisting her hands together between her knees and she glanced at the kitchen clock making its noisy progress as the minutes ticked past. Time to get to the point.

"We've seen Megan's emails to you. Why did you buy such an expensive ring for her? The one she was wearing. Clogau gold."

Sophie's eyes opened wider as she stared at Mandy and her mouth opened and then shut again. She swallowed and took a breath before replying.

"It was a gift."

Mandy could feel Josh tense but avoided any eye contact. Now for the truth.

"A very expensive gift for a friend. You may have inherited from your father," a nod from Sophie, "still, I can't imagine you giving gifts like that to all your friends.

197

Did you? Give all your friends expensive Welsh gold rings? I didn't notice anyone else wearing expensive jewellery."

Sophie bent her head and stared at the floor. They'd got her.

"Megan was blackmailing you, wasn't she? We've printed out her emails to you. There's a threatening tone to some of them." Mandy spread the papers on the table.

Sophie was trembling as she faced them. She opened and closed her mouth but said nothing.

Mandy pressed on with her questions. "She found out about the reason for your resignation and your affair. What did she threaten to do? Tell your mother? Inform prospective employers? What?" Her voice was harsh now, unrelenting. They had Sophie in a corner, and she knew it.

"Both. Mum would be furious if she knew although it was the job bit that really got me. I'd applied for a job with her firm and asked her if she'd put in a good word for me, as a friend." She swallowed. "She said she would at first. Then she started dropping hints about this dress that she'd like and how it would help her to be more presentable when she approached her boss. Then it was shoes, a jacket. I was caught in the web."

Now that she'd started to talk Sophie couldn't stop. It seemed she was relieved as the tension left her body and she almost slumped in the chair.

"When she asked for the ring, I told her that was it. No more. I was afraid Mum would find out. See my bank statements or something. She treats me as if I'm a teenager. Then Megan told me she was planning to go to Australia, and could I arrange a little get together for her. A reunion with the girls. She knew about the house in the Vale. She said it was perfect. I had to persuade my mother to let us have the party there. Another pack of lies. Then, then it all went awful, just a nightmare and, and I can't wake up." A sob.

"Were you aware that Megan was on medication and it would react with alcohol?"

"No. No. Megan could be mean and manipulative, but I'd never have harmed her. I haven't got the guts to do that. I can't even stand up to my mother. I escaped to London with Dad's help and blessing and then..."

"It all went to hell. Okay." Mandy had the feeling they had gained enough for one day. Sophie was a wreck. "Thank you for your time, Ms Grant. That's all for now. We'll be in touch."

Sophie seemed relieved and also exhausted. As they were leaving Mandy turned to her.

"Strictly off the record. A bit of advice. Find your own place as soon as possible. Live your own life."

Josh said nothing until they were in the car driving down towards Llanishen again.

"Should you have said that?"

"Which bit? The lying about knowing she was being blackmailed or the advice to leave home."

"Both, I expect, though the last bit more. She's a suspect, isn't she? Do you think she had anything to do with Megan's death?"

"I don't know if she could do anything to hurt anyone else. Gut feeling is that she's innocent. That girl needs to get away from her mother. As far as possible. The other side of the world would be good. Failing that, another city miles away. She won't be able to get on with her life, pick up the threads and move forward until she does that. Her bloody mother is a pain in the arse and a control freak."

Josh sort of grunted before he spoke. He'd made a link.

"The counsellor asked me if I thought Lisa's demands were a desire to control my movements and my life."

"Really? I thought those bods just listened."

"It surprised me as well. I hadn't thought about it and from Lisa's face neither had she. We've got homework to do as well."

"Bloody hell, Josh. One hundred lines, 'I must do better'," Mandy stole a glance sideways. Josh wasn't as frazzled as he had been so maybe the therapy was working. He blushed and half-smiled.

"Nah. We have to think of a minimum of three things we like about each other. Why we got married in the first place." He shifted in his seat, eyes fixed straight ahead. "That's easy for me but it must be hard for Lisa."

Oh God. He had a real chip on his shoulder. And she'd been picking on him, making him feel bad about himself. Time for a self-esteem boost.

"Arse. I can give you three straight off. No probs."

"Really?"

"Sure thing. You're honest, loyal and a truly nice person. What you see is what you get. No pretence. No bull."

Silence for a moment while Josh digested this.

"It's really nice of you to say that, boss."

"Come on, Josh. When have you known me to be nice? It's not in my nature. Add to that you're a bloody good copper. I wish there were more like you." Silence. Mandy coughed to cover the embarrassment she could feel coming from Josh. He wasn't used to praise. "We've got to do a detour. I need to pick up my niece and her friend from school and take Kelly to see her parents."

"That's the problem you had first thing? You said the girls were in trouble."

"Big problem. I'll tell you about it sometime. Let's just say it was the stuff parents never want to think of their kid being involved in." She changed gear and slowed down as they neared Rhydepennau. "Okay if I drop you here? Plenty of buses. I'll get back as soon as I can. Check through all the stuff on Megan's computer. Photos, history, finances, everything. See if she pissed off any of the others. I don't think Sophie is involved..."

"She's still not telling us everything, is she? I noticed she avoided eye contact a couple of times. Maybe we should have had her into the station? Sometimes that shakes them."

"And have the wrath of Withering descend upon us. You must be bloody joking. We can't do that to his goddaughter unless we have something more solid, or you want my head and your balls on a slab. Give forensics another prod, will you? We need something to get him on our side."

She stopped the car on Fidlas Road and Josh got out, giving a brief salute before slamming the door shut. Mandy's mouth was set. Now for dealing with Kelly's parents, although she suspected it would just be Mum. Dad seemed to be working away a lot these days. Made you wonder. On the other hand, she was a single parent, or the equivalent, and until this week it had worked out fine, hadn't it? Calm mind. Calm attitude and it would all be fine. Time for mild mannered Mandy while dealing with Kelly's Mum and then mad Mandy when she spoke to Tabitha later, although from the expression on Tabitha's face this morning it was more likely to be Mumsy Mandy this evening.

CHAPTER TWENTY-ONE

It was after two o'clock by the time Mandy got back to the station. As soon as she saw Olivia and Josh, she knew something had happened. She opened her mouth to say "what?" when she was aware of Superintendent Withers behind her. He'd been waiting for her.

"So good of you to turn up, Wilde. My office. Now."

"Sir?" Mandy caught Olivia's eye as she passed. The girl just drew a line with her finger across her throat. Sodding hell. Another bollocking. Mrs Bloody Ice Fucking Queen Grant had found out they'd been asking questions again and Withering was on the bloody warpath. Would she get out of his office with her rank intact? Would she even get out with her job?

Withers waited until Mandy entered the office. He slammed the door behind her, so the blinds rattled like teacups on a tray. She could smell his sweat, masked by aftershave, as he settled himself down behind his desk. He didn't ask her to sit, and she didn't dare take liberties while he was in that mood.

"So?"

Mandy frowned. What the hell was he expecting her to say? What was he thinking?

"Sir?"

"This Pritchard case. Why isn't it finished? Surely, it's a case of misadventure. Do you have any more evidence? Does my goddaughter have to go through any more stress waiting for a report on this... this debacle while you faff about for no reason?" He was fixing her with his "don't argue with me" face so Mandy decided to play safe.

"We are just pulling all the threads together, sir. We think Megan Pritchard was blackmailing Sophie. It seems she was quite manipulative. She's also been controlling Aisha to an extent. We've spoken to Sophie this morning. She's quite a nervous person, isn't she? Very much, how can I put it, under her mother's influence."

Withers said nothing for a moment and then almost deflated, sinking backwards into his seat. He indicated for Mandy to sit down. She did so, wondering what the hell was coming. He steepled his fingers and brought them up to touch his mouth. For once he seemed calm, contemplative. Dangerous. Withers in a temper she could cope with, but this was a calculating stare, like a lion stalking its prey. When he did speak his voice was low, measured, as if he were choosing each word with particular care.

"Diane Grant is a woman with high standards. Failure is not a word she will contemplate. She's a determined woman." He paused, almost as if he feared he'd said too much, and then changed tack. "I've watched Sophie grow up. An only child. Treasured but with high expectations. Nothing was too good for her; however, she was supposed to reward her parents by doing exceptionally well in whatever she was engaged in, academic or otherwise. They sent her to private school, engaged tutors, provided music, drama and elocution lessons to make her into something special."

He stared at Mandy, challenging. "And she is special. She's a charming young woman who did well at university. Her first attempt at escaping her mother's ambition was to go to London to work."

"I thought her father had encouraged that?" Mandy held her breath. Should she have interrupted? Withers concurred.

"Yes. He could see that Sophie needed to become more independent. When he died Sophie fell apart. I expect by now your investigation has uncovered what happened in London and why Sophie is back in Cardiff?"

"Yes, sir. I don't think Sophie is coping too well with her mother's dominance at present. We've tried to be discreet although there are still questions left unanswered. Sophie is very vulnerable, but I think she's still hiding something. I don't know what or why."

A raised eyebrow indicated that the superintendent was not pleased with that response. Maybe he expected Mandy to say that she thought Sophie was innocent of any involvement in Megan's unfortunate death. She couldn't do that. Not yet. Not for certain. How to keep him happy?

"We're pursuing several lines of enquiry at the moment, sir. We hope to have it wrapped up within a few days – as you wished."

He grunted in response. "You do that, DI Wilde. That girl has enough to deal with. She doesn't need all this hanging over her as well. Her mother is hopping mad and giving me a lot of earache. I might have a quiet word with Sophie myself if the opportunity arises. Now, get out of here and get on with it. Pronto."

"Sir."

Mandy left the office frowning in puzzlement. That was a change of attitude. What was the purpose of that conversation? Was he trying to get her to go easy on Sophie? Did he intend to become involved in some way? Take matters into his own hands. Surely not? Whatever she knew, or heard, about the Super, one thing was always clear. He was above board. No shady dealings or anything that would interfere with justice. She thought he was on Diane's side, though he seemed to be aware that she was the cause of much of Sophie's nervousness. He was supportive, almost paternal, towards the young woman. For that reason, he should be steering clear from the investigation, not giving them earache every five minutes. Bloody man.

* * *

It had been a difficult day and, with nothing urgent to follow up, Mandy went home early. She had a quick word with Kelly's Mum and promised a further explanation when she had got over the shock of knowing the danger the girls had been exposed to. There would be a few tears shed in that house this evening. No doubt about that. When she got back to Brithdir Street all was quiet. It was obvious that Tabitha had been busy. The hall tiles gleamed and there was a delicious smell of something cooking. Tabitha was sound asleep on the sofa, exhausted by all the drama no doubt. Mandy gazed at her with a mixture of love and frustration. How dare Joy leave her with this responsibility? How vulnerable the girl was. Half child, half woman. She had behaved responsibly. She'd supported Kelly. God knows what would have happened otherwise. A feeling of rage filled her when she thought of Gary, if that was even his real name. She'd like to do unspeakable things to him and his sort, preying on the young and susceptible.

As if aware, Tabitha stirred and her eyelids flickered. She opened her eyes and then jumped when she saw Mandy watching.

"I'm sorry. I must've fallen asleep." She yawned and pulled herself to a sitting position. "I've cooked something. I hope it's not burnt."

"It smells fine. Thank you for doing that."

Tabitha's eyes filled with tears. "I'm really sorry. I didn't mean to make you mad. You must be so angry with me. I mean, you never wanted to look after me and you've a busy life and I just get in the way and I'll go and live somewhere else if you want me to." She was sobbing now, shaking and gulping for breath as the words fell over each other.

Mandy sat on the sofa and pulled her into her arms until Tabitha's head rested on her shoulder. How could she stay angry with her niece when she was so upset? The poor kid had enough baggage without any more pain piled on top.

"Don't be silly, Tabs. I love having you here. Who else would do the washing up when I haven't the time?" She hugged her tight.

Tabitha made a sound somewhere between a laugh and a hiccough. She clung to Mandy, shaking with her head buried in her shoulder.

"Tabs, what happened was very dangerous and I'm disappointed that you didn't just call me. I'm here for you whatever happens, whatever you do. I trust you and I believe what you told me – but I was terrified. Please, don't ever do that again."

She was rocking Tabitha in her arms like a baby, and they stayed locked like that for several minutes. So much for reading the riot act. Mandy could feel the tears in her own eyes in empathy with her teenage niece who sobbed as if it was the end of the world.

At last, the sobbing calmed, and Tabitha raised her tear-stained face to Mandy's.

"Kelly's my best friend. I had to help her, didn't I? That's what friends are for, isn't it?"

The same words she'd said before. Mandy was reminded of Megan and her friends. What help had she given to her friends and what had they done in return?

CHAPTER TWENTY-TWO

SATURDAY

"Bloody hell." Josh didn't swear in the office very often, so Mandy wondered what had caused it. He was on the internet and at first glance over his shoulder Mandy thought he was surfing porn sites.

"What?"

"Bethan Rees. This is her website with some of the stuff she's been modelling. Not shy about her body, is she?"

Mandy peered over his shoulder and whistled.

"Bloody hell, indeed. These are a bit racy. It's not porn, still it's quite suggestive. As you say she's at home in her own skin. Oh well. Have fun. Let me know if there's anything we should be concerned about."

Mandy went back to her desk and started sifting through things again. Sometimes it was the fine detail that held the real clues. So, what did they know so far? She read back over the interviews and the forensics. Rishi had sent off some samples. Had he had those back yet? Would there be anything to help?

"Hey, boss. There's something here you need to see. Have a butchers at this." Josh was pointing at the screen. "She's got a troll. Just read some of these comments. They start about a year ago. Simple things like 'fat' and 'disgusting'. Then they become more frequent."

"Why didn't Bethan delete them?"

"She responded to a few of them, and it seems as if some things have been removed. See," he pointed, "her response here is, 'Why don't you leave me alone? You've got something wrong with you. There's nothing wrong with having a bigger body except in your sick head.' We don't know what the comment was or who's trolling her."

"How do we find out? Should we ask the cyber bods?"

"I can have a go if you like," said Olivia. "I can't say I'll find anything. If I don't, we can always pass it on to the techy team, can't we?" Olivia stood beside Mandy, viewing the screen and squinting through her specs. "Sorry. I'm a bit of a geek, like. I had a girlfriend who was into games and stuff and did a bit of hacking."

Mandy's sharp intake of breath gave an indication of her thinking. Olivia must have guessed as she continued, "Don't worry we're not together anymore and I didn't do any of the illegal stuff. I'll do a bit of tweaking and see what I come up with. Alright? Gimme an hour?"

"Sure. Anything else, Josh?" He shook his head. "Well, it might be worth a visit to Rishi to see if the rest of the toxicology report is back. Surely there's something, somewhere. Please somebody find a bloody clue."

While everyone was busy Mandy put photographs of the four suspects in front of her and studied the faces. Four clever and successful young women.

Which of you hated Megan enough to want her dead? Which one was the best actress? Who could lie with conviction? She went through it all again, putting the possible motives and alibis down in a table. Sometimes, she found it helped to have all the facts and thoughts in front of her as she thought about the problem. Would it work? Well, worth a try.

Aisha. Her earring was near the body. Fingerprints on the medication. Plus, Megan had guessed she was gay and was using that to control her. She was in bed with a migraine when Megan left the house. Was that deliberate to be removed from suspicion? Could she have spiked the drink and then left things to take place while she slept? Possible motives: professional and personal. She was manipulated by Megan and could gain from her death.

Bethan. Could she have known about the medication? Megan could have confided in her best friend. Or Nia might have told her. Megan's oldest friend. Slightly overweight and taunted by Megan because of it although seems happy in her own skin judging from website. Possible motives: Jealousy. Rage over being fat-shamed?

Sophie. Gave Megan expensive things to keep her quiet. Cowed by her mother. Megan knew how and why she'd lost her job. Sophie nervous. Did she organise the party in such a remote place for a purpose? Motive: Revenge for blackmail.

Siobhan. Megan had damaged Siobhan's long-term relationship with her boyfriend, Rhys. Despite reconciliation it must have caused distress. Has she forgiven Megan? Motive. Revenge.

Checking through her notes Mandy could see that the two main suspects were Sophie and Siobhan in terms of motive. However, there was still the circumstantial evidence linking Aisha to the scene. She stood to gain from Megan's death. Then Bethan. What was it Catrin Pritchard had said? Something about Bethan worshipping Megan. Had that relationship gone sour? Jealousy was a powerful factor.

Mandy stared at the list for some time before she got another piece of paper and wrote, Megan Pritchard at the top. What had they found out? Another list.

Plus points: Good fun. Generous. Hard working. Colleagues in work respected her. Ambitious. Driven to be the best. Took good personal care of herself. Fit. Well-toned. Liked nice clothes, shoes, jewellery. Reliable in work. Didn't drink.

Minus points: Could be difficult. Rift with sister, Nia. Demanding of friends. Duplicitous at times. Blackmailing Sophie, controlling Aisha – any of the others? Check. Despite being well turned out she was untidy. Expensive tastes but didn't spend on her surroundings. Manipulative. Could be nasty. Suffered from severe anxiety requiring medication.

As she read through it struck Mandy again that Megan Pritchard was a mixed personality. If she'd been a suspect in this case, she'd have been number one. Still, from what her family said Megan wouldn't deliberately take alcohol with her medication knowing it could lead to psychosis. Although death wouldn't always follow, it was possible. There was no evidence of suicidal tendencies they were aware of.

Typical Gemini someone had said and that was accurate. In life she had many positive qualities. On the other hand, she had damaging negative traits as well. Were the four women still in contact with her because of fond memories of their university days together? That bond of youth that never breaks for some people. Shared history.

"Boss?" Olivia had appeared at her side. "I've tried to trace the troll but there are numerous sources. It appears as though there are several people sending negative comments.' She shook her head a little. 'I think it's only one, I do. Someone with more computer knowledge than me. I've got so far but I'll go and ask the tech guys. One of them has a thing for me."

"Doesn't he know about your preferences?"

"Nah. What I do in my spare time is not his concern, is it now? I'll go and blink my eyelashes." She laughed, a loud laugh that seemed at odds with her diminutive body, then bounced off to find someone to help.

Josh came back just as Olivia was leaving. He gripped a sheet of paper in his hand and waved it in the air. Mandy waited.

"I've been to talk to forensics. See if I could persuade them to work a bit faster. Seems they've finished with the fingerprinting."

"Out with it then. You're so pleased with yourself anyone would think you'd fallen in horse dung and come out with a bag of gold."

"This is a game-changer."

"What have they got?"

CHAPTER TWENTY-THREE

Josh was grinning so much that Mandy thought his jaw would crack. Whatever he'd found out it must be good.

"So? Come on, Josh. Put me out of my misery. Fingerprints? A confessional note? A body part?"

"Nothing."

"What do you mean, nothing? What's that supposed to mean?"

"Everything has been wiped clean. No fingerprints. No alcohol residue in either the vodka bottle or the pop bottles or cans. A few crumbs in the bottom of the bag. Stuck in the folds so could have been missed. And..." he took a breath to prolong the drama of the situation, "no fingerprints on the bags either. Traces of bleach and other cleaning materials. Whoever did the cleaning up made a very thorough job of it. Wearing gloves, no doubt. No sign of those either."

Mandy's eyes lit up. "Too bloody good a job. You'd expect some residue of some sort. Lots of messy fingerprints. So, someone was aware there might be an investigation and decided to clean up after themselves. And who could that be, I wonder? I didn't see any rubber gloves in the kitchen or bathroom, yet those women had all been cleaning." Clever buggers. Too clever. It had backfired.

"You're right, Josh." Mandy stood. "This is a game changer. Premeditation or, at least, a cover-up operation afterwards. We need to find out which one of those young women cleaned up before the police got there."

She could see that Josh wanted to say something. His mouth was open, and he had a speculative expression on his face.

"Spit it out. What?"

"What if it was a conspiracy? What if they were all involved? Each of them had some reason to dislike Megan. What if they all had a hand in it?"

Mandy frowned a little while she digested that idea. "You're right Josh. That thought had crossed my mind at one point. It could be a set up so that they got their revenge. Both Sophie and Siobhan had strong reasons to want some harm to come to Megan. Blackmail and revenge. And they travelled to the house together. The other two not so much. Perhaps they didn't intend for her to die."

"You mean a trick gone wrong?"

"Yeah, maybe. We'll need to speak to them again. And I think we'll do some of the interviews here. Oh God. I'll need to take this latest development to Withers and run it past him. If his precious goddaughter is involved it's going to be shit hitting the fan big time. I'd better go and tell him."

Mandy squared her shoulders and patted her hair down before approaching Withers. His office door was open. She knocked. It seemed extra loud to her ears, and he peered up from the papers he was reading with a frown on his face. That wasn't a good start.

"I'm sorry to disturb you, sir. There's been a development in the Pritchard case. I thought you'd want to know."

The frown became deeper. He took off his spectacles, folded them and placed them on the desk. Mandy was aware of her own breathing. He may have been the concerned godfather last time she spoke to him. Now it was more as if he wanted to eat her alive.

"What developments? I thought the case should have been closed by now."

Mandy pointed at the door. "May I?"

A lift of the eyebrow and a nod. She closed the door and as soon as it clicked shut, he asked again.

"What developments?"

"We took the rubbish from Nythfa to see if there were any traces of anything else in the bags. Sometimes there are substances which cause allergies, that sort of thing."

"I am well aware of that, Wilde. So, what did you find?" His tone hinted at impatience.

"That's the problem, sir. We found nothing."

"It's not a problem. It eliminates foul play, doesn't it? If you were thinking her drink had been spiked with something."

Mandy's lips were dry and so was her throat. If only Sophie wasn't his goddaughter all this would be so easy.

"When I said nothing sir, I meant nothing. No fingerprints on the bottles, food containers or the bag itself. Everything had been wiped with bleach. The only thing missed were a few tiny crumbs caught in the folds of the bag."

Withers sat back in his chair. He opened his mouth and exhaled, long and loud.

"That rather changes things, doesn't it?"

"Yes, sir."

"So, what's your thinking now? In the light of these developments."

Oh God. She was going to have to spell it out. He wasn't going to like it.

"Well, it seems there was more to Megan's death than an accident. The clean-up indicates that either it was a conspiracy by all four young women to cover up or perhaps one or two worked together to cause harm to Megan. Perhaps they didn't realise what would happen or it was a deliberate attempt to harm her. Maybe whoever did this didn't mean it to be fatal."

Withers sat for a moment just staring at her. The chattering from the main office seemed louder than usual and she was aware of the humming of his computer. The moment seemed to stretch. Mandy could feel her hands become clammy. She'd put the problem in his lap now. What would he tell her to do next? She knew what she was going to do except it would be better to have the Super on her side. At last, he broke the silence.

"Right. First steps we need to talk to all of them again. It was Sophie who organised it wasn't it?"

Mandy nodded.

"Then we start with her. I suggest we hold the interview here. I'll tell Diane myself. Try to keep the peace. If Sophie's got anything to do with that unfortunate girl's death, then the sooner we find out about it the better. Agreed?"

"Yes, sir. What about Siobhan? She's in Chepstow and planning a return to Ireland soon." Mandy knew what she wanted to do about that little problem, although she figured some instruction from the Super would help smooth things for the team.

"You need to speak to her with some urgency then. If you can do that today so much the better. I'll go myself and speak to Diane, calm her down and make sure she doesn't put obstacles in the way. Arrange the interview with Sophie for tomorrow morning. Right. Let's get on with it."

He got to his feet and Mandy leapt into action. A little trip to Chepstow, with a side diversion to see Mr Norton, would be most welcome. She almost skipped into the room where Josh and Olivia were sifting through printouts of bank details, phone calls and rechecking notes from the informal interviews. Had they missed anything else? God, she hoped not, otherwise Withers would have her back on the beat faster than she could say murder.

* * *

Ross Withers sat for a moment after DI Wilde left the room. It was all a bit of a mess. Diane was just warming up nicely to his advances, or so he'd thought, and now this. Sophie was a bright young woman if a bit too highly strung and, much as he admired Diane's iron maiden attitude to life in general, it was having a detrimental effect on her daughter. Once this business was sorted, he'd have a quiet word with Sophie. See how he could help her to gain enough confidence to set herself up in her own place without undermining her mother. Diane would have more time on her hands in the evenings then as well so she might be glad of a male companion to escort her to the theatre and the opera. Yes, that would do well. Kill two birds with one stone as it were.

The latest evidence in the investigation certainly pointed to a cover-up. He'd bet his pension that Sophie had nothing to do with it. That didn't mean he could turn a blind eye. There was nothing Ross Withers despised more than bent coppers. If his goddaughter was involved in some way, then she'd be treated the same as anyone else in the same boat. God, he hoped that Wilde was wrong. That family had experienced enough bad luck for one year.

CHAPTER TWENTY-FOUR

They didn't ring ahead to find out if Siobhan and Rhys were at home. Mandy preferred the element of surprise and she had another item on her agenda.

"That bloke who assaulted me when we were down last time. You've got his details, haven't you?" She kept her eyes on the road knowing that Josh would have written everything down in the notebook in his coat pocket.

"Yeah, course. Intending to pay him a little visit too?" She could hear the teasing in his voice. No pulling the wool over his eyes.

"Might as well. As we'll be in the area." Mandy kept her tone light.

"Have you thought that your sister doesn't want to be found?"

"I think that's fairly bloody obvious. I don't know why. She says she's coming back, arrives in the country, meets a bloke on the bus and does a detour for months. Why? What's the bloody point?"

She could hear Josh move in his seat. He wanted to say something but was afraid to do so.

"Come on, Josh. Spit it out. What are you thinking?"

"Well, could be she's involved in something, well, you know, dodgy."

"Yeah. I've thought about that. Like drug smuggling or people trafficking or something. Joy has always played by her own rules. I knew I'd never be able to compete with that. Besides Mam would have bloody exploded with two feral kids to keep an eye on. I rebelled by joining the police." She laughed. It was a mirthless sound, false even to her own ears.

As they drove into Bulwark, Mandy kept her eyes open for any tall frizzy-haired women wandering around. Something told her that her sister was in the area. It upset her that her twin was avoiding detection. It was Tabitha who was suffering the most. Mandy knew she blamed herself for her mother's disappearance. When this case was solved, they'd need to sit down and have a little heart to heart. That and the heavy-handed talk about keeping safe they still hadn't had time for. Maybe she didn't need to do that one now. After all, the poor kid had been frightened enough, hadn't she? Kelly was the one who needed a heavy hand.

The front window of Rhys's house was open, and a low drumbeat could be heard as they approached the house. The music was indistinguishable. Nothing she recognised. Grunge. Mandy parked a little way back so that they didn't alert the neighbours to anything strange going on. Not that this was the sort of neighbourhood full of curtain twitchers like in that cul-de-sac where Sophie lived. In this area folk knew when to keep themselves to themselves unless it was to help a neighbour.

At the front of the house, she could detect the distinct sweet smell of weed. So, Siobhan and Rhys liked to get stoned. Interesting. She rang the doorbell and waited. They could hear urgent voices from inside then a faint click as the front door opened a little. Siobhan was a little wide-eyed as she stared at Mandy and then Josh. Her mouth opened but no words came out. Mandy wanted to laugh at the dumb expression. She'd had her own experimentation with weed and decided it didn't agree with her. These days a gin and tonic on high days and holidays was her indulgence. She got high from the buzz of the job. When had she become so dull, boring and middle-aged?

"It's okay Siobhan, we haven't come to bust you, or Rhys," she added as an equally bleary looking Rhys appeared behind Siobhan. "We just needed some clarification on a few points. I believe you're heading back to Ireland soon."

"You'd better come in," said Rhys, nodding towards the lounge. This time Mandy and Josh sat with Siobhan on the sofa and Rhys almost fell as he sat, crossed legged, on the floor. An ashtray with the remains of a joint stubbed out, sat beside him, yet he made no attempt to conceal it. The rest of the room was tidy, papers stacked on the table and everything in its place.

"Something has come to light which makes us believe that Megan's death was more than an unfortunate accident, so we need you to focus very clearly," Josh coughed at that point and Mandy knew what that meant. How could Siobhan focus when, from the dilated pupils and dazed expression, she was stoned? "We need you to think back to that weekend. After Sophie, was it, rang the police, what happened then?"

"They came back to Nythfa."

"Did you just sit and wait or have a cup of tea, breakfast? What happened? Anything that could give us more clarity."

Siobhan stared into space for a moment, her head wobbling a little as she considered the question.

"We'd had loads of coffee after Megan had walked out and the place was a bit of a mess. Sophie got into a panic as the photographer was coming again on Monday to do more shots for the house sale. She said we needed to tidy the place so that as soon as Megan turned up, we could leave." She sighed. "At that time, we thought she'd gone and spent the night in the pub or something. Sure, we'd no idea that..."

"It was Sophie who said the house needed to be cleaned?"

"Yes. She was frantic as we had glasses and empty packets everywhere. Ma Grant would have bust her stays. It was quite funny. Like one of those scenes from a film where the man living alone leaves half-full takeaway cartons and empty bottles all over the place." She glanced at her boyfriend. "Not that Rhys lives like that. He can be a bit obsessed with being tidy, sometimes." She gave Rhys a look of adoration, before turning back to Mandy and Josh. "No one would have guessed that five professional women could be such slobs."

Josh was taking notes.

"Who did what when you started cleaning? Did you have tasks set? Were you all involved with each room or how was it organised?"

"We all did our own packing." That made sense. "Sophie sorted out Megan's things. Changed the bed. That sort of thing. She said she'd go back later in the afternoon with her mother to do the last-minute things. Diane wanted vases of fresh flowers. The 'staging' or 'dressing' of the house had to be perfect."

That fitted too. Diane Grant was a control freak. A perfectionist. No wonder Withers felt sorry for Sophie, despite his attraction to Diane, or her money. Living with that expectation of flawlessness must be hell. Siobhan's forehead was creased as she concentrated on remembering the finer details.

"Did you see Megan's mobile at all?" asked Mandy.

A shake of the head. "No. She had it during the walk in the afternoon. She kept on checking how far we'd walked, that sort of thing. It would drive you to drink the fussing. She'd one of them top of the range iPhones in rose gold with a pink cover. I don't know where she put it. Sure, I just thought she had it when she left."

"Okay. So, tell me about cleaning."

"Em. Sophie and I did upstairs. Changed all the beds, cleaned the bathrooms, dusted and vacuumed the carpets. Hard going with a head banging like a toilet door. Usually now, you'd sleep off a hangover, but we didn't have the chance. Sophie was wound up to the nines, wasn't she, about her Ma and the house. I don't know why she suggested the house in the first place when she knew we'd have to play Mrs Mop before we left." Siobhan shook her head slightly as if she'd been caught in a cobweb.

"And who cleaned the rooms downstairs? The kitchen?"

"Well now, that was left to Aisha and Bethan. It was only fair they did their share of the work too. I don't know how they divvied it out. You'd have to ask them."

Aisha and Bethan. Alarm bells rang. They'd thought Aisha was innocent, but it was her earring in the field close to Megan's body. Was that really a coincidence? Plus, the fingerprints on the tablets. Had they missed something? Aisha was the one now with the big promotion. And Megan had been manipulating her, keeping control. Still, no evidence, other than circumstantial. Everyone said Aisha was in bed when the drama occurred. Then again wasn't Siobhan left alone in the house when the others went out to find a phone signal? Could she believe anyone?

"Remind me of the entrances to the house. Could someone have gone out without the others seeing her?"

A trick question. Mandy knew the answers. She had a mental floorplan of the house in her head, reinforced after the nocturnal visit with Olivia. She wanted to see what Siobhan had to say.

"Aye, suppose so. The dining room has the patio doors, and the downstairs loo is close to the back door. But we didn't go out that night. Megan was the only one who left the house. What are you thinking?" Siobhan frowned a little.

"I was wondering if anyone could have followed Megan out without the others knowing?"

Siobhan shook her head. "Aisha was in bed and Bethan in the loo. Sophie and me were stuck to the sofa, legless. We thought it was one of Megan's drama queen moments and that she'd be back within minutes.

225

It wasn't until the rain started to get heavy that we began to worry about her. Jesus, nobody knew that was going to happen." She waved her hands in front of her face as if to clear away the memory.

"Were you aware that Megan was taking anti-psychotic drugs?"

"God, no. Though it doesn't surprise me she was on something. Sure, she was more strung up than my Granda's fiddle. She was a laugh a minute, then she'd change just like that." She snapped her fingers. "You never knew where you were with your woman. I felt sorry for her, really I did. I mean, I know she caused hell for Rhys and me but at the end of the day it was all a bit pathetic."

Josh opened his mouth as if to ask something then thought better of it. Mandy blinked at him and said nothing. They may have to ask more questions, and under caution, if Sophie's account of the clean-up operation diverged from Siobhan's. At the back of her mind, Mandy had the worry that the four had conspired together to cause harm to Megan. They had time, not only to clear up any evidence, but to make sure their stories matched. Would they do that? And if that is what happened, who was most likely to break first? Sophie seemed the most vulnerable, though people were complicated, weren't they? Mandy was glad the Super was going to be on her side on this one.

"When is your ferry back to Ireland?"

"Another couple of days or so. I'm easy. I was going to book for tomorrow. Then Rhys is trying to organise his work so he can come back with me for a bit. I don't fancy being by myself." She gazed at her boyfriend, and he reached over to touch her hand, the devotion in his eyes saying everything.

Those two are so soppy, thought Mandy as she stood up and prepared to leave.

"Keep us informed of your plans. Things are escalating and we'll need to speak to you again. Don't leave the country just yet." Although it was said with the ghost of a smile on her lips, the tone was clear.

"Am I suspected of something then?"

"Let's just say that we're not convinced it was an accident. We're investigating other avenues."

Siobhan paled but made no further comments, rising to her feet and leading them to the door. A brief exchange of nods and Mandy and Josh were on their way again.

* * *

Siobhan crossed her arms over her body. The police were investigating. That DI was a hard one to read. Was she fishing or did she suspect something or someone? Was she saying it wasn't an accident? What else could it be? Nobody had left after Megan. Had they? Her head was a fog. Rhys had suggested a bit of weed to relax. Now she could feel the effects already beginning to wear off. It wasn't something she did on a regular basis. She preferred a glass of something alcoholic. Time to go and lie down and think back. She could remember bits and pieces of that night, but it was all muddled. Why? Many a time she'd had more to drink. And the feeling that she just couldn't move. That was dire. The memory of Megan's face flashed in front of her. She'd been manic. Screaming at them.

"There's someone out there. I know there is. Someone's watching us. We've got to get away. Come on." Megan had pulled at her arm, frantic, with pupils dilated and sweat on her forehead. "Come on, Siobhan."

She'd pushed Megan's arm off her with an impatient comment. What had she said? Oh yes. She remembered. "Don't be so daft, Meg. Do you think it's the wee people out there? Watch out for the banshee now, won't you?" Sophie giggled and Megan reeled away from them still ranting. They registered the slam of the door and couldn't be bothered to follow. That was the bottom line. They couldn't be bothered to follow someone who was disturbed in some way. What sort of a friend is that? A pretty poor one. Then again, what sort of a friend tries to steal your boyfriend and creates mischief for others? Whatever the police found out it wouldn't take away the guilt she felt.

Rhys had crawled on to the sofa and was snoring. He'd be asleep for a while. She hoped he'd wake up before Vincent called for his money. That guy gave her the creeps. Maybe she should warn him to stay away. The DI had said she wasn't interested in the weed, but that DS didn't appear happy about it. He might shop them to the local boys. Best get rid of the stash and Vincent too. Just as well they were heading over to Ireland. Break from the little circle Rhys seemed to have got himself into. Dodgy dealers. He didn't need that especially with the business escalating. He needed to break the habit and clear his head. They needed to get away from the storm that was brewing.

CHAPTER TWENTY-FIVE

Josh settled into the passenger seat. "He seemed laid back considering he was smoking weed."

Mandy laughed. "That's probably why he was laid back. I knew there was a strange smell under the fried food and that jasmine diffuser the last time we were there. That other stuff disguised it." She turned to face him. "You never smoked weed, Josh?"

"Once or twice maybe. You know, just to see." He wriggled a little, like a little boy caught doing something he shouldn't.

"Didn't we all? I know one or two in the force who still indulge from time to time."

"Really? But, that's illegal."

"Bloody hell, Josh. How naïve are you? There's probably a lot more goes on than we know about. Some of the undercover boys have to be part of whatever scene or gang they need to infiltrate. God knows what the hell they get up to. A bit of weed once in a blue moon is piss feed."

"Yeah, you're probably right. I just like to do it all by the book, if I can." He had that worried expression on his face. Sometimes she thought Josh was thirty going on eighty in his no risk attitude to life. Maybe his wife wanted to leave because he was so goody-two-shoes all the time. Bloody boring. Whatever was going on at home, she needed him on her side.

"I know you do, and it makes you uncomfortable sometimes when I forget what the book says. Deliberately. I'm not going to let a few rules get in the way if it gets results. Little white lies don't harm. I'd never do anything really off the wall. Scaring a witness into telling the truth is legit in my book."

A humph sound was the only response to that comment. Time to move on.

"Right. Now Mr Norton lives somewhere around here as well. Am I right?"

"Yes. East Crescent. Another cul-de-sac."

"Good. Did you manage to do any background checks on him?"

Josh opened his notebook. "Quick check. Vincent Norton. Thirty-eight. Caution when in his teens for possession of cannabis. Not even a parking ticket since although he's been involved in a few business ventures that are on the edge of dodgy."

"What sort of business?"

"Web ventures that make promises of big bucks then end up as disasters. He's always paid back any money. Just not got the head for it."

"Mmm. Could be Rhys's supplier? They live in the same area. Probably go to the same pub. Let's face it, Chepstow's not a big place. Should be easy to score if you had a mind to it. Wonder if that's why Joy took to him."

Mandy parked facing out of the close and they went and knocked on the door of number fifty-three. Vincent Norton's face dropped when he saw them.

"I ain't done nuffin. Whatever it is I know nuffin. Okay?" He went to close the door, but Mandy put her foot through the gap.

"We'd like a few words, Mr Norton." She flashed her warrant card and beamed at him as if he was her long-lost best friend.

"Arseholes." With a disgruntled sneer he opened the door and they followed him into a room, not dissimilar to the one they'd just left except this one was littered with old carrier bags, papers, empty boxes and dirty plates. Not exactly house proud then. They didn't sit. There was no-where obvious except an old armchair that had seen better days and an upturned box with an overflowing ashtray. Mandy had seen worse on her travels, still her nostrils flared a little at the fetid smell. Then she realised it came from an old dog who was asleep under a table in the far corner.

"You got a licence for the animal?" Josh asked.

Good on you, Josh. Get him on the wrong footing straight away. Vincent's sullen expression gave them the answer.

"How about your little side-line in dealing?" Mandy eyed him and then turned away as if seeking evidence of his supplies.

"Bugger." Limited responses from him. She turned back and raised her eyebrows.

"We have reason to believe you've been supplying Rhys Davies with cannabis. Can you confirm this, or do we need to get a search warrant?"

Mandy could feel Josh stiffen. Another of her little white lies that he didn't like. However, it worked. It loosened Vincent's tongue.

"I know Rhys. He's a mate. Met him in the local, like. I'd got some off another bloke and let Rhys have some. I'm not dealing. Personal use, innit?"

"And Joy Wilde? Did you supply her? She's a missing person and you have a connection with her. We'd like to know where she is."

Vincent gave her a lop-sided smirk. He wasn't so dense after all. He knew the real reason she'd come to see him.

"Joy ain't no missing person. Saw her two days ago, by the George. Cleaned herself up. Don't do nuffin no more. Told me she even given up the fags. Saint Joy."

"So, where's she living?"

"Dunno, luv. She was working in some care home. Said she'd found her vocation in life. Some vocation, eh. Cleaning up old people's shit. Star material that, innit?"

Mandy felt her jaw tighten and her fists clench. Wouldn't she like to punch his sneering face? She steadied her breathing.

"Thank you, Mr Norton. You've been most co-operative. We may need to speak to you again with regard to the cannabis or the local boys may be interested. I'd keep a low profile for a while if I was you."

As they walked out Mandy's head was spinning. Joy was alive, kicked her bad habits and working in a care home in, or near, Chepstow. Damn. They'd no time to do anything about that today. Maybe she'd be able to make a few calls. Find out where she was working. The puzzle still remained. Why hadn't she contacted them? Then a stray thought entered her mind. What if it wasn't her sister? What if someone had taken her identity?

That would explain a lot. It didn't explain how Vincent had mistaken Mandy for her twin. No time to deliberate over that one.

* * *

They were both quiet on the way back to Cardiff. There were reports of an accident on the M4 eastbound just after Magor, so Mandy took the old road, the A48, on the way back. On a normal day it would have been a pleasant, if longer, route except it seemed a number of people had the same idea. Traffic was heavy and they were soon reduced to a crawl.

"Just as well Sophie's interview isn't this afternoon," said Josh as Mandy groaned in frustration at the slow pace. Then, a complete stop.

"Now what?" Mandy clenched her teeth.

"I can see traffic lights up ahead. About three hundred yards or more. Probably more roadworks."

Mandy rested her head on the steering wheel for a moment before picking up her phone.

"I'm just going to ring Tabs to let her know. I thought we'd actually finish early today. More fool me."

Josh was peering out through the window trying to gauge if there was any movement ahead.

"Sorry Tabs. We're stuck in traffic. Not even near Newport yet. What? That's fantastic. Is there enough for three?" She nudged Josh and raised her eyebrows at him. "I might bring a stray home. If he fancies your chicken casserole and baked potato."

Josh gave a thumbs up.

"He says yes. Don't know what time we'll get there. We could probably walk quicker."

The car in front revved up.

"Got to go. We're on the move."

The journey should have taken less than an hour, but it was already early evening when Mandy pulled up at Brithdir Street. Josh seemed a little uneasy.

"You ready to get down with the kids? Any good at Xbox games?" Mandy was teasing him.

Within half an hour he was sitting with Tabitha on the sofa playing with the Xbox while Mandy prepared some vegetables to go with the casserole and opened a couple of beers. She figured they needed some time to relax. God knows what the next day would bring. Time was running out.

CHAPTER TWENTY-SIX

SUNDAY

Sophie Grant looked pale and fragile as Withers led her into the interview room. Her eyes darted from side to side, and she gripped her hands together until the knuckles showed white. That's how she'd looked the morning they'd gone back to Nythfa to tell them Megan's body had been found. Mandy could see her pulse throbbing in her temple. She knew this was serious.

Withers was professional to the letter, indicating where she was to sit and then sitting down opposite with Mandy at his side. His aftershave was almost overpowering in the heat of the small room and Mandy hoped she wouldn't gag. The sooner this was over the better.

"Now Sophie. First, we need to inform you what is going to happen. Do you want a glass of water or anything?"

Sophie nodded and Mandy went to get a bottle of water and a glass. She noticed that Sophie's nails had been chewed to the point that they were bleeding. She felt a shred of sympathy for the girl. Her gut feeling was that if there had been a deliberate attempt to harm Megan it hadn't been at Sophie's behest. That didn't rule out a cover-up after the event though. Sophie gave her a wan half-smile when she put the water down on the table. Withers started.

"You have the right to a solicitor if you wish and if you do not have a solicitor then we can arrange that for you. At the moment you are not being detained. This interview is purely voluntary. We are just trying to understand how, and possibly why Megan Pritchard died. Do you understand?"

Withers' eyes were full of sympathy and Mandy had a new respect for him. Despite his relationship as her godfather no one could doubt the professional manner he had adopted. Should he even be doing the interview? Considering the relationship, he should have made a declaration of interest but who was going to tell him to back off? Not Mandy, that was certain. She'd had her head bitten off more than once and there was no way she was going to suggest that he stood down and let her take charge of this. As if he was reading her mind, he cleared his throat and turned to Mandy.

"I believe, due to my relationship to the family, DI Wilde should conduct the interview." He turned to Mandy. "I just wanted Sophie to feel that I knew what was going on. I'll send in Jones to accompany you." He stood and gave Sophie a sympathetic look before he left.

Mandy thought she noticed an easing of tension when he'd left the room. Perhaps that was just her personal feeling, except Sophie also appeared less strained.

"Did you want a solicitor, Sophie?"

"I... I don't know. Should I? I haven't done anything wrong. I've already given a statement. What more can I tell you?" Her voice was strained as if she couldn't get enough air into her lungs. "I don't think I need a solicitor."

Mandy hoped Withers was watching the interview. In fact, she was sure he was. No pushing the boundaries today then. No upsetting the goddaughter. What was she? A witness? A suspect? That would be the first thing to establish.

Josh came in, acknowledged Sophie and took his seat beside Mandy. He had his notebook and pen and nothing else. Time to begin. He switched on the recorder, and they did the usual business of stating names. Sophie slopped some water as she lifted it to her mouth.

"We are trying to establish what happened just before and then after Megan Pritchard left the house, Nythfa. You've given us some idea of the events of that weekend, so we just want to go back over that to clarify some points. Do you understand?"

Sophie bent her head. "You have to speak for the tape," said Josh.

"Yes, I understand." It was a whisper.

Over the course of the next hour, they went over the events already recounted leading to the weekend and everything up until Megan left. Sophie's account didn't waver from her first statement and, despite her initial nervousness, she maintained control, shaking a little although meeting Mandy and Josh's eyes when she answered their questions. So far, so good.

"Thank you. You're being very helpful. We just need to fill in a bit about what happened after Megan left. You said that no one followed her, despite her obvious distress."

"Yes. I suppose we should have done something. It was about an hour later when the rain was battering down that we became a bit concerned."

"Where did you think she'd gone or why did you think she'd left like that," Mandy consulted her notes, 'screaming about how we were all going to be murdered or something.' That's pretty strong stuff. Hardly a joke, was it?"

Sophie pushed a strand of hair out of her eyes and shook her head. "We didn't think she was serious. She could be a bit of a practical joker at times. A bit off the wall, unpredictable."

"When did you decide to clean the house?"

The change of direction shook Sophie. A slight frown appeared over one eye and she tilted her head sideways. "The cleaning?"

"Yes. The house was spotlessly clean by the time the police arrived. I'm assuming that was done sometime after Megan disappeared and before you contacted the police. So, when and why?"

Sophie seemed to consider the question for a moment. "We had to leave the house spotless. Mum insisted that I made sure of that. The photographer was due on Monday morning. I knew she'd be running her finger along every surface to see if I'd done as I'd been told. We were in a sort of limbo. None of us could sleep. It seemed a good idea, at the time. Distraction, I suppose."

A knock at the door disturbed them. Olivia popped her head around.

"There's something you need to see, ma'am. A development." Despite the formal address Mandy could see Olivia's eyes were sparkling.

"Interview paused," said Josh as they followed Olivia back to the operations room, leaving Sophie time to reflect.

* * *

"What is it, Olivia? I can see that you're about to piss yourself with excitement."

"Rishi rang. The toxicology report is back. He says you'll want to know this. He's on his way up. Another game-changer was all he'd tell me. Oh, and the lab boys rang as well. Seems those crumbs had an unusual ingredient." She paused and grinned at Mandy who wanted to shake her with impatience.

"And? Come on Olivia. This isn't a bloody game show. What is it?"

"The crumbs had traces of cannabis. Someone had made special cookies." Her eyes were crinkled with mischievousness and Mandy knew, without asking, that Olivia knew exactly what effect that would have on anyone. No wonder they hadn't gone after Megan. They were all too stoned. Stuck to the sofa indeed. It would be funny if it hadn't been so tragic.

Withers appeared at the same moment as Rishi.

"What the hell is going on here? Why did you stop the interview? She's back to chewing her nails to the quick again." Withers was red in the face and Mandy wondered if he had high blood pressure. His mouth was a thin line of disapproval as he stared at them all.

Josh examined the floor and Olivia managed to get herself out of the way, slipping behind Rishi and making her way out of the firing line.

"A development, sir. Toxicology report which I've been told is very important." Mandy crossed her fingers behind her back. Please let it be something vital to the investigation. Her eyes met Rishi's as she tried, by telepathy, to convey her desperation. She needn't have worried.

Rishi was aware of the tension in the room. With a little cough and pulling his shoulders back so that he seemed taller than five ten, he said, "The toxicology shows something very interesting. It appears in addition to the antipsychotics and alcohol there was a further substance in the young woman's blood. She had ingested cannabis at some point in the evening. The mixture of all three proved fatal in this case. Had she been able to get to a hospital in time she may have survived." He raised his shoulders a little. "However, after her fall, she became unconscious and, as I concluded at the time, choked on her own vomit. Most unfortunate. A waste of a life." Rishi's eyes roamed from one to the other as they digested this information, then, making a little bow, he left.

"Well," Withers said, "there's still no evidence that she didn't do this herself."

"But the clean-up operation, sir. That's something, isn't it?"

"Something. Still not hard evidence. We need proof that Megan Pritchard either died by her own hand or by someone else's. So far, we've a lot of phantoms and dreams. You've got twenty-four hours to get some meat on the bones or we call it a day and report accidental death. Now, get in there and finish the interview so that poor girl can go home. You've no reason to keep her here any longer than necessary. Do you hear me?" Withers was almost shouting, and the spittle was gathering at the side of his mouth.

Mandy felt her stomach turn. Twenty-four hours to find out what had happened to Megan and to get justice for her. It wasn't long enough. They'd have to do their best.

When the Super had gone Josh exchanged looks with Mandy. "Well, that's added a new dimension. Who made the cakes or cookies or whatever it was with the magic ingredient?"

"We're going round in circles. We know Siobhan and Rhys partake of recreational drugs, so the spotlight is back on her now. I'm beginning to think it may well be a conspiracy. Let's get back in there and see if Sophie will break."

"But the Super–"

"Can go to hell in a handcart. He wants results and quick. The gloves are off. No more arsing around. Time to play dirty."

Josh trotted after Mandy as she marched back to the interview room, leaving Olivia standing with her mouth hanging open.

CHAPTER TWENTY-SEVEN

Mandy wasted little time getting to the point. She sat down, waited for Josh to switch on the recording machine and leaned forward a little towards Sophie.

"Why didn't you tell us about the cannabis?"

Sophie's eyes widened and she swallowed. Her face turned scarlet and her eyes filled with tears. She brought her hands up to cover her face and sobbed.

"I thought. I knew. It was…"

Mandy was in no mood to be sympathetic. She didn't know if Withers was watching or not, and her patience was running thin. She was going to get answers and to hell with the Super. He could string her up afterwards if he wanted, but time was passing.

"Did you know that Megan had eaten something containing cannabis?"

Sophie clasped her hands in front of her mouth for a moment and nodded.

"You need to speak up."

"Yes."

Josh made a puffing sound and Mandy leaned back in her chair.

"Why didn't you tell us this before? What did you hope to gain by keeping it secret?"

Sophie's eyes moved from Mandy's face to Josh's and then back again. She swallowed.

"It's illegal, isn't it? I didn't want to get into trouble."

Could you believe it? Trouble? The bloody girl was in trouble now and no mistake. Mandy took a couple of breaths to avoid losing her temper. That anger management course had some use after all.

"Obstructing the course of justice is getting into big trouble and that is exactly what you've been doing. Now. Let's get the whole story straight, shall we? Starting with who brought the cannabis? Whose idea was that?"

Despite the bland expression on her face, it was obvious that Mandy was angry. Her eyes held no warmth and her fingers drummed on the table. Sophie seemed to shrink into the chair as the realisation of her situation hit home.

"I don't know." She stopped as Mandy made a tsk noise and shook her head.

"How can you not know? It isn't as though you had a party for the whole of the Vale, is it? There were five of you. It had to be one of you unless it was your fairy godmother who just happened to leave a plate of cannabis cookies on your doorstep." Mandy's voice was rising with each sentence. "Someone passed them round. Someone made sure all evidence was removed, except, of course, from Megan's stomach. I want to know who, and I want to know now." Mandy brought her fist down on the table and some of Sophie's water splashed out onto the melamine surface.

Josh coughed and it was a reminder that sometimes a softer approach worked. Sophie was shaking and, remembering her fragility, Mandy closed her eyes for an instant before continuing with the interview. At least Withers hadn't interrupted, although she was sure behind the scenes he was fuming. Olivia would have made herself scarce if she had any sense or he'd take it out on her as a member of the team.

"I'm sorry," said Mandy, in a lower tone, "we're trying to find out what happened to your friend. It would be very helpful if you could cast your mind back. When were you aware you had consumed cannabis?"

"We had some brownies after the meal, while we were watching television. We'd had a bit to drink as well. It's all a bit of a blur. Someone said something about special cakes. They were really delicious. Then, when I tried to stand up my legs were all wobbly and we were all laughing at the programme, even though it wasn't funny."

Mandy indicated for her to carry on.

"When Megan started getting a bit het up, we laughed as well. We thought that was funny. Even when she stormed out of the door I couldn't move. I told the police we were too drunk to drive but, it wasn't just the booze. I've never been stoned before. Even in uni I avoided it. Some people were doing all sorts of stuff, especially near exam time. Uppers, downers, God knows what. I didn't."

There was something about this young woman that indicated she was telling the truth. Why had she concealed it until now? What was the purpose of that?

"You were aware you had taken drugs?"

"Not at the time. Well, not until everything started to become a bit spaced and I couldn't stop giggling.

Somebody said something like, 'Would you look at Sophie? If her eyes were any bigger, she'd pass as that bush baby.' We'd been watching a nature programme."

"And you didn't tell the police because you were afraid of getting into trouble. Did you think you'd be arrested for being stoned?"

It was incredible. How could someone so intelligent be so stupid?

"Was there also an element of cover-up?" asked Mandy.

"What do you mean?" A tiny crease had appeared between Sophie's eyebrows as she puzzled over the question.

"Try to see it from my point of view. A young woman goes missing from a remote house. Her friends don't raise the alarm for several hours. During that time, they clean the property to the point that all possible evidence is removed. No fingerprints on any of the rubbish, the only 'dirty' items a couple of crumbs containing cannabis. No one had mentioned using recreational drugs so what do we conclude?"

Sophie was blank. She gave a faint shrug.

"We think there was a conspiracy of some sort to cause harm to Megan Pritchard. You organised the party. You organised the clean-up. You omitted to tell us about the drugs that had a part to play in Megan's untimely death. You were being blackmailed by Megan to the tune of several hundred pounds. Possibly more than we know about. What would your conclusions be, Ms Grant?"

A gasp from Sophie indicated that she realised what they were implying. Her hand went to her mouth. Ghost-like pale before, she now appeared grey.

"You think I did it. You think I deliberately fed you false information, don't you?"

No response from Mandy or Josh. Sophie looked like a kitten stuck in a tree with no route of escape. Her bottom lip trembled. She took a sip of water, spilling a little on her hand.

"Sorry. I didn't mean to get in the way of any inquiry. I haven't told you anything that wasn't true."

"You omitted to tell us things that could have been helpful to our enquiries."

"What I told you is true. It was Megan's idea to have a reunion. I'm not sure how all the others felt about it. Then, when she said she was thinking of going to Australia, I suppose we all thought it might be our last get together. Even though we didn't really believe her. She was always making stuff up."

"Well, that turned out to be true," said Josh.

"Nythfa seemed a good idea. Cheap, a quiet spot so we could have loud music if we wanted and walks in the countryside. Pub nearby."

Mandy kept her eyes fixed on Sophie's. Watchful. Judging if this was going to be the full story.

"We all brought food and drink. Loads of it. I don't know who brought what as it was all piled in the kitchen at one point. We had a few bottles of bubbles, spirits and soft drinks. Aisha usually drinks fruit juice and Megan liked Coke. Siobhan and I picked up stuff in Carmarthen on the way back so no cannabis cookies from either of us."

That tallied with the statement she'd given at the beginning of the investigation and ruled them out, if she was telling the truth. Siobhan smoked cannabis. They'd seen that evidence. She could have brought cakes with her in her bag, hidden away.

"On Saturday evening we had some drinks and a sort of buffet in the kitchen. I can remember something about special brownies, but it didn't register. I didn't know what was so special. We'd had a pub lunch, so it was grazing really. I can't remember what we all ate as we were pretty wasted. Aisha had gone to bed with a migraine, and we watched television. I've told you all this before."

"Carry on. How long before the effects of the cake became obvious? Was anyone pouring drinks, or did you help yourselves?"

"Bit of both. After Aisha went to bed, I opened the last bottle of bubbles and poured that. Then I'm not sure. We had a load of savoury stuff. Aisha had brought some vegetarian stuff which I heated up and it was later when we had the cake."

All very vague. Mandy could have shaken her.

"Who said it was special cake?"

"I really can't remember. I was the one who said we'd better clean things up as Mum would be doing an inspection. I didn't realise it would make a difference to the investigation. I thought Megan had probably just gone and stayed at the pub or something."

"When she'd left screaming about being in danger? Do me a favour. Do you really expect me to believe that now? She was stoned. Someone deliberately laced her

Coke with vodka then fed her cannabis cakes. Someone who was well aware of the consequences."

Sophie put a hand to her throat and swallowed. "You didn't know Megan. She was always playing stupid tricks on people. And we all, apart from Aisha, had mixed the booze with the cannabis."

"But you didn't have antipsychotic medication in the mix. That's what made the difference."

Sophie stared at Mandy with a confused expression. She was exhausted and she would have a lot of explaining to do to her mother when she got home. They were getting closer to the truth though.

"So, the cleaning operation you say you organised. Did you come across Megan's phone at all? It's still missing."

Sophie shook her head.

"Okay. Cleaning. Who did what?"

"Siobhan and I did upstairs. There were new duvet covers and sheets in the airing cupboard. Mum wanted the place pristine for the extra photos, so we changed all that."

"What did you do with the dirty ones?"

"I put them in black bags in the boot of my car to take home to launder. They've all been washed and ironed now. We did all the bathrooms too. Aisha and Bethan cleared up downstairs."

That was what Siobhan had said. Had they conspired together? Worked out the story? That thought was still niggling away at the back of Mandy's mind.

"Who did the kitchen?"

"I don't know. I assumed they did it together. It was all sorted when we'd finished upstairs. By that time, we felt straight enough to contact the police." She blushed at that and picked at her fingers again.

"I thought you said Aisha was in bed with a migraine. How was she helping?"

"She got up in the middle of the night and wanted a drink of water. We were just about coming around to being able to move at that point. We told her about Megan. She joined in the clean-up. Honestly, if I'd known we'd never have... Mum's going to go mad over this." She swallowed. "Are you going to charge me?"

"That remains to be seen." Mandy tapped the table with her forefingers. "For the moment we expect you to stay within the country. If there's anything else you can recall, no matter how small or seemingly insignificant, you must tell us immediately. Understand?"

Mandy and Josh stood. Sophie remained in the chair.

"You can go now." Josh's voice was gentle, reassuring. Sophie inclined her head a little, rising to her feet. When they opened the door to the corridor, Withers was already there.

"I'll take you home, Sophie. And have a word with your mother."

He had a heart after all, at least for some people. It was unfortunate Mandy didn't belong on that list.

CHAPTER TWENTY-EIGHT

If Aisha Matharu was surprised to see the police at her door again, she didn't show it, inviting them in to her pristine house and even offering them refreshment. If she was the culprit, then she was a good actress. She indicated for them to sit down and sat on the edge of the tub chair, like last time, with her hands clasped between her knees. The interview should have been at the station but, after the last tense situation, Mandy didn't want to stir things up. Aisha had just come home from work and appeared every inch the young professional with her smart navy trouser suit and pale pink top. She opened the patio door a little to let in some fresh air. It had been another warm day and the air was stuffy in the house. A couple of sparrows pecked at the grass and somewhere outside a dove was cooing.

"How may I help this time?" Polite and to the point.

"Some new evidence has come to light and we're hoping you can help." Mandy watched for some reaction. Aisha's face seemed puzzled yet unperturbed by the news.

"New evidence of what, exactly?"

"We are now sure that what happened to Megan wasn't entirely an accident. We think someone, or more than one person, conspired to cause her harm. Perhaps the resulting death was not expected, nevertheless we need to get to the root of what happened. I know we've been through it all before but there are still some blanks to be filled."

Aisha pushed a stray lock of hair out of her eye and made a sound somewhere between a hum and a sigh.

"I haven't been able to get it out of my mind. If only I could drive. I was the only one fit to do anything. The other three... well, they'd overindulged. Not fit to do much for a while."

"So, when you came down for a glass of water in the middle of the night what did they tell you? What was said? Suggested?"

"Sophie was in a state, though there's nothing new there. I don't know how she survived in London. She was crying and said that Megan had gone off and not come back."

"Did they tell you that they'd ingested cannabis?"

"What? No way. No wonder they didn't want to go anywhere. Ingested. They'd eaten it?"

"In cake or cookies. Can you remember who brought anything like that?"

Aisha frowned a little as she tried to remember. "No. We all brought stuff and it was piled in the kitchen. We had a pizza delivered on the Friday night and a pub lunch after our hike on Saturday. Cannabis? Who?"

She turned away as Mandy asked, "Who indulged in recreational drug use?"

"I've no idea. I don't eat sweet stuff. I'm pre-diabetic. It runs in the family, so I need to be careful about what I eat."

Convenient. No alcohol. No cake. Access to the knowledge that Megan took antipsychotics. Earring at the scene. Circumstantial evidence. Being controlled by Megan. Was that enough of a motive?

"You said that Sophie was upset. And the other two? Were they the same? Did they seem distressed?"

"Siobhan and Bethan seemed concerned, but the thinking was that perhaps she'd gone to the pub and stayed there or something. At first, that is, then as time went on, we all became more worried."

"Who suggested cleaning up?"

"Sophie. She said we needed to do something to distract ourselves. We had to leave it in immaculate condition for the photographer so she said we might as well do it until it was a bit lighter, and we were a bit more compos mentos. It was pitch dark outside at that time. The idea was that come dawn we'd take a car out to where there was a signal and ring Megan."

That was new. No one had mentioned that before. Only about ringing the police. Josh was making notes.

"But?"

"No reply. Her phone was switched off."

"Did that not cause an alarm?"

"Not really. She'd do that if she was in one of her moods. Sometimes her phone would be off for two days."

Another note.

"By that time, we were very worried and rang the police to report her missing." The stare she gave Mandy was direct, almost challenging. "You know the rest."

Was it bravado or just annoyance? Mandy knew she needed to keep things smooth if she wanted any further information.

"We've spoken to Sophie and Siobhan about who did what in the cleaning process. What was your role?"

"Those two did upstairs and Bethan and I were downstairs." That tallied with what they'd already been told.

"Who cleaned the kitchen, or did you do it together?" Mandy watched to see if there was any change in Aisha's expression. There was not a flicker when she responded.

"I got all the plates and cups and stuff and took them to the kitchen. I put what I could into the dishwasher and left the rest there. Bethan said she'd sort it."

"Any food waste? On plates for example?"

"A bit. I hadn't eaten because of the headache and it made me feel a bit nauseous. I did the dusting and vacuuming in the other rooms and Bethan did the kitchen. She was very through with it. I think she took the food waste home. I recall her saying something about not wanting the bins to stink."

"Overzealous with the cleaning. My Mam's like that." Josh spoke for the first time and helped dispel some of the tension. Mandy was aware that she'd leaned forward in her seat and was staring at Aisha. Had they found their culprit? Did Bethan cause Megan's death? Or was Aisha lying?

"Did Bethan put the bag of rubbish out in the bin too?"

"I don't know. I haven't even thought about it. Does it matter?"

Mandy pursed her lips. She wasn't quite finished.

"One last question. Did you all go out in the car when it got light?

"No. Siobhan stayed in the house. She said someone needed to be there in case Megan came back."

Time to leave. Mandy thanked Aisha and they left. Outside the hedges were beginning to sprout and a kitten emerged from underneath and rubbed itself around Mandy's legs before dashing off again when a car started up.

As they drove out of Pontprennau she asked Josh, "Well. What do you think? She corroborates what we've been told about the clean-up operation. If Megan's phone was switched off, it's little wonder we've been unable to find it."

"I just remembered something as Aisha was talking."

"What?"

"When we went to speak to Bethan she was in Luke's flat."

"Yes?"

There were times when Josh was so slow about saying what he was thinking that she could throttle him.

"Bethan was baking a cake. I remember as it smelled divine. Chocolate something."

"Well, they say the way to a man's heart is through his stomach. Maybe your sweet tooth is of some use after all. You think she made the cannabis cookies? We need to speak to her. Next step Bethan Rees. That young woman has quite a few questions to answer." She changed gear as they entered Eastern Avenue and accelerated up to the fifty-mph speed limit. "You know the hardest thing about this case?"

"What's that, boss?"

"Motive. If one, or all those women, deliberately fed Megan alcohol and cannabis, what was the purpose? Why would you do that to a friend?"

"From what everyone's said Megan was an odd mixture of fun and generosity and spitefulness and jealousy. Sophie had a strong motive as she was being blackmailed, though she's a jelly baby. Siobhan also had strong motive if you count jealousy, but the other two? No idea. Especially Bethan. She's Megan's oldest friend. Been buddies since primary school. It's a mystery."

Mandy's phone was on the car pocket between them so when it rang, she asked Josh to put it on loudspeaker. Helen.

"Nia Pritchard's missing. There was a big row here this morning and she ran out. She was in a very distressed state. She kept saying, "It's all my fault. I did it. It's me to blame." She's not answering her phone and one of the neighbours said she was heading towards the Taff."

"Put out an APB for her. That girl has enough on her plate. We need to find her. And Helen…"

"Yes?"

"Find out if Bethan Rees is still with her boyfriend. We need to speak to her pronto. And see if we can get warrants to search the homes of Aisha Matharu, Sophie Edwards, Rhys Davies and Bethan Rees. And throw in Luke Wong as well."

"Sure. Will do."

The call ended. Josh asked, "Is that a good idea? Search warrants. I mean it's a bit drastic, isn't it? Heavy-handed."

"What the hell do you mean by that, Josh? We've a limited time to discover what happened to that young woman. If it means upsetting a few people, then tough shit."

Beside her Mandy could feel Josh stiffen. It was going to mean a confrontation with Withers, yet again. If Josh didn't like it. Too bloody bad.

"Where the hell has Nia gone, and why? What do you think she meant by that? "It's all my fault." She wasn't even there, was she?"

"Dunno, boss. Survivor guilt? She's alive and her sister's dead. The parents idolised Megan. At least the mother did, and it seems from what Helen said that the dad has had some sort of mini breakdown or something."

Mandy drummed her fingers on the steering wheel. She was deep in thought.

"You know, Josh, I saw Nia with Bethan the other day walking through Llandaff and chatting. They had to know each other if Bethan was friends with Megan from a young age. So, what if Nia is involved in some way? She could have given Bethan the bottle of Coke already laced with vodka. Maybe she wanted to get back at her sister for something? It's a bit outside the box though. And it's possible that someone entered the house and left the drink laced with booze at some point during the day."

There was silence for a moment while Josh digested that.

"Are you thinking that Nia could have gone to Nythfa during the day while they were out and planted the alcohol." He shook his head. "That is a bit far out, even for you, boss. How would she get in?"

"Come on, Josh. If you live in the arse-end of nowhere and you've forgotten your keys, what would you do? Chances are there's a spare key hidden somewhere. Under a pot, disguised as a stone, hanging by the garden shed. We didn't think about that one."

"So, Nia is consumed with guilt and tries to kill herself? I suppose that's a theory, although what about the cannabis cake?"

"Well, if your theory is right, we need to speak to Bethan Rees. Maybe that will throw some more light on things."

The phone rang again.

"It's Helen," said Josh, putting the call on speakerphone.

"Hi boss. Uniform have found Nia. She was down by the Taff, just wading in. Some woman spotted her and rang 999. She talked to her until the officers arrived. Nia's in a bad way. They've taken her to UHW."

"Did she say anything? Could they get any sense out of her?"

"Don't know."

"Right. Get yourself up there and see what you can find out. What about the parents?"

"There's a uniformed officer with them. I'll go back when I've seen Nia. Check they are alright. From what I could gather they are going to do a psychiatric assessment on Nia, but they'll have to wait until someone is free to do that."

"It'll be hours before they get anyone over from Llandough. You know that. Zip up there. See what you can find out and get back to me if there's anything significant."

They were almost at the station and Mandy was glad to be able to park outside. The seagulls were squawking and circling above their heads. Bloody birds. Breeding time so they were extra aggressive. The city was humming with traffic and Cathays Park was dotted with people taking advantage of a bit of sunshine.

They went up to the office to check with Olivia that nothing new had come in.

"The Super is on the warpath. He was ranting on about keeping a low profile and now it seems the press have got wind of something. He's not a happy bunny. I'd go out and stay out if I were you. He's already giving me the hot breath and flared nostrils."

"I wonder if it's worth a visit to Nia's parents. We still don't know half of what went on there. Definite tensions, Helen said."

"Well, their daughter had just died. I don't suppose anyone was feeling their best after that."

Mandy nodded. "We need to get some bloody evidence. Bethan Rees first. See you at the car in five. I just want to ring Tabs, tell her I'll be late yet again."

When she got down to the car park Josh was standing with his back to her. She could see the rings of smoke rising from him. Now the car would stink too unless he had some mints. Reminder to self. Always carry mints in the car for Josh. He didn't realise, of course, that the smell hung to him, seemed to seep out of every pore. She wondered if Lisa had noticed when they had their therapy sessions. Maybe they didn't sit close enough for her to register. Nobody could fail to notice the sallowness of his skin or the extra weight around his middle.

He stubbed the cigarette out when he saw her and pulled a packet of extra strong mints out of his pocket. His face spoke of misery and guilt. Mandy just raised an eyebrow. When they got into the car, she spoke to him.

"How are you with teenagers? Down with the kids? Fancy another meal with Tabs and myself when all this bloody song and dance is over? I'm not a bad cook when I've time. What do you like? Plain? Spicy?"

He seemed startled for a moment. She could see doubt mixed with apprehension in his eyes.

"I'm not going to poison you, you know. I just thought you could do with an evening out of your monk's cell. And if you could assure Tabs that I'm not going to ground her for life that would be great too."

"Er. Yeah. Fine, boss. I eat anything. I'm not fussy."

"Good. No fags. You'll have to do without for one night."

"Sure. I need to stop. I can't afford it anyway. It's just things have, well, got on top of me a bit."

Mandy didn't reply to that. She felt sorry for him, when she didn't want to shake him. He needed to get his head back in gear if he was going to keep his job.

"Right. Let's go and see what Bethan Rees has to say about her special cookies. Maybe she'll give me the recipe. I could make that for dessert."

She laughed as Josh opened his mouth to say something and then realised it was a joke. They made their way down to the Bay again and Luke's flat.

CHAPTER TWENTY-NINE

Luke wasn't pleased to see them. "Beth's not here and your boys have turned this place upside down. What the hell is going on?"

"Where is she? There's a team searching her place and they say there's no sign of her."

There was a hint of anger in Luke's eyes. "I don't know where she is and if I did, I wouldn't tell you after the mess you lot have made in here. What you searching for anyway?"

"Evidence. They find any cannabis here?" Mandy knew the flat was clean, but she wanted to unnerve Luke so that he might tell them something.

"No way. I don't do any of that stuff. I had a bad trip as a teenager, and it put me off all drugs. I don't even have an aspirin in the flat. Then your boys know that."

His lips curled in a sneer. He might not do drugs, but he didn't like the police either.

"When was the last time you saw Bethan?"

He shrugged. "Yesterday, maybe. We don't live together. She stayed here a couple of nights, like, after Megan. She was awful testy though. Nearly drove me up the wall. I work from home and it's a small flat. It was hard going with her at times."

"Has she not been back to work since the weekend?"

He seemed blank as he shrugged. "Don't think so. She called in sick and they said to let them know when she'd be back. She's been out a lot, walking like. Trying to chase her demons she said, whatever the hell that means."

Mandy and Josh exchanged glances. The need to speak to Bethan was becoming urgent. Luke must know something.

"Was she in contact with Nia Pritchard?"

"Megan's sister. Yeah. They knew each other. Well, they would, wouldn't they? I mean Bethan's been friends with Megan a long time. God knows why. I know you shouldn't speak ill of the dead, but that Megan was a piece."

"What do you mean?"

Luke seemed to find his feet fascinating as he moved from one leg to the other, avoiding meeting their eyes. "Well, she could be a right cow at times. Always on about Beth's weight and stuff."

Mandy could feel that Luke knew more. She had no way of getting him to open up when the priority was to find Bethan.

"Did Bethan have any communication with any of the other girls since Megan's death? Has she met up or had telephone conversations with anyone since then? It's important. We no longer believe that Megan Pritchard died by accident. We think it was a deliberate and malicious attack."

It was as if someone had struck Luke. The reaction was instant. He stepped back with a gasp. Then he tried to cover up his startled response by turning away from them.

Mandy was swift to respond. "If you know anything about Bethan's whereabouts it's your duty to tell us. If we find that you've been withholding evidence," she glared at him, "you could end up in court. I don't think that would be too good on your CV now, would it?"

"I don't know where she is. That's the truth."

They waited. There was a sense that he wanted to say more, so they gave him the opportunity to do that.

"Though, I did hear her talking on the phone."

"Who was she speaking to and what about?"

"I think it was the Irish one. Siobhan."

Just then Mandy's phone rang. She turned aside to answer it leaving Josh talking to Luke. As she listened Mandy's expression changed. When the call was over, she stared at Luke with a new intenseness.

"They've just found Megan's phone in Bethan's flat. Hidden at the back of a cupboard. That rather changes things, so anything you know you'd better tell us. Now."

Luke's bravado had disappeared. He didn't want to be implicated in anything. His words came out in a garbled mess.

"Hey. She's only been my girlfriend for about ten months. We met when she wanted someone to do her website for her. Those photos, well, I like a woman with a bit of flesh, so we sort of hooked up, like. She was all upset after the weekend. Seemed quite excited before she went, then a wreck when she came back."

He sniffed and rubbed a hand across his mouth and down over his chin. "I know she's been talking to Nia and Siobhan. Not the other two. Sophie and Aisha. She was talking to Siobhan about travelling to Ireland. I think Siobhan was going back sometime soon. I could be wrong, but it sounded a bit urgent to me. You know when someone's voice is not relaxed?"

"Do you think she went to see Siobhan?"

"I dunno. Swear I don't. You'd better ask Siobhan what it was about. I only heard a bit. Do you think she...?"

Tucking her phone into her pocket, Mandy stared at him. "If you remember anything else, you'd better tell us. I don't like having to ask the same questions twice. Not telling us something you know, or suspect, is nearly as bad as lying. Understand?"

Luke swallowed and made a grunting sound which they took to be an affirmative response.

"Anything at all," said Josh, as they left Luke was running his hand through his hair, lost in thought.

"What next, boss?" asked Josh when they were on their way down the stairs.

Mandy took out her phone. "Let's see what Siobhan has to say." A moment later she said, "No response. Get through to Olivia or Helen and ask them to trace the phones belonging to Bethan Rees and Siobhan O'Hare. And see if we can find Bethan's car. I wonder if Rhys knows anything."

Pressing the buttons fiercely, Mandy swore again. "Please leave a bloody voicemail." Then a beep and she said, "Mr Davies. DI Mandy Wilde. We need to speak to Siobhan. It's important. Ring me when you get this message."

They were about to drive off when her phone rang. Rhys Davies.

"DI Wilde. I've just had your voicemail. Siobhan has been gone since early morning. I had a bit of a night of it, so I overslept this morning. I haven't seen her. I heard voices and I thought I was dreaming. She's not answering her phone. I think it's switched off."

Alarm bells rang in Mandy's head. "Do you think she's gone back to Ireland?"

"Well, all her stuff is here. She's just taken her handbag. I'm a bit worried to be honest. It's not like her."

"And why's that?"

"It's out of character. We haven't had a row or anything. She'd never leave without telling me. And the voices I heard when I thought I was dreaming… they didn't sound too friendly."

"Did you hear what was being said? Do you think she was being threatened in some way? These voices. How many? Male or female?"

"Two voices. Siobhan and another woman. All low. No shouting or anything just a sort of hissing, if you know what I mean. Wait a minute. I remember something else. A car. There was a car engine revving just after that."

"Did you see it? Make? Numberplate? Anything?"

"No. Sorry. That's all. Is Siobhan in some sort of trouble? What's happening?"

I wish I knew. Mandy put a hand to her forehead and rubbed her temple.

"We just need to speak to Siobhan, so if she contacts you then please get her to ring us. It's urgent."

Mandy didn't care if they'd left Rhys Davies dazed and confused. It mirrored how she felt herself. What next? This bloody case was like a game of snakes and ladders. Up and down. No idea what lay ahead except possible redundancy. What a shitstorm.

"Seems we have ourselves two fugitives," she said to Josh.

"Do you think they're working together?"

"I'm damned if I know what to think anymore, Josh. Or what to do for that matter. We need to find those two before they do a disappearing act."

"Well, Rhys likes a bit of weed. Could he have supplied Siobhan or Bethan?"

"You mean a pre-planned 'let's get stoned' party? I really don't think so. Siobhan went straight to Nythfa with Sophie. They both said that. They stopped to pick up groceries on the way. And Pembroke is the opposite direction to Chepstow. Unless they're lying. I'm beginning to think they're all a bunch of bloody liars. I wonder how much truth there's been in anyone's statements."

"Back to the conspiracy?"

"Let's talk to Bethan first. See what she has to say about her award-winning cookies or brownies or whatever they were. And Megan's phone. If we can find her that is. And see if uniform can trace her car or her phone. Siobhan has hers turned off. I wonder if Bethan has done the same."

CHAPTER THIRTY

"Why did you want me to come with you, Beth? I mean you could just leave your car at the ferry port for the few days you'll be away. I didn't have a chance to tell Rhys where we are going. He'll be worried. I don't know why I had to switch my phone off."

Siobhan was puzzled. She didn't really understand why Bethan came to the house so early in the morning or what the urgency was. Rhys had been flat out. She didn't even leave a note. Maybe she'd send a text when they stopped.

"It's distracting when you're driving, things buzzing and ringing. I like to concentrate on the road," said Bethan. "And I'd rather not leave the car by the ferry. You can drive it back to Cardiff when the ferry leaves. You never know who's going to take a fancy and break in, or they might decide to tow it away or something."

"No, sure they wouldn't do that. Not if you leave them your details and stuff. Not that I'd know. This is a lovely road now, isn't it?" They had just passed Bridgend. "I love the way the sky lightens and gets bigger when you get away from the city."

"You're nuts. You know that, Siobhan. It's the same sky. No wonder you're a writer. Away with the fairies." Bethan shook her head and laughed.

"Did the police get back to you again? After you made your statement that is? They came to talk to me, and we were both stoned. I'd been so wound up that Rhys got some gear and the place stank of weed." She giggled. "The DI wasn't bothered though she said they didn't think that Megan's death was purely accidental. Pursuing other lines of enquiry, I think she said. God, she's a scary one that one, isn't she?"

"No. I didn't catch up with her again. I can do without all that." Bethan stared at the road ahead. Now they were past Bridgend it should be plain sailing. The ring road around Swansea was alright and after that the only possible delay could be at Carmarthen.

"She kept asking all sorts of weird questions about who'd brought the food, who cleaned up, was there a way to get out of the house without anyone knowing." Siobhan kept her eyes on the road. Bethan was driving a little too fast for her comfort. Maybe she should peer out of the side instead.

"She asked that?"

"Yeah. I didn't know what to say half the time. I mean, sure we all feel guilty as hell that nobody went out after her that night. I couldn't really say too much now, could I?"

"So, they don't go with the accident theory?"

"Seems not."

"You didn't tell her about the cake, did you?"

"No way. That stuff was lethal. My legs felt as though somebody was sitting on me. Jesus, you should have warned us first. I mean I'm used to a wee bit now and again but for somebody who didn't...did Megan have any of it?"

Bethan squinted at Siobhan for a second and gritted her teeth. Her foot pressed harder on the accelerator, her face a mask of determination as she overtook a lorry.

Siobhan gripped the door of the car. Was Bethan intent on killing them both? It didn't matter that much if she didn't get the ferry. There'd be another one in a few hours. It wasn't as if it was life or death. There was silence in the car as it thundered along the road. Something was very wrong. Bethan was behaving in an erratic way. She was usually so cheery, so positive about everything. Megan's death had changed her.

"I wonder when they'll release Megan's body. I suppose there'll be a big funeral," said Siobhan. "At home they lay the body out so that everybody can go and say their goodbyes. Then, they're buried quick. Before things start to disintegrate and smell, I suppose."

"Shut up."

"What?"

"I said shut up. I'm sick of hearing about bloody Megan. Truth is she was a right cow and she got what was coming to her."

Siobhan felt as though she was in a barrel thrown over the edge of a waterfall, hurtling down towards unknown dangers. Bethan was Megan's closest friend. They'd been friends before uni so why was she so bitter? And what did she mean by that? She'd got what was coming to her. Unless. The truth began to filter through Siobhan's confused brain. Bethan knew something. She'd seen or done something that had some impact on Megan's life. And death. Had she done something to her best friend? Siobhan's heart began to skip a beat as the danger of the situation she was in became clear. What to do? Stay calm. Find out more?

"Can we stop at the next services?"

"Why?"

"I need a wee and a coffee. In that order."

"Can't you wait? It's only about an hour more to Pembroke Dock."

"I'd really like to stop. Five minutes. I could ring Rhys. Let him know I'm okay." Siobhan tried to keep her voice even, natural, yet it sounded fraught, even to her own ears.

"I don't think you need to ring Rhys, do you? You can ring him when I get on that ferry."

Siobhan swallowed. She recognised that tone of voice. Threatening. Nevertheless, Bethan pulled up at the services at Pont Abraham. She turned to face Siobhan and leaned closer to her.

"You are going to go to the toilet and then back here to the car without speaking to anyone. I'll get you a Coke or something. It takes too long for them to make coffee here. I don't want to waste time. Remember. Don't speak to anyone. Your bag stays in the car. Understand?"

There was no doubt about the threat as Bethan's face had hardened, her eyes narrowed as she glared at Siobhan. It was hard but Siobhan held her stare, trying to act as if it was a normal conversation. What else could she do?

"Sure. That's okay by me. Toilets are not the nicest place to hang around. And I'd like an orange juice rather than a Coke. Gives me the belches."

Five minutes later they were on the way again. Siobhan had hoped to be able to pass a note or something to someone. It was impossible. Bethan had followed her in and waited until she was in the cubicle before going to get the orange juice. By the time Siobhan had finished in the toilet she was back with a bottle of juice in her hand, already opened. They said nothing on the way back to the car. She considered making a run for it, but Bethan worked out at the gym. She'd catch her in a second. Trapped.

As Siobhan settled down in the passenger seat, she wondered what Bethan had planned for her when they got to the dock. Her excuse for dragging Siobhan on the journey was that she wanted her to drive the car back to Cardiff. Was that true? If Bethan knew something about Megan's death, if she had done something... Siobhan swallowed. That put her in danger too. She gulped down the orange juice trying to focus on something else. Before long she felt her eyelids droop. She tried to speak although her lips felt too big, and she gave way to the blackness.

* * *

There was time to think on the way west and Mandy Wilde was deep in contemplation. It seemed as though Bethan Rees was responsible for Megan's death. Mandy didn't understand it. People changed as they grew older, drifted apart, married, had kids, moved to another part of the country, or another continent, except they had shared memories too. A history together, like siblings. After this little interlude she was

271

going to do some detecting of her own. Vincent knew exactly where her sister was hiding out, and why. He just needed a little bit of persuasion, like a knee in the balls. Not the sort of tactic the Super or Josh would approve of so best to keep it outside working hours. She'd have him for dealing and obstructing the police for starters if he didn't want to play kiss and tell. Joy was somewhere not far from Chepstow and Mandy wanted to know why. Tabitha needed her mother and Mandy had to know that her twin was alright.

"Have they alerted the local boys in Pembroke to keep an eye out for a blue Fiesta?"

"Yeah. They'll check all the cars boarding or queuing up to board. We've the registration details too. They've alerted all police cars in the area. She was last spotted outside Swansea. What if she ditches the car?"

"And how the hell would she get to the ferry then? She's on a limited timeframe."

"Do you think she knows we're after her?"

"I think that's likely. She knows we're getting close and it's a way of avoiding the inevitable. She's got herself into this. Now she's trying to escape."

"She'll need a passport and she can't stay in Ireland for ever."

"No. I think this is a panicked reaction. She's not thinking straight. Irrational. That's why I'm worried about Siobhan. Anyone heard from her?"

"No. Phone still switched off."

A buzzing indicated a call. Josh covered the mouthpiece and told Mandy, "There's been a sighting. Pont Abraham. Do you want the local police to stop her?"

"I don't think so. We know, or think we know, where she's heading. Unmarked car to follow at a distance. We don't know if Siobhan is an accomplice or a hostage. Let's not do anything to cause Bethan to go off the deep end."

"The Super will be pleased if we're right. At least it would let Sophie off the hook."

"We don't know yet, Josh, what happened. We think we know, but all the evidence is circumstantial. I don't think the CPS would bring charges unless there is more compelling proof that Bethan did feed Megan booze and drugs."

"We've got Megan's phone in her flat."

"She could say she found it, threw it into her bag at the time and forgot about it." Mandy shrugged. "We think she made the cakes, but it's all a bit vague. We think she spiked the Coke. Then again, no fingerprints so no evidence to stand up in court."

"You mean she could get away with it?"

"Yup. 'Fraid so. Shit, isn't it?"

Josh sighed, a long and weary sound. "Let's hope she tells all in that case or we'll be left appearing like idiots."

"And Withering will have a field day. He'll be hopping mad and sending us both back on the beat."

The forlorn expression on Josh's face made Mandy want to laugh although she wasn't so insensitive to his needs. "Don't worry. I'll take responsibility for any flack coming our way. You've just done what you've been told to do."

CHAPTER THIRTY-ONE

As they approached the ferry terminal, they could see the queues of cars waiting to board. They'd start rolling on to the ferry with their clinking and clanging in the next ten minutes. The air had a strange smell of sea and fumes from the waiting cars. An officer at the police barrier waved them down. Mandy produced her badge.

"DI Mandy Wilde. Have you got her?"

"No ma'am. No blue Fiesta with that registration number."

"I thought she was being followed. How did they manage to lose her?"

"Sorry ma'am. There was an incident in Pembroke town centre and all units were called to attend. A political demonstration got out of hand and people were hurt. It'll be on the news tonight."

"I don't give a… I don't care what's on the news. I'm looking for a woman who is possibly a danger to herself and others. Put out a call. Blue Fiesta. It must be in the area. Check anywhere cars are parked in the immediate vicinity. If she's going on that ferry she won't be far away." She turned towards Josh. "Come on. Let's take a little walk along these cars. Have a peep. She may have hitched a ride or changed cars."

As they walked up and down the narrow space between the parked cars Mandy's head was buzzing. She knew Bethan was close.

Foot passengers lined up, rucksacks on their backs. Off to enjoy a break in Ireland. Mandy envied them. What it would be to escape and just sit for a week, or even just a weekend. When was the last time she'd relaxed, really chilled out? Months? A year? Not since Joy had done a bunk and she was left with Tabitha.

Her phone buzzed. She listened and then gestured to Josh to join her.

"News?" asked Josh.

"They found the car. Parked in the hospital car park. Siobhan was in the front seat. Unconscious. They think she's been drugged. They've taken her into the hospital to check her out. It's not far from here. Very convenient."

"I suppose it shows she cares. Leaving her at the hospital gates as it were."

"Yeah. And drugging her first. How many of your friends would do that? She's here somewhere. I know it. She's got to be."

"There's another ferry later. Maybe she's waiting for us to clear and getting that one instead."

"No. She'd have to stick around the town for hours and people in these small places notice things more. All the police would need to do would be to alert the public and she'd be a target." Mandy shook her head. "No. If I was her, I'd be determined to get on that boat. Uniform all have her description and a photo."

"Yeah. One from the website, suitably cropped. Oh. I've just remembered something."

"What?"

"In some of those photographs she was wearing wigs. She had a blonde one and another in a deep red. I remember some of the captions. 'Gentlemen prefer blondes and blondes like fun' and 'Rev up your engine with a redhead'."

Mandy snorted with laughter. "Oh God, how corny can you get? So, we're watching out for a blonde, a redhead or a dark-haired woman."

"Of a certain size."

"They're starting to board. Let's get down there. Bit closer. Keep our eyes peeled."

The noise when the cars started boarding the ferry stopped any further conversation as cars, trucks and passengers began to move. It took less time than expected. Still no sign of Bethan. Then, as the stragglers approached the ferry, Mandy spotted her. She leaned closer to Josh and almost shouted in his ear.

"She's being riotous red today, Josh. Go get her."

Josh set off at a steady pace with Mandy following. She gestured to the uniform officers to be ready as they neared the footbridge into the ferry. Bethan seemed not to notice them and then, at the last moment, turned and sprinted away from the ferry through the remaining cars and towards the town. God, she could move. For a big girl she was agile, and Josh wasn't keeping up. Then a young PC, seeing what was happening, joined the chase. He managed to grab the rucksack she was carrying and pulled her down to her knees. Josh was panting as he reached her. Mandy wasn't far behind.

"Hello, Bethan. Nice to see you again. Going on a little holiday, were you? Well, we've got a few questions first. If you don't mind, of course. We've got a car to take you back to Cardiff. Your trip can wait, I'm sure."

Mandy raised any eyebrow. What would Bethan say? If she refused to come voluntarily, they'd have to arrest her. Although the evidence was stacking up, it was doubtful the CPS would press charges and she was reluctant to make a formal arrest without more proof.

"And if I don't want to come with you?"

"Well then, that would be a pity. Not wanting to help with our enquiries into the death of your best friend. That wouldn't be good, would it? It's in your best interests to come with us."

Mandy kept her face expressionless although she was tempted to cross her fingers. They waited.

Bethan scowled at her and said nothing. Her shoulders slumped and she allowed the officers to escort her to the car. Would they get any information out of her?

* * *

Mandy and Josh said little on the way back to Cardiff. Bethan was being taken in a police car. She appeared pale and tired when she got out at Cardiff and not as sure of herself as when they'd spoken to her after Megan's death.

"Am I under arrest or what?"

"What makes you think that you're under arrest? This is a voluntary interview. We just needed to talk to you. I'm sorry if we stopped your holiday but for now, we're still conducting enquiries about Megan Pritchard's movements prior to her death. You shouldn't have been attempting to leave the country while the investigation was ongoing."

Bethan was given something to eat and drink and taken to an interview room while Mandy caught up with the rest of the team.

"Anything new?"

Olivia shook her head. "We're still waiting for the tech guys to get back to us about the troll. They've got an IP address so it's just a matter of time, it is. We've been in touch with Pembroke Dock. The hospital say that Siobhan is fine. She'd been given some sort of sleeping tablets, herbal thing over the counter job and quick-acting, like. Probably in the drink that Bethan gave her."

"Has anyone taken a statement from her? What do we know about the connection? Was she aware of anything odd about Bethan's behaviour? We need leverage."

"Local boys questioned her. Their report will be emailed through later."

Olivia consulted her notes, reading the bones of the report from the police who had questioned Siobhan when she came around.

"They said Siobhan thought it was a bit strange that Bethan wanted her to go to Pembroke Dock. Some story about driving the car back to Cardiff. Bethan was acting strangely. A bit erratic, distracted by something. Then when Bethan started ranting about Megan and wouldn't let Siobhan ring Rhys, she got worried."

"And the tablets?"

"No mention. She says she felt sleepy after the drink. The guy who rang through said she seemed a bit woozy and was asking what had happened."

"There's still no evidence. That would be Bethan's way out. Siobhan could have taken those tablets herself. Her word against Bethan's. We need something more. Something to shake Bethan Rees, to get the truth." Mandy was chewing the inside of her cheek.

"Bethan took out most of her savings before heading off. Her rucksack had a wallet with two thousand euro inside. It doesn't look good," said Helen. "Maybe she'll say something now. She knows it's serious. Better she speaks up than ignore it all." It was an optimistic thought.

"We'll see. I've got a feeling this one will be a hard nut to crack. We've no real evidence against her. Nothing to hold up in court. We need to rattle her. Any word on Nia?"

Helen shook her head. "Mum said that she'd had a huge row with her sister after Megan caused the split between Siobhan and Rhys. Nia knew what Megan had done and it caused a rift."

"And Bethan? Any connection there?"

"Megan and Bethan started school on the same day. Mums got friendly and girls, too. Nia knows Bethan because of that."

"That means there's a possibility that Nia told Bethan about the effects of alcohol with the medication."

"Maybe that's why Nia had the guilt trip," said Josh.

"Mmmm. All speculation. Let's get a confession. If she's the one. Could be more than one. Even the lot of them. It's a tangled web alright. Okay. Let's go, Josh. See if we can upset her."

The interview room was bland. Grey walls and high windows. Nothing to cause a distraction. A table and chairs sat in the middle like a judge, waiting. Stale air. Bethan was on one side facing the door. She had a bottle of water with her. She looked up when Mandy and Josh entered the room.

"Should I have a lawyer?" Defensive, with an edge of something else in her voice.

"Do you want one? Do you think you need a lawyer?" Mandy stressed the word need. Bethan shrugged.

"Don't know why I'm here. What you want. I've been over it all with you before." There was no sign of warmth in her response. She'd taken off the red wig and her dark hair lay draped across her shoulders. She fingered a tendril of it the way young children play with their hair when thinking.

"Why were you running away?"

"Who says I was running? I was going for a little weekend break to Ireland. Siobhan's always banging on how lovely it is, laid back and all. I thought I'd go and see for myself. Not against the law, is it?"

"And the wig?"

"I needed to wash my hair, so it covered it up. I like the red wig. Sassy. Thought I'd be a bit more Celtic. I wear different wigs on the website. I'm sure you checked all that out."

She gazed at Josh, blinking her eyelashes then looking straight into his eyes with a slight smirk on her face, flirting. Mandy thought he'd blush, however it seemed he was hell bent on getting answers.

"With two thousand euro in your back-pack? Rather a lot for a just a weekend, isn't it?" Josh asked.

Bethan blanched and just shrugged her shoulders. The smirk was gone, and her eyes had lost the lasciviousness.

"Why did Siobhan go with you to the ferry port but not on the boat?" Mandy tried to sound conversational, more friendly, hoping for a chink in Bethan's armour.

"She fell asleep after we left Pont Abraham. She wasn't coming with me all the way. I was going to meet her next week when she went back to Ireland."

"So, it wasn't just for a weekend then?"

Bethan's eye twitched a little. Realising she'd made a mistake she tried to backtrack.

"Well, I might have decided to stay a little longer. I've holiday owed to me. No reason to rush back."

"Luke, your boyfriend, didn't mention it when we spoke to him." Mandy said.

A slight narrowing of the eyes before she answered. "He's not my keeper. He doesn't know everything. I don't have to do everything with him just because we're a couple, do I?" She glared at Mandy, removed her hands from the table and put them out of sight on her knee. She was beginning to become almost aggressive in her defence.

"Will Siobhan be able to corroborate what you've told us?" Mandy watched for a reaction. "She's still in the hospital but the local police have taken a preliminary statement. We should be able to talk to her soon. They said she was still a bit drowsy. Maybe she has a different version."

"I dunno what she'll say, do I? Now, I need to know what I'm supposed to have done." Bethan looked from one face to the other. It seemed she was becoming uncomfortable under their scrutiny.

They pressed on with the questions. Mandy took charge again.

"Do you have trouble sleeping?"

Bethan was a bit confused. A slight frown. "Sometimes."

"Guilty conscience, perhaps?"

There was a slight tightening of her jaw.

"You had herbal sleep remedies in your bag. That would seem to indicate some difficulty getting your eight hours." Mandy kept her expression bland. "And Siobhan had a similar remedy in her system. Is that what you put in her drink at Pont Abraham? We have video coverage of you both there."

Bethan sat upright in her chair. "No comment. I don't know what you are accusing me of, but I think I want somebody here to give me advice. A lawyer. Why have you been following me? What are you expecting me to say? I don't like this."

"You have every right to legal representation. That can be arranged."

A knock on the door and Olivia entered. "Ma'am. There's something you need to see. Right now."

"Okay. Bethan, I haven't finished with you. Someone will bring you a hot drink if you want, while we wait for your lawyer."

Bethan pouted. "What's happened?"

"It appears there's been a development. We'll be back. Meanwhile, perhaps you can reflect on the weekend. See if you can remember anything else that could help us find out what happened to your best friend."

CHAPTER THIRTY-TWO

"Well. What have you got?" Mandy's voice was sharper than usual. She hoped Withers wasn't about. She could do without him sticking his oar in and getting involved.

"The tech guys have found where the trolling messages were sent from," said Olivia.

"And?"

"It's an hotel in the city centre. Computers for guests in the lobby although the staff are a bit laid-back and will give you the code if you just go in and ask."

"That just tells us it was local. We need more than that."

"Helen and I went to see the manager while you were in the interview room with Bethan." Olivia's eyes were shining, and she could hardly stand still. "I think you need to see this. CCTV footage. We checked out the days when the messages appeared. Always sent around lunchtime or early evening, they were."

Olivia led Mandy and Josh to a small room at the end of the corridor where several screens were on display. Olivia sat at one of the desks and clicked a few buttons. "This is the day the first one appeared. About a month after the website was launched."

"Is that who I think it is? Zoom in." Mandy leaned closer to the screen. Josh too. "Bloody hell. Megan Pritchard. So, she was the troll."

"And some of the stuff she posted was not friendly at all," Josh said, "Vicious and nasty. They've managed to retrieve some of the archived stuff. Listen to this. 'You think you're great but you're a fat slag. Big tits and a HUGE arse don't make you sexy, silly cow.' And worse."

"Bethan wouldn't have known who it was. It's taken us a couple of days to find out." Mandy was puzzled. On the other hand, Josh was becoming quite animated.

"Luke. The boyfriend. She told us he was a techie. Set up the website for her. He'd have been able to trace it wouldn't he?"

"So, what do you reckon? Luke found out and told Bethan? Is that a motive? God knows. She seems on the defensive, though we've got nothing more." Mandy frowned. "Olivia, you carry on with trawling through that footage. Check the dates of the messages with the CCTV footage from the hotel lobby. We're not bloody there yet. Let's keep this one under wraps for now."

Helen came into the room. She was a bit flustered, cheeks pink and slightly breathless. "Legal guy arrived. I've introduced him to Bethan Rees. They're talking now."

"Right, give them a few minutes and then we go in. Helen, I'd like you to go and have a word with Luke Wong, Bethan's boyfriend. Ask him if he knew it was Megan who was the troll. And press him for answers. Let me know as soon as you find out. Have someone bring Siobahn O'Hare back here when she's fit to travel. We'll see if she's got more to say when she's pressurised. Maybe it was the two of them together. Shit, I don't know. Let's go, Josh. See if we can find the chink in her armour."

Mandy took a deep breath and straightened her shoulders before going back into the room with Josh. Keep it calm. Keep it smooth. See what she comes up with. Nice and easy does it.

Mandy eyeballed the lawyer and sat down. She had a file in front of her and took her time opening it and checking the contents. Then they took more time switching on the recording machine and going through the formalities. Bethan seemed tense and belligerent. She wasn't going to crumble like Sophie. Mandy looked her in the eye.

"I wonder, Ms Rees, if you could explain why Megan's missing mobile phone was hidden in your flat."

Bethan had her arms crossed over her body. "No comment."

So that was the game now, was it? Keep pleasant. Keep cool.

"We have Megan's phone records here." Mandy took out some papers and skimmed over them. "We know you sent a text to Megan the week before the reunion. It says, "This isn't a joke. It's not kind. Just stop now before it's too late." Perhaps you could explain what that refers to?"

Mandy saw something flicker in Bethan's eyes as she passed over the transcript for her to read. Bethan took her time and then pushed the paper away from her and shrugged her shoulders. "No comment."

"You do realise Ms Rees, that if we discover evidence that you had something to do with Megan Pritchard's death, and it went to court, then a jury would not regard a 'no comment' response favourably. Many people see it as a sign of guilt."

Bethan looked sideways at the lawyer who nodded.

"I can't remember every text I send, can I?" Still aggressive, but a response. Better than nothing.

A change of tack again. "Tell me about your friendship with Megan Pritchard. You've been friends since primary school, I believe."

"Yes, that's right. We were in the same group in school, and she lived close to my house, so we became friends. Our Mums knew each other. All good pals."

"And you both went to secondary school and university together. So, she was your oldest friend."

Bethan concurred with that although Mandy could see she was unnerved by the change in direction of the interview. She was blinking and not making eye contact.

"It must be hard to process that loss. Quite a shock."

Another nod, also wariness setting in. Was she was trying to guess what was next? Mandy watched Bethan shift in her seat a little. Good. She was beginning to feel uneasy.

"Did you go out together when you started dating and things?' Josh asked. "You know, teenage girls always have a mate."

Bethan met his eyes. "Yeah. The hot ones always have a fat mate. Makes them look better. Yeah, we went on the pull together. I was the fat bird no one wanted back then."

There was a touch of bitterness in Bethan's voice, despite the accompanying smile.

"But you changed all that with your modelling career. Quite an impressive website." Josh said.

Too fast, Josh. We need to slow down a bit. With an almost imperceptible nod in his direction Mandy took over again.

"Back to the phone. Where did you find it?"

"In the kitchen. She put it on the table earlier, before we had food that is. It was still there, after she'd gone out."

"And you didn't think to mention it or hand the mobile to the police? Did you tell your friends you'd found it? After all, the idea was to ring her first, wasn't it? Then, when she didn't answer, Sophie spoke to the police. That's correct, isn't it?"

"Yeah, well. It was an oversight. I shoved it into my handbag when we were clearing up and then didn't remember about it. I wasn't well." She leaned back in her chair, pretending to relax although Mandy could see a twitch in the side of her cheek. "When I got home to my flat, I put it into a drawer. I was going to give it to her parents. I forgot, didn't I?"

"You'd give it back after you'd deleted those texts from you, of course," said Mandy. "Have you remembered yet what they were about? What wasn't a joke? And why should it stop before it's too late? That sounds like a threat to me."

Bethan shook her head and pouted like a child. "No. Sorry. Probably something silly. Megs used to like playing silly tricks on people. Sometimes they weren't very funny for the person involved."

"Like photographs of Rhys naked in her bed."

Mandy didn't expect an answer and didn't get one either. Although Bethan's eyes opened a little wider, she sat, impassive, waiting for the next question.

"I think we'll take a break there. I've some other questions though so we aren't finished yet.' Mandy picked up the file with a fleeting gesture, a wave, towards Bethan's legal advisor. "Perhaps your solicitor can give you some insight into what's likely to happen next."

Bethan's whole body seemed to slump in the chair as Josh and Mandy left. A little progress but she was as hard to crack as toffee.

* * *

As soon as the doors closed after them Bethan turned to her solicitor.

"What now?" She hadn't even registered his name. To her he was just some grey-faced old bloke who wasn't going to be much help.

"That depends. I've seen the files. Circumstantial evidence. I don't think running away was a good idea. It makes you appear guilty. This other girl," he peered down at the file, "Siobhan O'Hare. What is she likely to say to the police? Did you drug her?"

Bethan narrowed her eyes at him.

"Why do you want to know? You in with that lot?"

"Because, Ms Rees, if I am to represent you and proffer advice, I need to be apprised of the facts in the case. Perhaps we'd better start from the beginning again."

She didn't like him. Didn't trust him. Still, she had to trust someone. And maybe he'd get her out of this mess. Co-operation was best. That was his advice. Okay, she'd co-operate. Nonetheless, there were things they didn't need to know. Things she needed to keep quiet about. Circumstantial evidence meant nothing, did it? She just needed to keep cool. She rubbed her forehead. Another tension headache. She had nothing to worry about. They had nothing on her, did they?

CHAPTER THIRTY-THREE

Olivia was still trawling through CCTV footage. She'd confirmed that all the troll's messages coincided with the dates Megan had visited the hotel. She was keen for Mandy and Josh to see the evidence.

"It was her. See, here's the last one. Megan visits the hotel, and a message appears on BethanOnFire.com. It was deleted not long after, so Luke was quick to deal with it but that's a nasty thing to do to a friend, innit?"

"Maybe Luke set up an alert or something every time a comment was posted. That way he could remove it before there was any lasting damage. Could he do that?" Mandy asked.

"Suppose. He's a techie. He'd have set up a firewall or something. Don't know how you deal with that stuff." Olivia peered over the top of her specs.

"It still doesn't tell us if he knew the source. If he realised it was Megan sending the messages."

Mandy stretched, reached up and massaged the base of her neck. The muscles were knotted with tension. If Bethan didn't confess, they couldn't hold her or charge her with anything, except possibly wasting police time. Somehow, Mandy didn't think, even if she knew she'd been drugged, that Siobhan would press charges. Withers would ensure Sophie was shielded from any charge of obstructing an enquiry. It would be recorded as accidental death or misadventure or something and there would be no justice for Megan. Her body heaved with a loud sigh.

"Oh, I think he knew," said Josh. "Stop the footage, Olivia. Wind back. Stop. Look who that is."

He pointed to a figure entering the hotel lobby just after Megan had left and going to the computer she had vacated. Mandy peered at the screen, squinting. Was it? Yes. Luke Wong. He knew that Megan was the troll. Had he told Bethan? She rang Helen's number.

"Yes, boss. Here now. Yes. He knew about Megan."

"We know that. We have him on CCTV. He must have discovered the location and then watched from a distance. He'd make a good copper. Ask him when he told Bethan and see what the reaction is. Make out that we know he told her and give him some guff about being an accessory. See what he says. Ring me back after."

They waited a few minutes. Josh fiddled with his phone and Mandy paced to the window and back. No sign of the Super. That was a blessing. There was enough tension in the air without him putting his size twelves in too. After a few minutes Mandy's phone rang. She listened to what Helen had to say without uttering a sound then, "Thanks, Helen. Well done."

Olivia and Josh waited. "It seems that Bethan was told, about two weeks ago, that Megan was the one leaving those awful comments. He says she was incandescent with rage to the point he had to take her phone away and calm her down. She wanted to deliver a mouthful of abuse. After that she went quiet."

"Did he say how she was when she went to stay with him after Megan was found dead?"

"Helen asked that too. He said she was quiet and kept saying, 'It shouldn't have happened.' He thought her reactions were strange and she didn't talk to him at all about the weekend."

"And Siobhan?"

Mandy shrugged. "Nothing to add on that score. Anyone heard how Siobhan's doing?"

Olivia shook her head. "You don't think she's involved as well, do you?"

"I don't know. We're still in the dark about what happened, but I think Bethan does know, which is why she wanted to run away. However, there are things you can't run away from, and your conscience is one of them."

"If you've got a conscience," said Josh.

As they entered the interview room again Mandy knew the case was hanging on a thread, tenuous like from a spider's web. Lies, deceptions, secrets and diversions had been the problem. Round and round in a circle. Time to break that circle.

Bethan appeared relaxed, if a bit tired. Weren't they all? It had been a very long day. Time to get reactions. Emotions, strong emotions like love and hate, greed and envy. That's what got people going.

She sat down and stared at Bethan, unblinking until Bethan averted her eyes.

"Right, where were we?' Mandy said. "We were discussing your close friendship with Megan. Buddies for years. What changed?"

Bethan frowned. "Changed?"

"Yes. When did you start to hate her?"

Bethan sat upright and made no response. Mandy continued to drive towards her goal.

"Was it when she called you fat in school? When she tried to steal your boyfriends? When she ridiculed you in front of uni friends? Posted stupid photographs of you on social media? Or was it when she trolled you, making those awful comments on your website?" Mandy opened the file, took out a piece of paper and started to read. "You're nothing but a fat slag. Think you're sexy? No man would want a pile of blubber in his bed. Are you trying to be a porno star? Big tits and little brain. Bitch."

Bethan was going red in the face. "Stop it."

Mandy ignored her and carried on reading. "Bethan's on fire. Lol. What a whore. A bitch on heat."

Bethan slammed her fist on the table making her lawyer winch. "Stop it! Stop it! All lies. She's the one that was the bitch. All my life. Every day since I was little, she taunted me. Bullied me. Made me think that if I did as she said, as she asked, I'd be her best friend. The truth is that Megan used people. She used all of us. She got what she deserved. She'd be so lovely, and you'd think she'd changed, valued your friendship. Really she despised all of us."

She was crying now, heavy sobs and tears streaming, mixing with mucus from her nose and mouth as she lost control at last. She rocked on her seat, arms wrapped around her body and shaking from head to toe.

Lowering her voice and leaning forward Mandy said, "Perhaps you'd like to tell us everything that happened on Saturday night."

The lawyer reminded Bethan that she didn't have to say anything. She shook her head at him.

"It wasn't supposed to happen. I never wanted her dead."

The tension in the room felt like a presence it was so powerful. Mandy knew that this was it. A confession, an explanation of events, would either clear the others of blame or lead to a conspiracy. Either way, if Bethan talked, then Mandy's persistence would be vindicated. Withers could go swing on it and the case would be solved.

"Tell us."

With a huge intake of breath, Bethan started.

"I was furious when I found out it was Megan who had been posting those crude comments. I wanted to confront her. Luke calmed me down. Said I'd just be feeding her attention seeking. He'd met her once. She made a play for him too. I sent her those texts, so she knew I knew. She didn't reply. Beneath her, I suppose. She was always posting photos on Facebook of people doing stupid things when they were pissed so I thought I'd put a little something in her Coke. See what happened. Pay her back with a few unsavoury photos of her own. I didn't know she'd go nuts, did I?"

"Nia, her sister, had told you she didn't drink because of her medication."

"She'd told me, but I didn't know how bad it would be." Bethan wasn't so calm now, as she continued with her explanation. "I knew what medication she was on. I'd checked it out years ago when we were in uni. I saw the tablets in her wash bag. Hallucination was one of the very rare side effects. I thought she'd just get a bit confused and stuff."

"Nia blames herself. I expect she thought that telling you was a breach of confidence. She wasn't to realise that you'd sussed it all out yourself." Mandy paused before continuing, "She was fished out of the Taff this morning."

A gasp as Bethan thought the worst. "She's not...?"

Mandy let the question hang in the air for a moment. "No. Someone caught her wading in. Hauled her out. She's in a pretty bad way. Full of guilt. I think telling her that her sister's death was not connected in any way to anything she said to you will help with her recovery. Did anyone help you with this trick you intended to play on Megan? Who was privy to your plans?"

"No one. I didn't even tell Luke. It's been hard keeping it to myself." She made a sound somewhere between a sigh and a sob.

Now that the truth was out the aggression had gone. Instead, she slumped in the chair. Beneath the makeup, Mandy could see the shadows under her eyes. Not much sleep over the past week then.

"You spiked Megan's drink and then to add to the mixture you baked some cannabis cakes. Who supplied that? Was it Rhys Davies?"

"What? You crazy or something? No way. I know Rhys has the odd smoke. Always did in uni anyway.

296

But dealing? That's a step of the imagination." She shook her head. "No, I hung around the university. Kept my eyes open. It didn't take long to find some stuff. There's always some dodgy guy hovering about wanting to sell his gear. Thought you lot knew all about that."

It was a sneering remark. Mandy suspected the drugs team knew that too, and most of the students in Cardiff.

Bethan gave a shuddering sigh. "I don't know what I thought would happen. We hadn't had anything that strong since uni days, so it knocked us all for six. What I told you was true. I was sick. I knew Megan was getting a bit paranoid though when Siobhan and Sophie said she'd gone out," she swallowed, "I was worried."

"Why didn't you go after her?"

"I told you, I was sick. Throwing up something awful. By the time I'd got myself sorted she'd already been gone a while. I walked down the drive then but there was no sign of her. And it was hammering it down. We waited until dawn, cleaned up and then went out to find a mobile signal."

"Nobody could get through to Megan as her phone was in your bag, switched off. So, as we've said before, Sophie reported her missing." Mandy waited a moment. "Did any of the others know what you had planned to do? Or afterwards? Did you tell any of them what you'd done?"

"God no. I couldn't tell anyone. It was a joke. I thought if we got some daft photos of Megan losing control it would stop her making life uncomfortable for us. I mean, she had a go at everyone at some time. Sophie was a wreck. I don't know what hold Megan had over her. Aisha was wary as well. As for Siobhan, well I don't know how she was able to forgive her for that business with Rhys. Catholic upbringing maybe. Forgiveness and all that."

So, not a conspiracy. Just Bethan acting on her own behalf. A joke? Hardly that. Revenge for a lifetime of bullying. How different their lives would have been if Bethan had stood up to Megan when she was younger. Years of resentment and fear bubbling away under the pretence of friendship; for both women.

"When you cleaned the kitchen, you made sure there was nothing to point to anybody being responsible by wiping everything down. No evidence of fingerprints on the vodka bottle or anything else. I expect you put some stuff in your car as well. We didn't think about that possibility after we found the body." Something to remember for the future. Even when things seemed straightforward it was better to be over-zealous than to miss something. She wondered if the Super would agree.

"How did you know that?" Bethan asked.

"It's one of the things that alerted us to the idea it wasn't accidental. If you'd left everything as it was, there would have been nothing too suspicious. Megan could have taken the drink and drugs herself."

Bethan was stricken. "She wasn't supposed to die. It was an accident. Can't you see that? I didn't mean her to die. I'm not a murderer. I wish I could bring her back. She shouldn't have died. Not there. Not in a field alone."

Her voice had risen in volume, and she was shouting and crying at the same time. Lost control.

It was over. A confession. Mandy had been right after all. Her gut feelings had led her in the right direction. Despite it all she couldn't help feeling sorry for Bethan as well as Megan. Both clever young women whose friendship had always been somewhat toxic. Both lives ruined. And the families too. What would happen to those friendships now? Would the Pritchards be able to forgive? Nia would need support. That was certain. And Bethan. The jury would decide on guilt and the judge on punishment, although it was clear that Bethan would do time.

* * *

"So, that's it." Ross Withers had appeared as if from nowhere not long after they left the interview room and Bethan had been formally charged. He was smiling, full of benevolence. "Well done, Wilde. I had my doubts, but you proved you were right."

Mandy gave him a cold stare. It could go further, other implications uncovered during the course of the investigation.

"What about the others, sir?" A conspiracy of silence had stopped them finding out the facts earlier. None of them had lied, nevertheless they'd withheld information that could have made a difference. If they had known about the cannabis it could have saved time in the investigation. Would the Super acknowledge that?

"Do you have evidence linking the others to Megan Pritchard's death? Has Ms Rees implicated any of them?"

"No, sir."

"And the O'Hare girl. Any evidence she was in collusion with Bethan Rees?"

"No, sir." Mandy had her mouth open, ready to add to the conversation. Withers didn't give her the chance.

"Then I suggest we call it case closed. Well done." There was no warmth in his congratulations now, and Mandy knew she was not forgiven for upsetting the Grant family. She hoped Sophie would have enough strength of character, now the mystery was solved, to leave home again. She needed to regain her independence and her confidence. Perhaps, now there was a vacancy at Megan's firm, she'd get a job there. Stepping into a dead woman's shoes. Siobhan and Rhys would head off to the sunset, well, Ireland anyway, and Aisha was off to London. Mandy wondered if they would ever meet up again or if the events in Nythfa would rip those fragile friendships apart. Only the future would tell.

* * *

"What do you fancy for dinner this evening? Or shall we go out? I hear that new Italian on Crwys Road is good."

"Or I could cook." said Tabitha, with concerned eyes, eager to please.

They hadn't had the talk Mandy had planned about cyber stalkers. She had hoped Josh would do that one.

In fact, Mandy had said little about the Kelly adventure which seemed to upset Tabitha just as much. She kept trying to make amends. There had been no sign of Kelly either. That was predictable as she'd been grounded for at least a month. Her parents were horrified at the possible outcomes of that escapade. Pontypridd police had found Gary and his mate, and they'd been arrested for grooming offences. To Mandy's surprise, they'd also managed to track down the youths who had taken Kelly's purse. The item had been recovered and they'd also been charged. Justice in action. It didn't take away the memory of that awful evening for Tabitha. All she was guilty of was being a good friend for Kelly. Mandy hoped that their relationship wouldn't end up like Megan and Bethan. A tragic waste.

"Let's have a takeaway for a change. Something unhealthy and full of useless calories. I'll ask Josh to join us although I did promise him a home-cooked meal," said Mandy.

She went out to the kitchen to get the menu. She rang Josh and spoke to him and then went back into the lounge where Tabitha had curled up in the corner of the tub chair.

"Well, there's a surprise. Josh is on a date night... with his wife."

"Oh, that's nice. Do you think they'll get back together?"

"I hope so. He's been moping around like a hen without an egg all week. I just hope he doesn't decide to leave the force. It wouldn't be good for him. He loves the work."

"Like you do." All sincere and big eyed. "I think when I get a job, I'll go for something that has less to do with dead bodies."

"Not a mortician then?"

They both laughed. The police force wasn't for everyone, that was for sure, and Tabitha would find her own path in life, without or without her mother's presence. Joy. Absent but always with them as well.

All those problems could wait. Right now, it was time to relax with her niece. Mandy thought about Nythfa. All that wealth and all that unhappiness. She preferred her own little nesting place.

THE END

Printed in Great Britain
by Amazon

70999275R00184